Outstanding praise for Kim Wright

THE UNEXPECTED WALTZ

"Captures our fear of the unknown and the tender joys of coming into one's own."

—*Booklist*

"The novel has everything I look for in a good read: intrigue, interesting characters at a crossroads and a comfortable authority that allows me to surrender to whatever happens next."

—*Charlotte Observer*

"A moving tale of a middle-aged widow learning to spread her wings and live again. . . . It feels genuine, as new beginnings and second chances aren't always perfect and fairy-tale like, even if outward appearances suggest otherwise. With strong characterization and a cast of intriguing secondary characters, the story dances its way through all the right steps."

—*RT Book Reviews*

"It is an all-too-rare experience for me to browse the first page of a new book and become instantly hooked, as I was with *The Unexpected Waltz*. Happily my obsession with reading this delightful story never waned. Readers at all stages of their lives will identify with smart, funny, self-deprecating Kelly. We find ourselves urgently needing to join her, by turning yet another page, as she examines her life with painful honesty and then takes steps to change, mapping out a better future."

—*Bookreporter*

"Wright sketches the ballroom world with a wry and knowing eye. . . . It would have been easy to camp up the world of ballroom competition, but Wright takes it seriously, seeing the sequined silliness but also the longing and striving behind it."

—*Wilmington Star News*

LOVE IN MID AIR

ALSO BY KIM WRIGHT

Love in Mid Air

The Unexpected Waltz

THE CANTERBURY SISTERS

Kim Wright

G

Gallery Books

New York   London   Toronto   Sydney   New Delhi

G

Gallery Books
An Imprint of Simon & Schuster, Inc.
1230 Avenue of the Americas
New York, NY 10020

First Gallery Books trade paperback edition May 2015

GALLERY BOOKS and colophon are registered trademarks of Simon & Schuster, Inc.

For information about special discounts for bulk purchases, please contact Simon & Schuster Special Sales at 1-866-506-1949 or business@simonandschuster.com.

The Simon & Schuster Speakers Bureau can bring authors to your live event. For more information or to book an event contact the Simon & Schuster Speakers Bureau at 1-866-248-3049 or visit our website at www.simonspeakers.com.

Interior design by Davina Mock-Maniscalco

Manufactured in the United States of America

10   9   8   7   6   5   4   3   2

Library of Congress Cataloging-in-Publication Data is available.

ISBN 978-1-5011-0076-5
ISBN 978-1-5011-0080-2 (ebook)

To my mother, Doris Mitchell,
who made so many journeys possible

It is better to travel well than to arrive.

—Buddha

ONE

You know that old Chinese curse that goes "May you live in interesting times"? I've always thought the modern-day corollary was "May you have an interesting mother." Because I was cursed the minute I was born to the impetuous, talented, politically radical, and sexually experimental Diana de Milan.

The "de" was her idea. "Diana Milan" wasn't big enough to hold her. She needed to stretch her name with that small but exotic middle syllable—the chance to make her life roomier and looser, a way to give her something to grow into.

As for me, my name is Che.

I know. It's utterly ridiculous and it's not even a nickname. I was named in honor of the Cuban revolutionary Che Guevara on the day after he was executed by a Bolivian firing squad. My mother always claimed it was the shock of his murder that sent her into labor, but that's just one more piece of her intricate personal mythology. According to my father, I was two weeks overdue and labor was induced.

My birth marked the first and last time in my life that I was late for anything. If I had been born on September 24 as predicted, I would have entered the world as the somewhat sugary, but ultimately tolerable, "Leticia," in honor of the maiden aunt who'd left my parents the apple orchard on which they built their first commune. But by lingering in the womb too long, I was branded Che de Milan, a name better suited to a revolutionary than a wine critic, and ever since then I've made it a point to arrive places twenty minutes early.

MY MOTHER became religious late in life, after she had already lost one lung to cancer and my father to a sudden stroke. And I don't mean religious in the drum-beating, breast-baring, goddess-channeling manner of her youth. Oh no. Diana de Milan never did anything halfway. When my mother turned to God, she twirled several times *en pointe* and leapt in the air like a ballerina. She went back all the way to her spiritual roots— which in itself is ironic, for she had always proclaimed Catholicism to be her own curse, one she'd spent a lifetime trying to outrun. But now there were spots in her last remaining lung and she'd begun to crave a very specific deity, the one she called "the God of my childhood." Diana spent the last seven months of her life in a nursing home run by the local parish, a gloomy Gothic building that looked like the establishing shot of a horror movie. I don't think I ever went there when it wasn't raining.

For the nuns and priest running the place, she was a true prodigal daughter. They didn't seem to mind that she'd marched for every liberal cause known to mankind or that in her youth she'd written a briefly infamous memoir on the joys of bisexuality. In fact, I think all that made them like her better. The bedfuls of sweet old ladies at the nursing home, women who had spent their entire lives working bake sales and bingo halls, were mostly ignored, while the more sinful patients were treated like celebrities. The priest would come and get my mother each morning for mass, as if it were a date. He would roll her wheelchair down the chapel aisle himself.

As the cancer continued its slow but relentless march through her body, Diana began to entertain fantasies about a miraculous cure. She was especially obsessed with the idea of going to Canterbury. She wished to kneel at the shrine of Thomas Becket, a place reputed to be the site of all sorts of spontaneous healings, offering hope to the blind, the lame, the infertile. Even lepers. She never asked if I wanted to go, just as she'd never asked if I wanted to come along on any of her half-cocked adventures, but I suppose that at some point in those agonizing last few months I must have agreed to take her there. Anything to keep her spirits up, and besides, on some level I think we both knew she'd never make that trip. She barely had the strength to walk me to the elevator after my visits, much less to hike the rutted trail that stretches from London to Canterbury Cathedral.

"Sixty miles, more or less," I'd told her once. "So it might be out of reach. At least for now. Maybe someday, when you're stronger. Definitely someday."

Yeah. It was a lie of the rawest sort, but it's hard to be honest in the presence of the dying and it's hard to be honest with your mother under any circumstances. So when your mother is dying, the effect is squared and you enter into the most bizarre netherworld of bullshit. Words just start coming out of your mouth at random, because you're willing to say anything you think might get you through a particular moment. I once found myself reciting the capitals of the fifty states to her, in alphabetical order.

And when I did that, somewhere between Denver and Dover, she'd turned in her hospital bed and looked at me. Looked at me like she had so many times before. Like I was a surprise, some sort of eternal mystery, and she couldn't figure out how I'd happened to show up here in the middle of her life.

YOU'D THINK that Diana's death would have marked the end of the Canterbury guilt trip. But three weeks after the memorial service, when I received the urn filled with her ashes, there was a note attached.

If you are reading this, she had written, *then I am at last and truly dead. Per our agreement, you must now take me to Canterbury. Do it, Che. Take me there. Even if you're busy. Especially if you're busy. It is never too late for healing.*

Now that was strange, even by Diana standards. Not just the funny lawyerish language of "per our agreement," but that bit about "never too late for healing." By the time your body has been incinerated and swept into an urn—which was surprisingly heavy, by the way—it would seem that any opportunity to rally was pretty much kaput. My mother had spent most of her life mildly stoned—first on the cannabis that she cultivated among the apple trees and later on the morphine that the nuns doled out along with steady drips of Jesus. But I didn't think even Diana believed it was possible to be recalled from the grave.

The urn had been shipped to my office. Delivered UPS, along with a case of twelve new Syrahs that a fledgling vineyard had sent for me to sample and possibly review. My newsletter, *Women Who Wine,* goes out monthly to thousands of restaurants and wine shops and a mention from me can mean sales for a new label, especially if the review is positive. Few of them are. I am known across the industry for my discriminating tastes. I do not approve of many things, so when I do give a wine the nod, it counts.

I took the twelve bottles from their shipping crate and then unpacked the urn, struggling more than I would have guessed to free it from the well-padded crematorium box. In the bottom I found the book about Canterbury that I'd given Diana for her last birthday gift. It was one of those big square coffee-table kinds and she'd had trouble even holding it. I'd sat beside her in the hospital bed, the book open across both our laps, and read it aloud to her like a child. The routes you could walk, how a priest—Anglican this time—would give you a blessing when you entered the Cathedral, how he would even kneel to wipe the dust of the trail from your shoes. She'd loved that part. The book listed quite a few medical miracles that had allegedly been confirmed at the shrine and explained how those clever medieval monks had begun mopping up Becket's blood seconds after he was murdered, certain that each drop contained potential magic. Or at least potential profit.

Magic born of murder. Money born of both. It had struck me as odd, even sinister, but Diana had nodded in satisfaction, the way you do when the last piece of a puzzle finally drops into place.

SO HERE I am. Blinking, as if I've just awakened from some sort of trance. I sit back in my office's one chair and consider the lineup of items on the table. The wine, the urn, the book, the note. The handwriting is thin and shaky, hardly recognizable as my mother's, and like it or not, I know I'm stuck in my promise. I've always been an only child, and now I'm an orphan as well, and the time has pretty much passed for having children of my own. Not that I ever particularly wanted such a thing. The bumper sticker on my Fiat reads, I'M NOT CHILDLESS, I'M CHILD-FREE, but still, to find myself utterly alone in the world, at least in terms of blood relations, has hit me harder than I would have guessed.

Diana died so slowly that somehow I thought I would skip this part, that I had finished all my grieving in advance. But I hadn't counted on there being so much difference between *going* and *gone*. *Going* is busy. *Going* has tasks involved with it—meeting with doctors and social workers, snaking your way through the system to find an empty bed in a decent place, cashing out mutual funds and putting furniture in storage. *Going* demands many visits, and at times, during them, you begin to think these Judas thoughts. You think that it would be better for everyone if she weren't still here, so trapped and suffering, and you imagine that when you get that final call, it will be a relief.

And it is, at least at first. But after a week or so, life goes back to what people call normal, and only then do you start to realize that *going* was easier than *gone*. It's only then that you face the final silent emptiness that's at the heart of every human death, and it's not just a matter of the extra hours that suddenly appear in the day, strangely difficult to fill, it's also that there's nowhere to put the mental energy that circles around the space your mother once occupied.

And Diana occupied a lot of space.

I stare at the urn. We want our mothers to see us for who we really are—or at least that's what adult daughters always say. *Why doesn't she understand me?* we agonize. *Why does she never even ask what I think?* But when our mothers try . . . when you get that occasional weak, tentative question, that unexpected "And how are you?" always uttered at the end of a conversation that was largely about her, inserted after the hanging-up ritual has begun—you realize that understanding wasn't what you wanted after all. You shut this pallid attempt at real conversation right down, you say a quick "Great, Mom," and tell her you'll be there on Sunday as always. But then comes the day when your mother is finally dead, not dying but dead, not fading but invisible, and you know that she is absolutely not, never will, flat-out is not going to ever get you . . .

So here we have it. Twelve bottles of Syrah, none of which I'm likely to enjoy, a book about a cathedral I don't want to visit, a shaky command, and an urn of my mother's ashes. I pick up my phone and press the button at the bottom.

"Siri," I say. "What is the meaning of life?" The little purple microphone flickers as I speak.

And then she answers, *I don't know, but I believe there's an app for that.*

Great. I've reached a point in my life where my own phone greets me with sarcasm.

EVEN AFTER the arrival of the ashes and my mother's strange note, I'm not sure I would have made the decision to go to Canterbury. Not if something else hadn't happened the same day.

It came in the form of another letter, this one delivered not by UPS but by general mail, sent not to my office, but to my condo. I had arrived home from work and dropped the six untasted bottles of wine and my mother in the foyer, then snapped a leash on my Yorkie, Freddy, so I could take him straight out for a walk. Since my keys were still in my hand, I circled by the mail station to see if there was anything in my box.

I don't check my mail every day. I bank online and no one writes letters anymore, so I doubt I drop by the mail station more than once a week. And even then there's usually nothing more than ads and pleas for charity. I'm saying something to Freddy, who's a jumper and a barker, as I slide the key into the box and swing the little silver door open and . . .

Suddenly I'm engulfed in bees.

It takes me a minute to realize what's happening. One stings my hand, just in the fleshy part of the palm between the thumb and first finger, and four or five more swarm out behind him, swirling around my head. Freddy is going nuts. The mail has dropped at my feet, the heavy thud of newsprint circulars and some flyer informing me that I can provide Thanksgiving dinner for a homeless man for just ninety-two cents. And then the strangest of all possible things falls to the ground beside them—a personal letter. I look down at the envelope in a kind of frozen shock and recognize the handwriting on the front as my boyfriend Ned's. Why is he writing me? We Skype every other night at eight, right on schedule, and of course we text throughout the day. He sometimes sends a card, but this is clearly a letter. The envelope is long and businesslike, with the address of his law firm in the corner.

I swat at the bees and another catches my shoulder, reaches me through my shirt, while a third is trapped in my bangs. It doesn't occur to me to run, but it occurs to Freddy, and his leash pulls from my hand. I am screaming, batting at the bee in my hair. I'm ordinarily not much of a screamer—this may be the first time since childhood that I've let go with a total shriek—and then I hear the blast of a car horn, the echoing squeal of tires.

Our lives can sometimes turn in a moment, just like this. A stab to the palm, the slide of a leash, a letter that falls at our feet.

Don't worry. Freddy wasn't hit by the car. There's darkness in this story, but that isn't it. The car was driven by one of my neighbors, a woman with dogs of her own, and she has managed to stop in time. She jumps from the driver's seat, shaken and crying at the close call, and grabs the leash. Freddy is happily leaping, and this woman and I are both babbling. *The bees,* I say, *they came from nowhere. They were in my fucking mailbox. The dog,* she says. *I almost didn't see him. He came from nowhere, just like the bees.*

My hand is throbbing as I take the leash from her. *I'm so sorry,* I say, as I bend to pick up the mail. I tell the dog I'm sorry too. He strains against his collar, unperturbed, only wanting to finish his walk.

Put ice on it, the woman tells me. *Scrape a credit card against your skin to make sure the stingers are out. And take a Benadryl, just in case. Thank God,* she says. *Things could have been so much worse.* She says this over and over.

NO DOUBT you're way ahead of me on all of this. No doubt you've seen what was coming from the minute you learned that the letter was sent from an office. Maybe it was his name, Ned, so minimal and careful, or the fact that he's a lawyer, or maybe you even picked up on the bit about Skype as evidence that we live in different cities, which everyone knows is the relationship kiss of death. But I was still preoccupied with the stings and the dog and the fact that I looked like an irresponsible fool in front of my neighbor. I crammed the letter in my jacket, threw the rest of the mail in the trash, and took Freddy on the long loop, the one that goes around the man-made lake and through the landscaped woods.

It was not until hours later, when I was in bed with the lights off and almost asleep, that I even remembered Ned's letter.

I turned on the bedside light, to the dismay of the dozing Freddy, got the letter from my coat, put on my reading glasses, climbed back into bed, and ripped open the envelope. Three pages, typed and single-spaced, followed by a fourth one containing numbers. An estimate of how much it would cost one of us to buy the other out of our vacation cottage in Cape May.

And that's how I learn what you've undoubtedly already figured out.

That I am being dumped.

THE GIRL Ned is leaving me for is named Renee Randolph. He wants to make sure I know the facts right up front. He isn't going to make excuses or pretend she doesn't exist. He respects me too much to go through all the standard stuff about us growing apart or how it isn't me, it's him. He wants, he says, "no artifice between us." We are far too good friends for that.

They met in a gym, he explains, and then adds that this fact will probably amuse me. I can't imagine why, until I remember that he and I met in a gym, or at least the workout room of a hotel, each of us on side-by-side treadmills. And at that point I begin to skim. I can't seem to keep reading from left to right in any sensible fashion—I hold the paper in front of me and words and phrases swarm up from the page one by one, like a thousand little stings.

This woman, this Renee, it would seem she has a bad husband. Worse, she has a bad foreign husband. He comes from one of those countries where they divorce you for having only daughters and then they try to kidnap the daughters. She lives in fear, he writes, never knowing when this man will appear, or send some sort of heavily armed emissary on his behalf. The teachers at her children's school have been instructed not to let the girls leave the campus with anyone but Renee.

Yes, she's got a bad husband and then she trumps that by being sick. Something is wrong with her. She has some unpronounceable disease—more of a syndrome, really, the sort of thing that's tricky to diagnose, the sort of thing they decide you must have when you don't seem to have anything else. But this syndrome, this illness, it may require him to give her . . . I don't know, something. Something vital. A cornea, his bone marrow, access to his most excellent health insurance. My heart.

She needs me. The words float up from the page, accompanied by their silent echo, *and you don't.*

He's right, in a way. Since we met six years ago, each of us on a business trip, walking side by side on those treadmills, staring up at CNN, Ned and I have had a partnership, a friendship sweetened by an almost epic sexual compatibility. I liked it and I thought he did too. The way we left each other alone through the week to work, but how on vacations we would meet in so many interesting places—Napa, Austin, Miami, Montreal, Reykjavík, London, Key West, Telluride, and Rome.

When we bought the cottage in Cape May we put sunflowers on the table and a hand-braided rug on the floor. Our furniture was old, good wood but old, and we painted each piece burgundy or moss green or Dutch blue. Van Gogh colors, that's what Ned called them. It was a perfect little world, made complete by a couple of carefully planned imperfections, the kind you throw in just to make it clear that you aren't, you know, Those Kind of People. Each Sunday morning we would walk down to the corner café for two copies of the *New York Times* so that we could sit at our table, racing each other through the crossword. We were well matched. Sometimes he won, sometimes I did.

Was I in love? I think I was. I must have been. It was a very modern sort of romance, or at least that's what I told myself as I traveled back and forth, always in some car or train or airport. And we laughed . . . dear God, Ned and I laughed all the time.

And when you laugh that much, when you finish every puzzle at precisely the same time, when you look up across the painted table and your eyes lock in satisfaction . . . it has to mean something, doesn't it?

I'm sure I loved him on the weekend that we bought Lorenzo. Lorenzo was a lobster. We got him from one of those roadside places where the signs read "FRESH" and they have a bunch of hand-drawn pictures of smiling seafood. He was packed in ice and Styrofoam, his claws bound shut with big rubber bands, and I had begun to feel regret over the whole idea before we'd even managed to pull Ned's Lexus back on the road.

"Do you think it can breathe in there?" I'd asked, and Ned had said, "Lobsters don't breathe."

Well, that's ridiculous. Everything breathes, in one way or another. But I didn't say anything and after a mile or two Ned said, "If he needs anything, it would probably be water."

Of course we were silly to be so concerned about the welfare of a creature that was hours from its execution, but I knew even then that we'd never bring ourselves to boil Lorenzo. You can't boil something you've named. We went ahead and made several more roadside stops, collecting our lettuce and tomatoes and lemon and herbs and sourdough bread, and by the time we pulled into the driveway of the cottage, Ned had already taken to talking to the lobster, pointing out landmarks we passed along the way, as if Lorenzo were a weekend guest. We made the salad and opened the wine and even set the big pot of water on the stove to boil, but it was a lost cause. We ended up snipping Lorenzo free from his bands and tossing him into the bay.

"You know," Ned said, raising his wineglass in salute as Lorenzo drifted out to sea, "we need to stop thinking of this place as an investment and start thinking of it as a home." The next weekend we went out and bought Freddy.

Now he says that he wishes me the best, but the best is what I thought we had. No, "the very best," that's what he writes. That he wishes me "the very best of everything." According to him, I deserve nothing less.

Is he telling me the laughter didn't matter? Nor the friendship, nor the sex? We worked crosswords together, for God's sake. We had a lobster and a dog. He's the only man I ever dated that my mother liked.

But evidently that's all out the window now that he has found his wounded bird. Now that he has stooped to rescue her, now that she is fluttering in his hand. And he has written to inform me that he has never been happier.

I think, he writes with a killing simplicity, *that she may be The One*.

Yes, he capitalizes it, lest I miss the point. The. One.

I LIE there in the dark for hours, my heart pounding, my legs numb. He will call me on Monday, the letter says. We have many things to discuss, but he didn't want to drop them on me unawares. That's why he has written in advance, to give me time to absorb the news. Which, of course, is utter crap. He sent the letter because he didn't want to hear me wail or cry or attack him with questions. When did this happen? How long has he known her? Were there times when he came from her bed to mine, and did she thus win him slowly, in tiny incremental ways, or was her victory over me accomplished in one swift stroke? And which answer would be harder to accept?

It's almost light when I emerge from my bed. I open another bottle of the Syrah, slosh some in a juice glass, and go to my desk to turn on the computer. For a minute I fight the urge to google the girl, to learn all about Renee Randolph, but I stop myself. She is undoubtedly beautiful. Beautiful and tragic is such an appealing combination, the natural stuff of romances, while average-looking and tragic is just . . . average-looking and tragic. Certainly not compelling enough to drive a man to upend a life as pleasant and convenient as the one Ned and I shared. So she must be beautiful. Nothing else would make sense.

I take a long, slow draw of the wine and consider the search line where I've typed REN. What could Google possibly tell me about this woman that I would find comforting? If she is more accomplished than me, that will sting . . . but what if she's less accomplished? Somehow that would be even worse. Finally I delete REN and enter PILGRIMAGES TO CANTERBURY instead.

What I'm thrown into, of course, are sites devoted to literature and history. Articles about Chaucer and Becket and Canterbury's reputation for miracles. I sit back in annoyance as the scholarly articles roll by and while I'm waiting, my eye falls on a copy of my alumni magazine, which has languished for God knows how long on my desk. In the back they always list guided tours and I've noticed them before, in a passing sort of way. I've always thought it would be nice to have a professor lead your group through museums, battlefields, and palaces. To have someone there to point out the important things. It's easy to imagine how these trips would be appealing for lonely single women, those sad souls who have reached middle age with enough money to travel but no one to travel with.

I scan the catalog by the glowing blue light of the computer screen and soon enough, there it is: the name of an art professor who escorts both groups and individuals through southern England. She looks like just what I need—pale, serious, academic, disinclined to asking personal questions. I send her a quick email, telling her I need to walk the Canterbury Trail ASAP, top to bottom, from London to the steps of the Cathedral. And then I google how to transport ashes on an international flight.

Evidently the dead are a sizable segment of the travel industry, because the answer pops right up. The urn must be carried onto the plane, not packed in a suitcase. It must be scanned and taken through security and I will need a note from the crematorium confirming that the contents are human remains and not something like plutonium. I must be prepared for the fact that security can open the urn at any time if they wish, that small bits of my mother might fly out onto the airport carpet or dirty the hands of a TSA agent. Or perhaps I might choose to eschew the urn altogether, the site suggests, with a gentle but pointed hint. Transfer the ashes to something less heavy and likely to trigger the scanning machine. Like, for example, a ziplock bag.

I always meant to take my mother to Europe, but my travel was so often for business or I was meeting Ned in some romantic place. And of course she was busy too, fostering misunderstood pit bulls, walking for Amnesty International, framing houses with Habitat . . . Then she got sick. We let all our chances pass, Diana and I, and now at last she's coming with me, but she's coming in my carry-on bag. I put the wine down, thinking that it's bitter, but I know I'm being unfair. I've been drinking while thinking of something else, which is the cardinal sin of wine tasting, for everyone knows how easily emotions can trickle from the mind to the tongue. Has the wine gone bitter, or have I?

The sun is up. I rise and leave my desk, the juice glass still in my hand. I pour the remains of the Syrah into the kitchen sink and look down at the dark-red stain. In my email I told the professor that I could be in London as early as Sunday and I would like a private tour. It probably costs a fortune to hire a personal guide, but all I can think is that I need to be gone, long gone, before Ned calls to apologize and explain again about how he just couldn't help himself, how no man can resist a woman in need. The desire to escape feels huge within me. In fact, if I don't get out of here right now, I'm not sure what will happen.

I pick up my phone and try again. "Siri," I say. "What's the meaning of life?"

A pause and then the answer: *I Kant answer that. Ha ha.*

Ha ha. She's quite the hoot, that Siri.

TWO

They did a study once on why so many people cry in airplanes—whether it's the silence, the isolation, or perhaps just some primordial fear of leaving terra firma.

I think it's because airplanes are the closest most of us come to enforced meditation. On the runway, in that small, trembling world between here and there, we have nothing to do but sit with our thoughts. Of course, once the plane is airborne, there are a thousand things to preoccupy us—movies, Kindles, games, puzzles, drinks, that slim but seductive possibility that our seatmate could turn out to be our soul mate. But during takeoff and landing, we're on our own. We cannot avoid the vast lonely prairies that exist inside our own heads.

At first, it seems luck is with me on the flight. No one is sitting in the aisle seat, so I'm able to stretch out and sleep. We land early; so early, in fact, that Heathrow doesn't have an empty gate ready for us. While we wait for an opening, I pull out my phone and check my messages. Most of them are predictable—work and ads and notifications from Facebook, Instagram, and Twitter. But one of them is from the college professor

I've hired as my guide, and the subject line reads *Slight change of plans*.

Slight change of plans? That's not good. In my experience, there's no such thing.

I look out the airplane window at the rain-washed tarmac, a tremor of anxiety working its way up my spine. Even the brief time I spent researching this trip on my computer taught me that walking the Canterbury Trail isn't nearly as easy as it sounds. It's more a matter of walking what's left of the Canterbury Trail. The original pilgrim route followed an even more ancient Roman path, but now this old and holy road has been broken by the demands of modern life. The trail is slashed in several places by a major highway and the pieces left intact weave largely across private land, through farms and orchards and even the backyards of rural homes. Since the trail belongs to the National Trust, the owners of the land knew they must cede the route when they bought the property. Presumably they are used to Americans with backpacks and blisters and broken hearts stomping past them in the mist. But Google warns that following the path is tricky. The markers are few and subtly placed, making it nearly impossible to tell where the trail breaks off and takes up again.

Bottom line, you need a guide.

But it would seem I've already managed to lose mine. She is emailing me from a gurney in a hospital ward, where she lies awaiting an emergency appendectomy.

"Can you believe it?" she writes.

No, I can't believe it. No one has an appendectomy anymore. She may as well be telling me she's succumbed to bubonic plague. But then, in suspiciously complete and grammatical prose for a woman who is allegedly in the grip of agony, she offers me a solution. One of her fellow teachers at the university, by luck, is leading an organized tour to Canterbury that will be departing London this very afternoon. A classics professor, highly regarded in her field, quite young, almost a prodigy. And she assures me that I needn't worry that I am crashing someone's party. The women in the group come from all over America and have booked their trip through an outfit called Broads Abroad, which caters to the solo female traveler.

The solo female traveler. I guess that's what I am now.

"It's the perfect solution," the professor writes, but I'm not convinced. I don't want to talk while I walk. I don't want to bond with other women, to tell them my troubles, which, while agonizing, are also—let's face it—pretty clichéd. And once I've been forced to tell them my stories, politeness demands I must listen to theirs and I bet they all have dead mothers and bad boyfriends too. My phone has adjusted to the local time, which is not quite seven a.m. I gaze out into the ugly foreign morning and consider my options.

Maybe I should just take the train to Canterbury. Dump Mom and get the hell back to Heathrow, and with any luck I could be on a return flight to Philly tonight. It wouldn't be a true pilgrimage, not in the step-by-step sense, but it would fulfill my promise. And that's what this is about, isn't it? Putting the period at the end of a sentence. Hitting TAB and starting a new paragraph in my life. Saying goodbye. Ridding myself of ghosts. There is absolutely no reason to make things harder than they have to be.

The plane at last begins to move toward an open gate. I look down at the message in my hand.

The Broads Abroad. Jesus. The name doesn't sound promising.

BY THE time I take the Heathrow Express into the city, the rain has stopped and the morning has turned pink and gold. Oil-slick puddles shimmer like Monets on the sidewalks and the air feels fresh. I emerge from Paddington Station and head in the direction that my phone assures me is dead east, the autumn leaves crunching beneath my boots as I walk. *London moves at a different pace than American cities*, I think, stopping on a street corner to change hands on my suitcase. The bustle is more muted. The tempo more civilized and humane. I don't like it.

How long has it been since I've eaten? Too long to remember, which isn't good, so I dip into the nearest café. Order the "standard" without thinking and am greeted with the eternally confounding British breakfast of baked beans, mushrooms, and tomatoes. But I realize I'm hungry once I smell it, perhaps truly hungry for the first time in days. As I work my way through the plate of food, I read the email from the professor once again, this time in a calmer state of mind.

The Broads Abroad are meeting at the George Inn for luncheon, she writes. *It's near the site of the Tabard Inn where Chaucer and his pilgrims began their journey five hundred years ago, but the Tabard burned somewhere along the way in some sort of brothel fire. The George is of the same ilk and era and thus a suitable spot to inaugurate a pilgrimage.* Those are the precise words she uses—"ilk," "era," "inaugurate" and "pilgrimage"—and I wonder again that a woman on the brink of surgery would take the time to write such a wordy and persuasive note. It is a British trait, evidently, this chipperness in the face of adversity, this compulsion to wax about medieval history while bent double in pain.

Take the tube to London Bridge Station, she advises, *and you'll find the George no more than a ten-minute walk away.* I eat my beans and look at a map I grabbed on the train. It's a considerable distance from Paddington to London Bridge, but then again I have hours to kill and after being cooped up on the plane, a long walk might do me good. I don't intend to actually join the group, of course. At least not without a little reconnaissance. She says there are eight women on the tour, counting the guide, and a party of that size should be easy to spot. I decide I will observe them from a suitable distance and try to gauge how annoying they are before I make my decision. If they seem okay, I will approach them. If not, I can catch the train from London Bridge to Canterbury and scatter my mother alone.

ACCORDING TO Wikipedia, Chaucer's pilgrims began their journey in Southwark, then a sketchy part of London. Southwark was outside the city limits, the medieval equivalent of a suburb, and thus beyond the reach of the law. The district was filled with prostitutes, thieves, and drunkards.

Now it's full of tourists. The entire London Bridge area, in fact, is a hub of amusements designed for foreigners on holiday. The bridge itself, as well as the dungeon and the tower and several full-size reproductions of sailing ships, which are moored and bobbing on the Thames. People are even walking the streets in costume, handing out flyers for museums and tour buses, and I am barely within Southwark when I'm accosted by a man dressed like Sir Walter Raleigh. I know he's Raleigh because he makes a grand gesture—steps back and bows, taking off his shabby red velvet cloak as if he might lay it across one of the rather sizable puddles that have formed on the street. I guess the idea is for me to walk over the cloak like the original Queen Elizabeth, but I shake my head to show him this isn't necessary. To show him that, despite the fact I'm wearing a backpack and dragging a suitcase, I'm not your typical American tourist. No matter how gallant he pretends to be, I will not follow him back to the dock and pay ten pounds to tour his boat. He's got the wrong sort of fool entirely. To emphasize my independence and busyness, I step directly into the puddle.

He smiles.

"Fare thee well, milady," he says, his voice rising a bit on the last syllable, as if it were a question.

Is he mocking me? Is "Fare thee well" Elizabethan for "Fuck you"? I've always suspected that British men consider themselves wildly attractive to American women, and let's face it: they have a point. They know we love them for their accents . . . that a British man can be pimply, broke, and rude, and yet an American woman will fawn over him, favor him without question over one of her own countrymen. But what is a woman supposed to say in response to "Fare thee well"? Is it "Fare thee well as well," which doesn't make a lot of sense, or is it more proper to say "Thank you" or "I'm fine"?

I look back over my shoulder as I walk away. Sir Walter Raleigh is already unclasping his cape for another tourist. Someone more appreciative, more feminine and helpless and lovable. She is giggling and her friends are taking a picture as she steps, one tentative foot hovering in midair above the moth-eaten red velvet. He bows before her, his plumed hat in one hand, her fingertips in the other. She is smiling in a way that suggests she will give him ten pounds. Smiling as if she would gladly give him anything he asked for.

Even with the long walk, I get there early, nearly an hour before the women are due. The George Inn is not quite what I envisioned. Dark, yes, with red trim on the windows and copper pots, all that sort of inn-ish nonsense. But it's larger and more upscale than I would have guessed and crowded, apparently with locals as well as tourists. I take a seat at the long oak bar and order my first drink. My state of mind is probably best illustrated by the fact that I think of it precisely like that. As "my first drink."

RESTAURANTS ARE the churches of my generation. These are the places where we congregate to confess our sins, drink wine, search for glimmers of hope, and most important, find community . . . or at least a momentary sanctuary from our loneliness.

And if the George Inn truly were a church, this bar would be its shrine. I gaze up at the rows and rows of brightly colored bottles, all carefully lit from behind, as if they are jewels on display in a museum. Or maybe books on a library shelf. No, not quite. Not books. Because books contain stories of things that have already happened and the liquor bottles on these high shelves before me hold stories of what is yet to be. Lovers who have not met, swords still in their sheaths, journeys that may or may not be undertaken. *And this goblet*, I think, looking deeply into the one in my hand . . . *something unexpected waits for me in the bottom of the glass. Some story will begin when I take my last sip.*

Almost two hours have passed and, obviously, I'm drunk.

The group of women I've been waiting for entered some time ago and took a long, picnic-style table near the back. I can't hear their conversation from this distance, but I can see their reflection in the mirror behind the bar. They don't seem to have the awkwardness one might expect to find in a group of strangers who are about to spend six days together. They are talking and laughing, adjusting their chairs. They have shucked their coats and scarves, and raised the large beer-stained menus to their faces.

And good luck with that, I'd like to tell them. I've eaten, but just barely.

The leisurely quality of European service has always annoyed me. All around me, plates sit unbussed and glasses unfilled. Credit cards lie uncollected on their black folders and yet the young man tending the bar before me leans back against the wall with his arms folded across his chest, staring thoughtfully into space. I want to inform him he'd better hurry up, that I have somewhere else to be, but of course that's a lie. I have absolutely nowhere else to be. No one on earth—save the owner of the dog kennel where I left Freddy and the college professor who, even as we speak, is slipping under the dark waters of anesthesia—has the slightest idea where I am right now. No one even knows what country I'm in. I am expected nowhere, by no one, and the free time yawns before me like a mouth. If I'm not careful, I might fall in and be swallowed on the spot.

The eight women have arranged themselves with four on one side and three on the other, with the head of the table claimed by a woman who is clearly one of the youngest in the group. In fact, I'd call her a girl, midtwenties at best. Thin and dark with a low ponytail and an air of natural dignity. Evidently she's the classics professor, the academic prodigy, and thus the leader of the tour. Suitcases and backpacks and purses are piled around their chairs and the group is drinking steadily, stopping every few minutes to toast something, most likely the beginning of their journey. Something about them seems strangely out of control from the start, but they're the most animated table in the whole pub and I think there's a foolishness in our lives— how we women make such a business of finding men, cajoling them, seducing them, taking care of them, and all the while on some level we know it would be so much easier, in some ways so much more fulfilling, to just allow ourselves to . . .

Quick, I tell myself. *Think a new thought.* Type it over the last one and hit ENTER again, because I'm right on the verge of becoming That Woman. You know the one I'm talking about. That woman who has been recently burned and who has now sworn off men. The one who has to flag down everybody she passes on the street and tell them about what the bastard said when he was walking out the door and all the ways she's been done wrong. The woman whose bitterness shows on her face, who walks through the world with clenched fists. The sort who shakes her head impatiently at Sir Walter Raleigh. I need to change my thinking, to pull my eyes from this long, bright table of laughing women and back to the other people in the pub.

There's a game I play when I get like this. I look around whatever room I find myself in and try to figure out who are the most attractive three men in the place. It doesn't matter if a man is married, or way too young, obviously gay, or in some other way unattainable, because the point of the game is not to approach him or even to smile and flirt. The point is simply to notice that he's out there. To remind myself that attractive men are everywhere.

The most obvious choice here in the George is one of the waiters, another figure I've been following in the mirror. He's not languid like most of them, but rather intense and full of energy. His eyes dart around the room, slipping from table to table as he walks among the diners, putting some things down and picking up others. There's a calculated bit of stubble on his chin and he wears a white shirt and jeans with a stone-colored apron tied around his waist like a cummerbund.

The second attractive man is not so obvious. I have to twist in my seat and really study the room before spotting him, sitting at a table of businessmen. Closer to my age and actually a little goofy looking, with his eyes too large behind his glasses. He has a deep cleft in his chin and dimples and he has what my father used to call a hail-fellow-well-met quality. Like he would insist on picking up the check for everyone, even people he doesn't know. Not handsome, exactly, but there's something in his face I trust.

Okay. The third one. That's harder yet again, but finally I settle on the man sitting right beside me. Balding, or perhaps it is just that he has clipped his gray hair so short that at first glance it looks as if there's nothing there. It gives him the air of a Roman senator in one of those lavish BBC productions, the air of a man with power. He is thin—not with the thinness of a man who is naturally slender and has been so all his life, but rather thin like someone who's been sick and is now slowly finding his way back toward the light. I've seen the same expression on people in Diana's nursing home—those in the rehab wing, the recovering ones, the lucky ones, those who have bruised their shoulder against the dark wall of death but somehow survived. They have this same wary look. He wears a navy V-neck sweater, which I like, and he notices me noticing him. Of course he does. The fact that I play this game often has not made me particularly good at it.

"You're an American," he says.

An interesting comment, since I don't believe I've spoken since he's arrived. "How did you know that?"

"You smiled at the waiter. That's what you Americans do, you know. You smile at everyone."

He says it as if smiling is some sort of character fault. Despite the fact that this is a gross oversimplification, and this irritates me, I find myself smiling at him the whole time he's speaking. We each flick our gaze to one another's hands, note the absence of rings. He looks at my iPhone beside me on the counter. Freddy is my wallpaper, which I suppose tells this man my whole story, or at least as much as he needs for present circumstances. A woman with a dog for her wallpaper is a woman without children, without a husband. I scratch my hand. The bee stings are still itchy, especially this one so inconveniently located in my palm.

"And what do you call your little dog?" he asks.

"Freddy," I say, and for some reason just saying the name out loud makes me want to weep. *I'm exhausted,* I think. Burned out by that half-assed plane sleep and now drunk as well and lost somehow, carried on the wings of fate to this strange pub. So when he furthermore asks what brings me to London, he's probably expecting a simple answer, maybe just a single word like "business" or "holiday," but instead I find myself telling him the whole story. The urn, the bees, the cancer, the appendectomy, the Broads Abroad. I run my fingertips around the edges of my iPhone as I talk, and perhaps I should say I tell him almost the whole story because I skip over the part about Ned. It's too humiliating and if I were in a restaurant back in the States I wouldn't even be talking to this man. I would be on Twitter, or checking email, alone in my virtual office, so I suppose it's a bit of a small miracle that I've even noticed he is here. Hell, it's a miracle that I've even noticed I am here. And yet I still hold my phone in my hand as we chat, just as I always do, even when it's turned off, even when I am out of range or low on bars. It's my talisman, and I clutch it like a Christian holds her prayer beads, my fingers restlessly flicking over the edges.

"So you've brought your mum's urn with you," he says. He has a habit of pinching his lower lip between his thumb and pointer finger when he finishes a sentence, although he also has that same odd cadence that Sir Walter Raleigh had, where every statement sounds like a question, and every question sounds a bit like a statement. It's a British thing, I suppose. The raised note at the end of the sentence implies uncertainty, but also a "haven't you?" that confirms he already knows the answer to the question he just asked. It's incredibly distracting, or maybe it's his eyes, which are clear and gray-green and a little crinkly around the edges, that are distracting, or more likely it's just that I am even drunker than I thought.

"Not the urn," I say. "It's heavy and it requires more paperwork to get it through airport security. I've got her in a ziplock bag."

"Your mum's in a ziplock bag?" he asks, and I can't tell if he's shocked or amused.

"Enough of her. The gesture is symbolic, after all."

"Then why are you taking time to walk the whole trail? It's rather long, isn't it?"

"Sixty miles."

Now it's his turn to smile, but more with the eyes than the mouth. "I meant in a proper measure."

I stop and think. "About a hundred kilometers. They say it will take five days, which sounded like way too long until I got a look at these Broads Abroad people. The ones in the corner, the long table. They don't look like brisk walkers, do they? In fact, they all look drunk."

He twists in his seat and studies the group but makes no comment on their sobriety, which is probably several notches higher than my own. *I sound like a total bitch,* I think. *Why is a man like him even talking to me?* The most obvious answer is that I possess a faint echo of Diana's attractiveness—I have the same long legs and long neck, prompting comparisons to giraffes and colts or even sometimes swans. The same coloring, reddish-gold hair with blue eyes, and, when I am careful not to tan or freckle, my pale complexion makes the resemblance between us even stronger. Everyone says it is a beautiful and unusual combination, but I do not guard this birthright with the same zeal Diana employed. She wore wide-brimmed hats on the commune in the days before sunscreen and rinsed her hair with cider to bring out the sheen. That is the smell I most associate with her, the lingering whiff of apples, still there even after she would leave a room.

"You know, a train runs from London to Canterbury at least twice an hour," the man says, turning back from his survey of the Broads Abroad table to face me. "Hardly necessary to cross the route step by step, is it?"

"So I just barrel down to Canterbury, toss my mother's ashes in the direction of the Cathedral, barrel back, and I'm on the plane home to the States tonight, is that what you're suggesting?" It's nothing more than the plan I considered myself this morning, sitting on the tarmac, so I don't know why my voice has suddenly gone all sharp and accusatory. I hate it when people quote me back to myself.

He raises his palms in surrender. "I'm only saying that it's an option. It's hardly April out there, and you don't look like you're particularly longen to goon on a pilgrimage."

Okay, so he's smart. Or at least smart enough to remember that "longen to goon" bit from the prologue to *The Canterbury Tales*. And he also has a valid point. The short dark days of November are a strange time to undertake this sort of walk. A true pilgrimage should commence when the trees bud in the spring.

It should earmark the start of something, not the end, and all around me things seem to be coming to a close. I'm as brittle as a leaf fallen from a tree. If someone brushed against me, I might crack.

"Your phone," he says, aware that he's upset me and changing the topic. "You never put it down."

I'm not sure if that statement is intended as an observation or a criticism or even if it matters, because once again I feel myself bristle. "There's no way of knowing how long I'll have a good connection. Once we get on the trail . . ."

He looks at me as if to say, "But you could talk to me because, after all, I'm right here in front of you," and that annoys me too. I don't know this man, and I guess you're thinking that at this rate I never will. That I'll never slow down or open up enough to know any man, but I haven't come to England to chat up strangers in bars, have I? No. I've come for a very specific mission, and it lies in a different part of the George.

I look at the group of women behind me in the mirror and then I finish the last swig of wine and rummage through my backpack for my credit card. My wallet is under the ziplock bag with Diana's ashes. Even from the afterlife, she nags me. *Take a chance*, I hear her say. *Go on, baby, 'cause what's the worst that can happen? You waste a week? That's nothing in a world where people waste years at a time, waste decades without ever thinking of it. Hell, most people waste their whole lives.*

"I've offended you," the man says.

"Not at all," I say, snapping my bag shut. "In fact, I should thank you. I've just been dumped, you know, two days ago back in the States. A man I was with for years—we even bought a cottage together and painted the porch—he up and left me for a wounded bird and now I have to start over, even though I'm at a god-awful age. Forty-eight, neither here nor there, too old to start over and too young to die and I don't know what's supposed to happen next. Plus I'm drunk and being a bit of a bitch, which I guess is obvious, and I know I haven't been the easiest woman in the world to flirt with. But I do appreciate you for trying."

"A wounded bird?"

"Oh, you know. One of those women who flap around and make little cheeping sounds." I wave my hands to illustrate.

The eyes crinkle again. "You don't strike me as much of a wounded bird."

I don't? I feel like I'm flapping and cheeping all over the place, like I'm weak and abstracted and dizzy, like I'm getting ready to tumble to the pub floor and just lie there until someone comes to sweep me away. But it pleases me that it doesn't show. I glance down at my phone, on which a new message has just popped up. Odd. It's the middle of the night in America, so I can't think who would be texting me. But then I see that it's Ned. He must have called and not gotten an answer or maybe he's been calling, over and over, out of guilt, for the past two days and now he thinks I've gone and jumped off a cliff or something. I put the phone down on the counter and wave my credit card at the waiter.

How are you? he has texted. *Where are you? We really need to talk.*

When I look up from the phone the British man is still watching me, his head cocked to one side. It's a look Freddy gets sometimes. "So it's off with you, I take it? Leaving now, is that the call? And you're sure you won't stay for just one more glass of wine?"

I shake my head. "Sorry. It looks like I'm about to take a very long walk."

THREE

Apparently my sick guide took the time to text her colleague, for I seem to be expected at the Broads Abroad table. The hostess introduces herself merely as Tess, without mentioning any of her academic titles or accolades, and stands to shake my hand.

"I wasn't at all certain you would join us," she says. "But nine makes our party more complete, does it not?" A strange remark. I try to think of something that naturally falls in units of nine, but I can't.

"What's the most women you've ever taken touring at a time?" asks a pretty blonde woman with an almost ridiculously symmetrical face. She reminds me of Grace Kelly, which is probably the effect she intended, for she's twisted her hair into a twist at the nape of her neck, a style that no one wears anymore. Looking at her, it's hard to understand why it ever fell out of fashion. Already I've forgotten her real name. I was introduced to everyone when I approached the table, but it's hard to absorb eight names at once, even when you're not woozy and under emotional duress.

"Twelve's the limit the touring company will allow," Tess

says. "We pride ourselves on giving every guest individual attention. This isn't one of those packaged jaunts where I'm waving a
little yellow flag and screaming out facts as we walk."

"Twelve counting you, or twelve tourists?" the blonde
woman persists. I can't imagine why this matters to her. Maybe
she's hosted a lot of dinner parties and has had to be concerned
with such things, or maybe she's superstitious about the number thirteen.

"Twelve not counting me," Tess says, "and at Broads Abroad
we think of you as our guests, not as tourists. Which makes me
your host, and not your guide."

"It takes thirteen to form a coven," another woman says.
She's sitting at the end of the table, has loudly pronounced her
name to be Valerie, and she looks a bit mad. Her hair is parted
badly, straight down the middle except for one great zag halfway
through, and her makeup is smeared. If I were to be charitable
I'd assume she'd flown the red-eye in from the States, just as I
did, but that's probably true of most of the women at the table
and none of the rest of us look quite so blurry. At least I don't
think I do. *Valerie,* I repeat to myself, hoping to keep at least
one of them firmly centered in my mind. I once had a doll
called Valerie. It's a charming name. It doesn't suit her.

"Hostess?" I say to Tess. "I assume that's in honor of the
fact that Harry Bailey was the host in *The Canterbury Tales*?" I
don't particularly like myself when I do this. These little pseudo
questions are common at wine tastings—a display of knowledge
disguised as an inquiry—and I notice the table has fallen
slightly more silent since my arrival. I guess I'm a bit of a buzzkill.

"No, we use the term 'host' on all our tours," Tess says, "no matter where we're going. But I'm glad Che has brought the subject up, because this is as good a time as any to discuss your collective expectations for our little adventure. Each group has its own personality, you know, its own dynamic. Some wish to hold more to the *Canterbury Tales* theme than others." She shrugs, her narrow shoulders rising and falling in her starched oxford shirt, and it amazes me not only that she would wear white here in this boisterous pub, on the brink of a long walk, but also that she would have managed to keep herself so pristine during this long siege of eating and drinking.

"What do you mean?" asks another woman. The only black person in the group, which should have made it easier to remember her name, but I can't think of that one either. She has the rangy, easy quality of an athlete and she sits back in her chair, one ankle resting on the other knee. Her boots are expensive, that mellowed sort of Italian leather, and she's ordered a salad, with the remains sitting before her on the table. A rookie mistake in a British pub. Who knows, this may have been the first salad that's ever left the kitchen. It looks like they just threw together a pile of sandwich toppings—shredded lettuce, white onion, pickles, a bit of a sad tomato, sprinkles of olive.

"Tradition has always demanded that pilgrims travel to Canterbury in a group," Tess says. A hush has fallen over the table and we have unconsciously taken on the postures of schoolgirls, shifting in our seats and watching attentively as Tess folds her slim white hands before her. "The surface explanation is that the trail started a trade route between London and the port of Dover, and thus attracted robbers. A lone traveler might have been beset at any moment along his journey and there was safety in numbers. In other words, the spirit of fellowship so long associated with Canterbury began as a matter of pure survival. Am I boring you yet?"

Eight heads shake no.

"Most of the pilgrims, like Chaucer's characters and like us, did not know their fellow travelers before their journey began," Tess says. "They called each other 'companions,' from *compagnons,* an old French word which was not in wide English use at the time. They didn't need it. Before pilgrimages came into fashion, most people stayed at home, rarely straying from the village of their birth, and thus not coming in contact with many strangers. 'Companion' means 'someone you eat with,' nothing more and nothing less. But the idea of breaking bread with new people, those whom one had so recently met . . . The conversations that must have arisen along the trail and this sense of a shared mission . . ."

She shakes her head, as if stunned at the wonder of it, as if she has no trouble at all imagining the excitement of the medieval pilgrims leaving the gates of their villages, turning their backs on the small and familiar, setting forth to find death or salvation, or both. She must be a good teacher. She's probably given this speech a hundred times and yet she's not jaded. The everyday miracles of life have not yet been lost upon her.

"But of course here in our happy party of nine we are not all strangers, are we?" she continues. A rhetorical question, for she knows the composition of the group better than anyone. "There are two pairs among us. Jean has come with her daughter . . ."

And here she nods toward Grace Kelly, who yes, of course

is Jean, I remember now, and a teenage girl at the other end of the table. Becca, she turns out to be, and I find it interesting that she's not elected to sit beside her mother, not even at this first meal. Of course she's much younger than anyone else at the table, save Tess, and most likely has been dragged on this trip against her will, just as I was swept up in so many of my own mother's madcap adventures through the years.

I feel a surge of sympathy for the girl, who, now that I look closely at her, has the same sort of all-American prettiness as her mother. Or at least the potential of it. But where I let my resemblance to Diana slowly erode throughout years of neglect, Becca seems to be trying to consciously obliterate any similarity between her and Jean. She has dyed her short, spiky hair a cartoonish shade of orangey-red, has bitten her nails to tiny turquoise-painted dots, and is wearing glasses so heavy and dark that I wonder if she really needs them. They seem like an affectation, a prop, like Sir Walter Raleigh's red cape, a way for you to know what game our young Becca is playing the minute you meet her. The glasses and the hair all but scream *I am not my mother. You make that mistake on point of death.*

Jean smiles and flaps a well-manicured hand in the direction of her daughter. "Yes, Becca and I have been planning this trip for years," she says. "My younger two are boys, both athletes with all the practices and schedules and tournaments that come with that sort of life. It's hard to get some real mother-daughter time, so when her fall break rolled around . . ."

Her voice trails off. Becca says nothing, so Tess smoothly weaves back in. "And we have a pair of friends from Texas," she says. "Claire and Silvia . . ."

Now these two are an even odder duo than the mother and daughter. Because you expect daughters to boomerang off their mothers, to assert themselves by trying to be wildly different. But friends are often similar, and these women seem to share nothing. It's hard to tell if they are even close in age, although somehow I suspect they might be, that their friendship is one of long standing. If they were in an ad, Claire would be the one who'd been wise enough to purchase the two-hundred-dollar skin cream and Silvia would be the one who had not. Claire is blonde like Jean, but icily so, silver instead of gold, almost Nordic, and her face is so flawless that she's probably had work done, but done so well that you can't quite be sure. While Jean comes off as a woman who has graciously accepted the mantle of her fifties—your most serene highness of some minor kingdom—Claire is edgier, almost hip. I want her earrings. I want her scarf. When I get to know her better, I suspect there's a good chance I might want her life.

Silvia, in utter contrast, is worn and weathered, like a woman who spends her days training dogs or maybe even breaking horses. Something outdoors in the brutal elements of Texas. Age spots dot her forehead and temples, the splotches undimmed by makeup, and she seems to be locked in a permanent squint. It's difficult, keeping track of three women who are so close in age or at least far enough north of me that the actual number hardly matters. And yet they are all different and I need to stop for a moment and figure out how. Okay. If Jean is warm and golden and Claire is cool and silvery, then Silvia could be called bronze. Solid and matte, less pricey than the other two but more durable, a woman who has been tested by time, who has a sheen rather than a shine. I look at their hands for confirmation of my theories, for hands are the purest indication of a woman's way of life, the one part of the female anatomy that cannot be frozen, dyed, lifted, sucked, or tucked, although I'm sure they're working on a way to remedy even that. Jean's hands are plump and soft, with oval pink tips and a wedding band cutting into the flesh. Claire has the square, dark nails of a city manicure, a single oversize amber ring. Silvia's hands are utterly unadorned and unpolished, as if she has recently been digging in a garden. As if she is accustomed, in fact, to ripping potatoes from the black earth.

Okay, so the older three are straight enough in my mind, but Jesus, all these names. I forgot half of them the moment I heard them, and I can hear the accusatory tickle of my mother's voice in my ear. *You never listen, Che,* she would say. *You never slow down long enough to really listen.* So I make up a series of my little mnemonics to help myself keep it clean. Becca broods but Jean is genteel. I dare not ask Claire if that's her real hair, and Silvia sits in the sun. Our host is Tess, no more, no less.

From the end of the table vile Valerie speaks up again. "You asked us how much we wanted to make this trip about *The Canterbury Tales*, right? Does that mean you expect us to tell stories as we walk?"

"I don't expect you to do anything, but storytelling is certainly an option," Tess says. "Some groups enjoy it."

"I like the idea," says Claire, and there are nods of agreement from around the table. "But how do we decide what sort of stories to tell?"

"Chaucer's pilgrims told romances," Tess said. "They challenged each other to see who could best articulate the nature of true love."

"Love," I hear myself blurt out. "Are you sure we want to spend the whole trip talking about that?"

"Your stories can be about whatever you choose," Tess says. "I'm just describing the tradition. And of course, in Chaucer's time they were talking about courtly love, which is quite different from what we think of as love today. Courtly love was a bit—I suppose 'forbidden' is one way to say it. Forbidden love."

Forbidden Love sounds like one of those romances you only buy online, for your Kindle, because you can't bear the thought of someone seeing the cover. I think I know what Tess is really getting at—there was a lot of adultery in *The Canterbury Tales*—but most of the other women look confused, so Tess takes a dainty sip of beer and tries again to explain. "Courtly love was spiritualized and pure but always thwarted in some way. The object of your desire was married to another, or not of your social class. Perhaps they were even dead. But the point is that your great love was somehow unreachable, so you are doomed to worship them from afar, knowing that your passion would never be consummated."

"Depressing," mutters the Athlete, licking a fingertip and picking up a fleck of olive from her plate. "Why bother to play a game you can't win?"

Tess smiles. "It does sound rather dark, doesn't it? But the medieval mind was already—well, some might say it was already clouded by an unhealthy preoccupation with religion, with realms both above and below. So Chaucer and his pilgrims were ripe for an obsession with the unattainable."

"But weren't some of the stories in *The Canterbury Tales* dirty?" I say. "All this stuff about belching and farting and affairs with the neighbor's wife?" I got this off Google, the same place where I picked up that Harry Bailey was the name of the host, but the other women are openly staring at me now. I showed up late and I hate true love and I know way too much about Chaucer, that seems to be the general consensus of the table.

Tess nods. "Exactly so. Yes. Right again. As they sat together in this inn, or one very much like it, the pilgrims may have made a pledge to tell tales of courtly love. But once they got on the trail and began walking and talking and getting to know each other, all sorts of stories came out. Some rather surprising and . . . yes, bawdy, just as Che says."

"Bawdy," Jean says thoughtfully, as if she's unsure what the word means.

"Well, I like the idea," says Valerie, making an ineffectual attempt to fluff her matted hair. She's evidently one of those people who thinks that if she keeps repeating herself, her opinion might count as two votes. "We can tell whatever stories we want. How people get through . . . Oh, you know, all of it. Love. Death. Having the rug pulled right out from under you just when you think you're set. How you keep your heart alive in the middle of this fucked-up world. You know, everything."

The 6:42 express to Canterbury is sounding better by the minute.

Becca's lips are pushed into a pout. "I don't know why the stories have to be so heavy," she says. "There's nothing wrong with just telling a simple love story, is there?"

"Of course there isn't," her mother says. "But in the original

Chaucer, wasn't there some kind of bet?" Everyone is nodding. We've all read the same Wikipedia articles.

"More of a contest," Tess says. "The host declared that the pilgrim who told the best tale would be treated to a feast at the expense of the others when they returned from Canterbury."

"Then let's do that," says the Athlete, whose name I still can't recall. "I love contests."

"Who won?" asks another woman. This is the first time I've heard her speak. She's small, and her hair is as black as if someone has drawn it on with a Magic Marker. She has a rough voice that echoes Jersey, or Long Island, or maybe one of the lesser boroughs, a voice that brings to mind mobsters and pasta and TVs sold from the back of a van. Something about her seems familiar, although maybe I'm just thinking that I know her type. "In the real book, I mean."

"No one won," Tess says. "They never reached Canterbury because Chaucer abandoned the tales halfway through." She wrinkles her nose. "Some say he died. Others say he just got tired of the project and switched to other work. Either way, most of the pilgrims' stories went untold."

"Then it's decided," says Claire, and I think she's smiling, but her face is so taut that it's hard to tell. "We will each share a story, and I think we should follow the example of the original pilgrims and challenge ourselves to explore the nature of love. Tess will judge which one of us comes closest to the mark. Must the stories be true?"

"She's hoping the answer is yes," says Silvia, and I swear that when she throws back her head and laughs, she all but whinnies. "Go ahead, darling. Tell them how many husbands you've had."

"Just four," says Claire, her tone kind of coy and teasing. It's the kind of voice most women save for when they're talking to men, not each other, but I don't think she can help herself. She reminds me of Diana. Seduction is her default mode. It's like she has some sort of sexual Tourette's. "Is that a lot?"

It's four more than I've had, but Silvia isn't finished. "And tell them how old your present boyfriend is."

"Age isn't an issue between us," Claire says airily, so evidently he's a freaking child.

"I don't think we should say the stories have to be true," says Jersey. "I think we should say they can either be like reality or we can make them up, or it can be a little bit of both, and it's the teller's choice. Whatever she wants."

Becca glances at her mother and her mouth gives a little twist. I can't quite read her expression, but there's some problem brewing between them. Of course, there's always something brewing between a teenage girl and her mother, the only question is what. Maybe they've argued at some point about the suitability of a particular boy—or perhaps they've argued about the suitability of a girl. It's hard to say. Becca has an androgynous look, a sort of carefully calculated rebelliousness, but I imagine that's typical of girls her age, so I'm probably reading this part all wrong.

"I'd be happy to serve as judge," Tess says. "So here are the rules. The stories don't have to be true, or autobiographical. And yes, the nature of love is a worthy theme, but don't imagine that all the stories must be romantic, or noble. You might tell a tale of the most foolish thing you've ever done for love, or one in which the lovers give up everything for each other, or even one in which they never meet. And since our time together terminates in Canterbury, the winner shall be declared there and treated to a marvelous dinner by the others. I know just the place." Her voice and manner are that of a teacher giving an assignment, and when she finishes, I almost expect her to clap her hands. "Shall we draw lots to see who goes first?"

"I've never understood that term," Valerie says, probably speaking for us all. "What are lots and how do you draw them?"

"Shortest straw?" asks the Athlete.

"No," says Tess, "for that implies the loser goes first, and the right to tell the opening story of the journey is a great honor. You shall all draw cards. Highest begins."

With this, she extracts a blue silk bundle from the backpack at her feet, which, when unwrapped, reveals an oversize and elaborately decorated deck of cards. It looks nearly medieval itself, the figures hand-drawn and faded, and I wonder what else Tess has in that pack. Leading these tours must require the host to be a veritable Mary Poppins, able to entertain, instruct, and comfort at a moment's notice.

The deck goes around the circle, each woman selecting a card. I look at mine under the corner of the table, surprised to find that my heart is beating a bit faster. I don't want to go first. It seems like too much responsibility, as if the first story might set the tone for our entire pilgrimage. But I wouldn't want to go last either, so I'm relieved to get an eight of hearts. Right in the middle of the lineup and thus probably safe.

"Now turn them," says Tess.

The cards turn. The winner/loser is Jean, who has pulled the queen of diamonds. It seems appropriate to her, just as I suppose a middling amount of love is appropriate to me.

But Jean is unfazed. "This is easy," she says. "I can tell the story of my husband. Because I was married to the perfect man."

Well, that's quite a statement. It seems to strike the whole group mute for a moment and it's the sort of remark that implies way more than it explains. The fact she said "was married" instead of "am married" proves she's no longer with this man . . . and since she's proclaimed him to be perfect, divorce isn't likely. Jean must be a widow, and judging by the calmness with which she has spoken, this is not a fresh wound. Her husband died years ago, that's my guess, which means not only that Becca is the daughter of a perfect man but she was half-orphaned sometime during her childhood or early adolescence. No wonder she seems so angry. The oldest, the only girl, her most likely family ally lost just when she needed him most.

"You're talking about your first husband?" asks Claire.

"My only husband," Jean says firmly, and Claire frowns, as if wondering how such a thing is possible.

"But the rest of you are married?" she persists, looking around the table, and I realize we're all trying to define each other as quickly as possible, based on whatever criteria leaps to mind. For Claire the primary distinction seems to be among those who are married and those who are not, and I feel the customary tightness in my chest that I always get whenever the M-word arises. The assumption is that everyone gets married sooner or later, even the doughiest and dullest and most hopeless. The people you see walking around Walmart at three in the morning usually have someone with them.

As it turns out, Silvia in the sun is married and so is the black Athlete. Tess and Becca are single, but it's okay because they're young. Claire has been to the altar a hundred times, that's been established, and the Queen of Jersey says, "I'm married," and then adds "more or less." So there's a story there—I guess we'll hear it soon enough—and Valerie says, "I'm a spinster." Of course she would say "spinster." Of course she would claim the most loaded possible word, all Quaker and Amish and witchy, and she would furthermore say it ironically. Making sure we all know she's chosen this lesser-taken path, which we understand being a spinster is hip.

They look at me next, so I blurt out, "I was married once, but so long ago that it's like it hardly happened."

It's a good lie. I know, because I've told it many times before and no one has challenged me. People are comfortable with divorcées, far more comfortable than they are with the spinsters of the world, and I've now been evoking the ghost of this discarded husband for at least ten years, ever since I rounded the bend of thirty-five and being single suddenly began to feel abnormal. I've given him a name, Michael. A height, "shorter than me," and a profession, architect, sometimes even adding, "He worked on big public buildings like airports, that sort of thing."

"So shall we settle our bill of fare?" says Tess. "A van is waiting outside to drive us to our first inn and tomorrow, bright and early, we will begin the trail."

Bill of fare. Love it. So British, so old-fashioned and cute.

This is what we're paying for. There are murmurs of agreement all around, credit cards being produced, scarves being retrieved, the scrape of chairs being pushed back. A hum in the air. A sense of departure. Should I throw in my lot with this group of women? For we've come truly to the point of no return, I suppose. If I'm going to catch the train to Canterbury on my own, I should leave now. If I'm going to the airport, and back to America, then I should have left thirty minutes ago. I look around the table. A companion is someone with whom you eat—a rather random and not particularly high standard of friendship, but what the hell. If history has taught us anything, it's that no woman should journey to Canterbury alone.

JUST AS Tess promised, a van is waiting for us, parked in an alley behind the George, near a Dumpster in a position that is undoubtedly illegal. The young man leaning against it looks like a hood. Pimply and lanky, a cigarette dangling from his lips. But the moment he sees Tess approaching, all of us behind her dragging our bags and packs over the cobblestones, he straightens up and flings the cigarette to the side, suddenly all pep and service. There's an art to loading this many suitcases, ranging from a stylish bag with LOUIS VUITTON emblazoned on the side, probably Claire's, to a nearly shredded military-style knapsack, probably Becca's. But the young man gets them all wedged in with a practiced ease.

Fitting in the women proves trickier. We hesitate at the door of the van, no one quite willing to go first. I want to redeem myself as a good sport, so I step up and struggle my way to the back row, with the Athlete right behind me and Valerie, still chattering, trailing her. The black-haired Queen of Jersey takes the seat in front of us, along with Jean and her daughter, leaving Claire and Silvia in the best position, beside the door and only two to a row. Tess slides in the passenger seat beside the driver, who has been introduced as Tim.

Valerie wants to talk. She wants to know where I've come from, why I joined them at the last minute, what brings me to Canterbury. My initial scan of the situation has convinced me she's pretty much the last one I want to befriend and God knows how long we're going to be wedged in this van. So to discourage her I say I want to read my email before we leave the city. It isn't totally a lie. Just as I said back in the George, I suspect phone service will be spotty in the country, so this may be my last chance to check in for days. I should text something to Ned and at least let him know that we won't be talking tomorrow. I'm responsible like that, even when I've just been dumped.

But when I wiggle my purse up to my lap, I can't find my phone. I dig systematically through every compartment in the bag, my panic slowly rising with each zipper I pull and pouch I explore. And then the mental image pops in my head. Me putting the phone down on the bar beside the closely cropped man when I signed my bill. I must not have picked it up again.

"I've left my phone," I call out. "I think it's back in the bar."

This is a minor-league disaster, of course. We have edged from the parking lot and are on a city street, our journey underway. Who knows how hard it will be to change direction on these small, confusing, one-way roads and wind our way back to the George. And I'm in the worst possible part of the van to climb out, the left-hand seat in the very back. Five or six women will have to move to set me free. I've already joined them late, with my weird name and bad attitude, and now I'm starting off the trip by being a mondo pain in the ass.

"Use mine," says the Athlete, slipping her backpack to her lap, and managing the transfer far more smoothly than I did. "Call the restaurant and see if they have it."

"Are you sure? Roaming is expensive."

"No problem. I bought one of those programs with unlimited travel minutes." As she unzips her backpack to take out the phone, I glimpse the undeniable glint of a gold Godiva chocolate box, nearly hidden in the folds of a scarf. So that's her formula. Order a salad when you're in public and pick at it in the most ostentatious manner, giving little side lectures on antioxidants and organic farming as you go, making sure everyone at the table understands you're a paragon of health and self-control. But then at night, alone and in bed, I bet she hits the Godiva and hits it hard.

The Athlete pauses for a minute, as if she is as surprised to find the candy box there as anyone, then hands me her phone. "Go ahead," she says. "I have unlimited time. Really."

Tess calls back the number of the George and I type it in, but it's busy. I try again. Busy again.

"I'm so sorry about this," I call up to the front of the van, but Tess is chirpy. She knows her job.

"It's easier to turn back than to wait for the line to clear," she says over her shoulder and then she murmurs a few low words to the driver and the other women hasten to assure me it's no big deal, we'll just pop right back. It's too early in the trip for any of us to be rude to each other, or even honest, and when Tim stops the van in the street dead in front of the George, everyone is cheerful about climbing out and making way for me.

I'm breathless when I get to the door of the pub, my heart pounding, my mind already racing. Everything I need to function in the world is in that phone. Contact information for everyone I work with, my plane reservation back home, my bank accounts, my compass and camera and bills and music and games and step counter. If I lose that phone, I will be utterly adrift. It will almost be like I never existed.

The laconic bartender is still in the exact position where I left him, leaning against the wall, arms folded. I spew out my story. Describe the phone, with its vineyard-themed cover, the picture of Freddy on the screen. Point out where I was sitting. Mention the man who had dined beside me, who I had the sense was somewhat of a regular. But there is no phone. He looks beneath the bar and in the back to make sure, even goes to talk to the hostess, but returns empty-handed.

"How can it just be missing?" I ask him. I can hear how shrill my voice is. I am right on the cusp of screaming. "What in the name of God am I supposed to do now?"

He leans back against the altar of liquor, his arms once again crossed over his chest. "You could buy a new one," he says.

"You don't understand. It isn't the phone itself. It's what was on it. My whole world was in that phone. I'm not even sure how I'll get back to America now."

He shakes his head. "No need to panic, miss. You can't really lose anything anymore, not the way they have it all fixed today. Everything you need is in the cloud."

"It's just that . . . are you sure you didn't see it?"

"Here you go," he says, reaching into his shirt pocket. "Use mine and call yourself."

"But roaming charges . . ."

"Quite all right. No one will answer. We're just listening for the tone, aren't we?"

Good point. I struggle for a moment to remember my number and then thumb it in. The phone rings . . . and rings. My ringtone is church bells, and I'm not sure why. Perhaps it was the default mode and I never bothered to change it. The young man turns down the sound system behind the bar and he and I both listen, intently, for church bells.

No luck. I hear the click and then my own voice on the outgoing message starting and I hang up. The bartender shrugs. "So it would seem to be gone, eh miss? Poor luck."

"Yeah," I say. "Exactly. Poor luck."

FOUR

For the first night of the trip we stay in a little town near the start of the trail, which has a carved wooden statue dedicated to the Canterbury pilgrims in the village square. The next morning we all take turns posing beside it, our walking staffs in hand. My camera was on my phone, so I have to rely on the others for my shot.

The two pilgrims in the statue have differing facial expressions. One of them is solemn and sorrowful, his gaze lowered to the ground, while the other's head is thrown back with a knowing smirk. The carving is relatively new, according to Tess, so I suppose the figures are meant to represent a contemporary view on why various pilgrims might have taken to the trail. For some it was a mission of penitence, and for others, more of a spring break road trip—an excuse to get the hell out of town for a while, the proverbial change of scenery, a chance to drink, carouse, or bed a wench from another village.

The Athlete's name has turned out to be Steffi. She takes my picture when my turn comes and promises to email it to me. I have no doubt that she's the kind of woman who will do exactly whatever she says she will do, but we haven't yet set a foot on the trail, and she's already getting on everyone's nerves. She keeps peppering Tess with questions about how far we will walk today, how much elevation we will gain, and our approximate pace per hour. She has one of those Fitbit things strapped to her wrist and she consults it every few minutes, even though Tess has patiently explained that exercise is not what this particular walk is about.

"Each group must find its own pace," Tess says, "and the first day out is always a bit of an experiment. I'll be able to give you a greater sense of the numbers this evening, when I see how far we've come."

It's a rather incomplete explanation. This is Monday, and we know we have five days to walk the trail before a pilgrim blessing awaits us in Canterbury Cathedral at three o'clock Saturday afternoon. Not to mention that our nights in various inns have been prearranged along the route. In order to meet those obligations, it would seem that Tess would have to have some sense of how far and fast we will walk. Steffi jumps on the discrepancy at once.

"So you adapt the route based on the speed of the group," she says, her voice disapproving. Even a little frantic, like I imagine mine was when the bartender back in London told me he couldn't find my phone. "If you can see that we're slow, you cut off part of each day's walk, is that how it works? So you're saying there's a chance we won't see it all?"

In the past eighteen hours I've learned not only that Steffi is black and female, which of course is obvious, but also that she's a doctor whose specialty is heart disease in women. *She's used to fighting,* I think. *Used to taking every step along the path, climbing every hill, and it chaps her ass to no end to think there's something out there somewhere that we might miss. Even if what we miss is just a few miles of farmland that look precisely like all the others.*

I start to say something, to tell her not to worry about it, that walking fifteen miles a day isn't any more likely to purify your soul or challenge your body than walking ten, but then I stop myself. I'm still the outsider. And not just because I missed the opening lunch at the George, but because I missed dinner last night as well. By the time we'd gotten there and unloaded the van it had been nearly dusk, and the fact that I'd flown the red-eye the night before had caught up with me. I'd begged off of joining the others in the pub, and climbed the narrow stairs to my small, nunlike room, my suitcase clanging behind me with every step.

I'd snatched a banana from a basket on the registration desk but when I sat down on the bed to eat it, I saw that it was dusty. Perfect. Evidently that fruit was intended as decoration, not as an invitation for the guests of the inn to randomly pillage. In fact, by fishing a banana from the bottom of the bowl I may have messed up the symmetry. Maybe the whole arrangement was now off balance, with apples and pears tumbling to the floor left and right. *Crazy bloody Americans,* the innkeepers were undoubtedly thinking. *If we don't lock them in their rooms at night, they'll probably eat the shrubbery off the lawn.*

I showered and put on my nightgown, exhausted but with the sense I'd have trouble falling asleep. Normally I use my phone to wind myself down at night, reading articles from links on Twitter, checking email, playing Angry Birds. When I'd gone to the window and looked out from my high little room, I could see the whole village, such as it was, with a smoky autumn dusk settling over the town. A single human was visible: the vicar, walking from the church in his robes, weaving his way among the listing tombstones. And I wondered how I'd come to be here, in this place I hadn't even known existed until a couple of hours before. How I had found myself surrounded by strangers, with no clear way back to the airport or America or anything real, and as I looked at the village it had suddenly struck me that, without my phone, I couldn't even call for help. The only thing I might have done was open the window and scream . . . but there was no one to hear me but the vicar and I had no idea what sort of assistance a vicar could provide.

A cat was there too. He'd come to the window and was looking at me with exasperation, pushing at the panes of glass with his paw. Evidently I was in his favorite room. I cracked the window open—no screens—and he slid silkily through, then claimed his place on the lumpen little bed. *Okay*, I thought. *Here's what I don't have. I don't have a mother, or a lover, or a phone, or any fucking clue of why I'm here, where I'm going next, or what any of this means. But I do have a cat and a dusty banana and a vicar across the way, so let's see what comfort I can derive from these small certainties.* And maybe I could read. I could hold a book in my hands. If memory served, the feel of a book was generally quite soothing. I'd passed a bookcase on the landing, halfway up, crammed full of whatever had been left by the inn's former guests, the titles pointing this way and that.

So I'd crept halfway back down the stairs and looked through the abandoned paperbacks, finally choosing a techno-thriller with a screaming black and silver cover, the sort of thing I would never read at home. And sure enough, along with the purrs of the cat, the book put me right to sleep. In fact, it was the best night of rest I've had in as long as I can remember and I needed it, although now in the light of day, the other women are all chatting easily among themselves and I'm the one who still isn't sure of their names.

"Jean has the first story," Tess is saying to Steffi, who seems nearly panicked at the thought that there is some field some-where in England we're not going to tromp through. "So she will be the one continually walking and talking, which can be rather draining, even for someone who is fit. It's hard to say what rhythm she will fall into, and the one who tells the story is the one who establishes the speed of the group. That's an unbreak-able rule of Canterbury—that the listeners adapt to the story-teller, and that each story demands its own pace. For listening is a bit like a dance, isn't it? You move to the music of the mo-ment. I'm sure you understand."

"I'm sure you understand" is what you say to people who clearly don't, but as she speaks, Tess glances pointedly from Steffi to Jean. Jean knows how to dress for her body, so she looked slim enough yesterday in the George, but now, in boots and pants and the harsh light of day, it's obvious she's heavier than she first appeared. In other words, Steffi is just going to have to get a grip on herself. With Jean as our storyteller, we're not going to be breaking any land speed records this first morning.

"And we won't walk single file," Tess says, this time turning to speak to the whole group. "If we march in a straight line, like good little soldiers, the one in the front won't be able to hear the one in the back, and vice versa. So we shall travel like true pilgrims, walking abreast."

Great. Now the Broads Abroad are the Broads Abroad Abreast. The furrow in Steffi's brow deepens. She's probably thinking that walking in a clump will slow us up even more. She'd be better off unclipping that Fitbit right now and flinging it into whatever cosmic black hole has sucked up my iPhone. Otherwise she's going to spend the entire trip in torment.

"And the route won't be especially picturesque until we're farther out from the city and the landscape opens up," Tess continues, speaking as if we're walking out of New York. The town seems utterly picturesque to me, kind of like the front of a jigsaw puzzle box. But Tess is pointing into the distance, toward a vista of rolling hills in colors of sage and moss and gold. The light is already beginning to grow slowly around us.

"I may walk in circles around the group so I can keep up my pace," says Steffi. "Promise you'll speak up if anyone finds that irritating."

And so we start. We move down the sharply pitched road that leads from the town toward the fields, our boots skidding a little in the pebbles. Becca hangs back and I find myself dropping a bit away from the clump of women too, falling in step with her.

"Don't you want to hear your mother's story?" I ask, even though I know it's a loaded question. Diana's ashes are jostling along with me in the backpack. I debated keeping the ziplock bag in the suitcase and sending it ahead with Tim to the next inn down the trail, but then decided that to do so would be to defeat the whole point of the trip. She wanted to walk to Canterbury, not ride in a van to Canterbury, so it would seem that her remains must come along with me, pressed into their own little pouch.

Becca shoots me a sour look. "I've heard it."

I bet you have, I think, because I realize, maybe more than the others, that whatever we're about to hear from Jean is not a spontaneously told story, but a tale that she has recited many times to many listeners, a narrative that has been polished and sharpened through the years. This is why Jean was not alarmed at the idea of going first. She's more than ready. And Becca has heard it all so many times before that she's gone numb to the meaning. The girl has long ceased to be able to distinguish fact from fantasy in her mother's pet stories, even if they're about events she herself witnessed, even if the events happened to Becca as much as they happened to Jean. My mother collected family legends too—stories of how my parents came to Aunt Letitica's orchard and cleared the land, stories of how my father built the first cider press with coat hangers and the shell of a broken washing machine. The pond in the back, so bountiful that sometimes fish leapt unprompted into rowboats. How much I loved that pond, how I could swim before I could walk. Could I really swim before I could walk? Did the fish really leap into rowboats? Does it matter?

Most families have their official stories, I imagine, and they tell them to each other over and over, each repetition reassuring both the speaker and the listeners that the world is an understandable place. I suppose you could even argue that the very act of telling a story is an act of faith, for it advances the belief that life truly has a beginning, middle, and end. The belief that we're all headed somewhere, that the seemingly random events of our lives mean something, that tomorrow will be more than just a repeat of yesterday, all over again.

"Here's the gate," says Tess, as we step off the country road and turn toward an open field. A small blue tile nailed to the fence shows a stick man walking with a staff and a pack on his back. Google was right. A trailhead like this would be easy to miss.

"So this is where the official route to Canterbury begins?" Steffi asks, her voice doubtful. I think we were all expecting something more.

"Our feet are now on the path," Tess says as we step, one by one, over the muddy ditch and through the gate. She nods at Jean. "So begin whenever you wish."

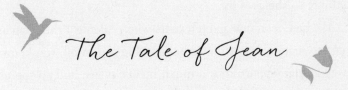

The Tale of Jean

"My father didn't think Allen was good enough for me," Jean says. "That's where it all starts. Maybe that's where all love stories start. Daddy could be like that—critical, always measuring everyone around him, and so of course Allen was determined to do what he could to prove him wrong. He said he would provide for me and the kids, provide not just adequately but spectacularly, that's what he always said. That he would not be content until our children went to the best schools and I didn't have to work and we lived in a house . . . in the sort of house that even my father would have to acknowledge was a fine place."

But here she pauses, as if doubting herself already. "Of course it wasn't just that. I don't want you to think Allen was some sort of workaholic, one of those men who rose at dawn and left with a briefcase. He was always there for us, especially on Sundays. Those were our family days. Isn't that true, Rebecca?"

"This is your story, Mom."

"So it is. But where do you start the story of a marriage? I could tell you how we met. It was on a boat, on one of those cruises around New York Harbor, which is silly, but if I go back that far we will be halfway to Canterbury before we finish the first story, and that won't do, will it?" Jean pushes back a strand of her golden hair with a nervous little titter, but no one says anything, so she goes on.

"We had been married ten years when Allen got the chance to go to Guatemala with his company. He was in oil, you know. It was a huge opportunity, a much higher salary, and on top of that there was an additional cost-of-living stipend that they paid anyone willing to live out of the country for eighteen months or longer. The stipend was so generous we knew we could bank virtually all of his salary. This was our chance, and you don't get many. He knew it and so did I. Most of the men didn't take their families with them on these assignments, or at least not those going to Central America. Guatemala could be unpredictable in those days, especially if you got away from the tourist areas. Americans were often the target of kidnappers, and we had heard of one family . . . Well, we knew the people, actually, at least in a social sense, and they had a daughter, just fourteen . . ."

"Skip that part, Mom," Becca says. "No one needs to hear it."

"You're right. It's a dreadful story. Suffice to say Guatemala was not always safe for Americans who were known to be rich, and all Americans were rich by Guatemalan standards. Allen wanted me to stay in Houston with the kids, but I couldn't bear the thought we'd be separated for so long, that the children would only see their father two or three times a year." She sighs. "So it was all my fault in a way, you see, everything that happened while we were down there. Because I was the one who insisted we pack up and go with him. Even the dog. Even Taffy. He was supposed to be for the boys, this big bounding golden retriever. But he always slept on your bed, do you remember, Rebecca?"

Becca doesn't answer. She's evidently thrown in the towel. Decided to force her mother to tell this guilty tale on her own, for better or for worse.

Jean lets a beat pass, then continues. "We had so much to take and we had the dog, so we drove. It took forever and it seemed with each mile of road we put behind us that we were leaving more of the world we once knew. I think I began to realize, somewhere in the southern part of Mexico, that it might have been a mistake. It always works like that, doesn't it? You get these little glimmers now and then that you've lost your way, that you've somehow gotten on the wrong road, but by the time you realize it . . . there was no turning back. I'd pulled the children out of school, leased the house. Everything we owned was in that U-Haul."

She pauses midstride and automatically we all match her rhythm, stopping to adjust our backpacks, bending to pull wrinkles out of our socks. We've walked just long enough to realize what's chafing, which of our clothing or packing choices may have been a mistake.

"But that's what makes a marriage a marriage, right?" Valerie says. "What holds it together? Doesn't every couple get to a point somewhere in Mexico and you realize it would be even more trouble to turn back than it is to go forward?"

She's probably right. It sounds right. But none of the married women say anything and the silence just sits there like a brick. Finally Valerie shrugs. "I'm only guessing," she says. "I'll always be single . . ."

Okay, another beat. Another awkward moment, all of us standing in a circle, facing each other for once, scratching and stretching and drinking water, and here out of nowhere Valerie feels compelled to announce not just that she's single—which puts her in the same category as me and probably several of the others—but that she'll always be single. That's completely different, and a rather extraordinary thing to say. Such a matter-of-fact closing of a door, and marriage is a door that sooner or later almost everyone walks through.

Maybe she's gay, I think. *I should try to like her better.*

But Jean has bristled at Valerie's comment. "I never seriously entertained the notion of turning back," she says, a bit snappishly, as we all re-heft our packs and resume the trail. "I had made the decision to follow my husband and that's not the sort of commitment a woman breaks. And besides, Guatemala turned out to be wonderful in its own way, at least when we first got there. We had a bigger house, much larger than the one in Texas, almost an estate, really. The owners before us had named it Paradiso Blanco, and there was all sorts of security. There was even a school within the American enclave, although there weren't many children and I don't think the kids liked it much. They missed their friends back home, and I missed mine, but we did have the servants. Five of them, counting the chauffeur."

Suddenly, out of nowhere, she laughs. "When I say it that way, it all sounds very grand, doesn't it? Like we were characters in a movie with a cook and a gardener and both an upstairs and downstairs maid and of course Antonio, the driver. He's the one I'll always remember best because he was always with us. Allen said it wasn't safe for me to drive. So I didn't, and when I finally got back to Texas, it was almost as if I'd forgotten how. I remember sitting in a car that first time, sitting there in the driver's seat behind the wheel. It had been two years, maybe a little more, and for a second I couldn't even remember how to crank it. I hadn't truly forgotten, of course. Driving is such an automatic thing, like swimming or breathing, but at first . . . well, the point is that Guatemala was a different world, and there was good and bad in that. Allen left every morning after breakfast with the driver and then Antonio would come back and take the kids to their little school. He had to drive them, even though it was just down the street. The level of fear was that high, you see, and then Antonio would return again, in case there was someplace I wanted to go."

Another pause. Her face is red and she is panting gently.

The chore of walking and talking has taken something out of her, just as Tess predicted it might do. Jean is a woman who unravels easily, I think. The sort of woman who might come completely apart if you found a certain thread and pulled it.

"Of course," Jean says, regaining her poise, "the trouble with Antonio waiting on me is that there was never anyplace to go or anything to do. Five servants sounds like a fine thing, until you have five servants. So I flitted around the house all day and then somehow, at some point, I heard of a church that was doing a ministry in the dump. For there are these enormous garbage piles, you see, in the cities of Central America, and people actually live in them. Whole families, from grandparents to infants, and it's appalling, but that's how they live, scavenging among the garbage for food and clothes, anything they can use for shelter. This church had plans for a clinic and a school."

"Mom," Becca says sharply. "That isn't part of the story."

"Isn't it? I'm not so sure. Because that's something else I blame myself for. Everyone warned me that it was dangerous to work with the ministry. The other women who lived in the enclave tried to tell me. *You go through those gates,* they'd say, *and you take your chances. If there's anything you need from the outside, can't you just send your driver?* For some reason they never suffered with the isolation like I did. They were happy with the situation, or at least happy enough, and they played bridge and had dinner parties and changed clothes three or four times a day. You would have thought we were living in one of those British manor houses in an Agatha Christie mystery—you know, one of those books which start out so peaceful and then someone gets knifed? But the point is that the other wives were far more clever than I was. They found ways to fill their days. Are there manor houses near here, Tess?"

"A few," Tess says. "Old family estates."

"And are they lovely?"

"We could stop at one if you like. There won't be much to see in the gardens this time of year, I'm afraid."

"I would very much like to tour the gardens."

"Come on, Mom, focus," Becca says. "You've been talking for twenty minutes and nobody has the slightest freakin' idea what this story is even about."

"It's about how I killed my husband," says Jean. "Or rather, how he died trying to protect me. Me and Rebecca and the boys."

"That's not what happened, Mom."

"Of course it is. Where was I? Where in the story, I mean."

"You found yourself in a land that managed to be simultaneously dangerous and boring," Tess says gently. She must be used to prompting people in their stories, used to nudging them back onto the trail of the narrative when they have wandered off.

"And it was all my fault," Jean says, blinking back tears. "Allen knew from the start that the kids and I shouldn't come with him, that a family like us would be a target. But yet there I was every morning, traipsing around the trash dump dispensing gloves and cartons of milk and these bizarre comic-book Bibles. They had the strangest and most distorted images of Christ. I remember thinking that they had drawn him to look like an Incan, all short and squat and actually rather frightening . . ."

"Don't blame yourself," someone says. I turn my head to look. Silvia, squinting into the distance as always, looking past us to something only she can see. "Those people had nothing, and you were just trying to help."

"Yes, trying to help, trying to give the kids milk and trying to give myself something to do," Jean says. "I was hardly Mother Teresa. Because that's what originally drew them to us, you see, the sight of our stupid limo going back and forth between Paradiso Blanco and the dump. The license plate was 487, I remember that too. The Americans always had low numbers. No, volunteering with this church was just one more thing I did wrong, one more thing that caught their eye. Or maybe they would have found us anyway. We had the driver, of course, and the children are all so blonde . . ."

All the children used to be blonde, I think, looking at Becca's shock of Crayola-colored hair. The girl is right—her mother's story is rambling and nonsensical and yet my heart is pounding slightly and not just with the effort of getting up that last hill. Tess's promise has come true . . . now that we are a couple miles out of the village, the land has opened up around us. The world seems bigger, as if God has exhaled, and the meadows stretch in every direction. Clumps of sheep graze here and there, but the land is otherwise empty, gone fallow with the season. There are no signs of human occupation. No houses or cars or power lines or farm machinery. It could be 1515 instead of 2015. There's nothing to place us in time except ourselves, our hiking boots and backpacks and shiny water bottles. And of course, Jean's story.

"There was a kidnapping attempt?" Tess says, still trying to coax Jean along.

Jean nods brusquely and makes an effort to pull herself together. "Of course, of course. Of course that's where this all has been going from the start. But it didn't happen the way you think. The attack wasn't against me or the children. They followed Allen instead, very late one night when he and Antonio were out in the car."

"Where were they going?" Jersey girl asks. The short one with the coal-black hair and surprised eyebrows, Angelique, they call her, and I must find a way to remember that name. Angelique. She looks like an angel who has sprung a leak. I imagine her sputtering across the sky like a released balloon, making rude noises and doing loop-de-loops in midair. Not my best mnemonic image, but it will have to do.

"I was just getting ready to ask the same thing," Valerie says. "If the city was so dangerous, then why would your husband go out in the middle of the night?"

The question seems to pull Jean up short. "I really don't know," she finally says. "Allen often worked late. And his job took him all over the city. It's not like it is here . . . not like it is in America, I should say, or here either, probably." She fiddles with her scarf, which is tied at her neck bandana-style, even though it isn't a bandana. Even though it is silky and delicate and probably expensive. Jean's French twist is not so smooth today. We haven't been walking that long, and the knot of hair in the back is already half undone.

"We could slow down," Tess says, "or pull up entirely and have a proper rest, if anyone wants to. There's no schedule. No particular place we need to be and no particular time we have to arrive."

Jean shakes her head impatiently. "The minute you drove

through the gates of our enclave," she says, "you were thrust into immediate poverty. That's the part I don't think I'm explaining right, what I'm not helping you to see. Guatemala isn't like here or like America, where you have to work to get yourself into serious trouble. Down there, one thing is just smashed up against another. You could go from sanity to insanity within the course of a city block, from the school where my children wore their little blue uniforms to a street corner where a woman was trying to sell her baby. I don't know why Allen went out that night, not exactly. But he was far across the city, somewhere near a bridge . . ."

At the word "bridge" she falls silent and we walk a bit with no one talking. Steffi finally stops circling us like a border collie and pulls up breathless, ready to hear the end. *We've come to a bridge*, I think. *Now something is going to have to go off of it.*

"I'm afraid I've left out a piece of the story," Jean says. It seems to me she's left out a rather large piece—like the actual story—but she goes on. "When businessmen were robbed, which was a common event, the bandits would take their wallets. Not just for the money or for the credit cards, but so they would have their identification, with their addresses. And then they would know where they lived with their families. Sometimes other things were in the wallets too, like pictures of the children, or the wife. One man was even foolish enough to have written down all the security codes to his house and put the paper in his wallet. That's how they got that poor teenage girl. Her father had been robbed at gunpoint and within hours, while he was still down at the police station . . . even that quickly . . . even though it was still daylight when they came . . ."

"Seriously," says Becca sharply. She has sped up now, is walking slightly ahead of the clump, and she calls back to us over her shoulder. "I thought we agreed not to talk about the teenage girl."

"And so we won't," says Jean. "But my point is that back then, maybe ten or twelve years ago, if you had a man's wallet, you had his life. Much like phones are today." She looks at me apologetically as she says this, but I've already thought of everything that could happen. Already imagined whatever London thug swiped my phone happily going through my online banking accounts, draining one after the other, charging meth on my American Express. "And so Allen always said that no matter what happened, they would never get his wallet. He said that he would die before he gave up the wallet."

It's a funny thing about this story, I think. Jean claims she is telling it as a tribute to her late husband, and she furthermore has made the grand pronouncement that she will start off our trip by giving us an image of the perfect man. But nothing she has said so far has given me any sort of image of Allen at all. I can only conclude that he was the sort of person who tried to do the right thing. A man who would probably still be alive if he'd followed his original impulse and left his family back in Houston. Yet, beyond that, he is strangely absent from his own story—a shadow, someone who comes and goes at all hours in a limo with darkened windows. Faceless, voiceless, and I suspect that even his children remember him mostly for the money that he left behind.

"Two cars blocked off the bridge," Jean is saying. "One on one side and one on the other. I got all this from Antonio. They roughed him up a bit, but let him live. He was one of them. Once they had the car stranded over the water—and I knew that bridge, you know. I drove over it every day on my way to the dump. The water was so polluted, so full of . . . of things floating down the river. But that's where they stopped them and pulled Allen from the car. He gave them all his money, of course. He wouldn't have been that foolish. Antonio said he dropped it at their feet and said, 'Take everything. Just leave me in peace.' But when they reached for his wallet—"

"He threw it over the railing into the water," Becca says. "And they shot him right there on the bridge."

Her voice is dim and cold. It has the slap of finality. The cold dim slap of a wallet hitting the water beneath a Guatemalan bridge, ten years ago, very late at night.

"Yes, he threw the wallet and they rolled him off after it," Jean says, her own voice as dreamy as her daughter's is clear. It's like she's watching a movie in her mind. A movie she has seen many times, with dialogue she knows by heart. "It wasn't until the next day they recovered the body. But by then . . ."

We have stopped at the crest of a hill and she looks around, as if surprised to find herself surrounded by so much beauty, safe and secure in the middle of an English meadow. "We went back to the States as soon as we could. The insurance money was astounding. Much more than I would ever have dreamed. I remember that when they told me the amount, my head began to buzz. I was looking at the lawyer, who was saying that the payout would be double his normal policy because he'd been killed while on foreign assignment, but the buzzing drowned everything else out. His lips were moving but I couldn't hear him.

And the money from that insurance policy has kept us beautifully ever since. Even my father had to admit this. That Allen did a superb job of providing for his family, even from beyond the grave."

And there we have it. A tale of the perfect man. Rich and dead and utterly self-sacrificial. Jean's face is splotched with tears, but it strikes me that she's told us no more than the story of a redshirt in a Star Wars movie. A minor character who must die early so the plot can advance. I glance at the others, but it's hard to read their faces beyond the sort of polite respect that such sudden and violent widowhood would seem to demand. Becca's hood is pulled low, obscuring her eyes. The moment is awkward. We've come to the end of the first story, told by a woman eager to share it. Should we clap? As stories go, it seems like a bit of a failure, since I don't believe any of us is feeling the degree of emotion we expected to feel. *That teenage girl who can't be spoken of,* I think. *The one who was kidnapped, likely raped, and maybe murdered. She's the real story here.*

"Well, okay then," says Valerie, bringing her hands together in a loud, ringing clap. "One down, seven to go."

It's an extraordinarily glib remark under the circumstances and Silvia recoils as if she's heard a gunshot. I catch her eye. *This fat fool,* we both seem to be thinking. What's she doing here? What could Canterbury possibly hold for the likes of her? She will be the pilgrim among us who tells the story with all the farts and belches, that's for sure.

"I'm sorry," Angelique says to Jean, but it's hard to say whether she's sorry that Allen is dead or is just trying to cover up for Valerie's rudeness. The rest of us murmur things. Make cooing sounds, the sort of monosyllabic noises of sympathy that are expected after this sort of confession. We must sound like a chorus of birds.

The only one who seems utterly nonreactive to Valerie's crudity is Jean herself. "What are those?" she asks, pointing in the distance. "Those vine things all stacked to look like wigwams?"

"That's the remnants of the hops harvest," Tess says. "We'll see any number of them along the route. Hops and apples are the primary crops of the region. When we stop at the inn for lunch you will find plenty of beers on the menu that are brewed locally, if you'd like to try them."

"They're lovely, aren't they?" Jean says vaguely, staring down at the meadow before us, her tears still unwiped. "They don't quite seem real."

FIVE

Despite the fact that the main street of the next town seems deserted, the pub parking lot is nearly full. We make our way single file through what Tess calls "the smoking garden." A dozen men and a couple of women are huddled around picnic tables and plastic chairs, puffing away furiously.

"As you can see, the structure is humble," Tess says, making a sort of game-show gesture as we enter the small room. A bar at one end and a bar at the other, low ceilings, exposed beams. "But this is precisely the sort of place where Chaucer's pilgrims might have stopped along the route. Remember this room when you get your first glimpse of the Cathedral, and it will be easier to understand why everyone who saw it was so dazzled. Why the legend has remained so strong for so many years. Most of the people who traveled there had never even seen a building with two levels, so the grandeur of a place like Canterbury . . ."

She breaks off, and we all know what she's implying. We are modern women, accustomed to vaulted ceilings and wide doors, grand spaces encrusted with riches of every sort. Canterbury will not stun us as it stunned the original pilgrims. Mankind will never be quite so stunnable again.

"I bet we'll still be dazzled," Valerie says, choosing a chair at the end of the table, just as she did back at the George yesterday. "I bet the magic of Canterbury is just as strong as ever."

"The sticker on the door said they have wi-fi," Steffi whispers as soon as we're seated. "Which is hard to believe, considering we're about twenty-eight miles from nowhere. Do you want to use my phone to check your mail?"

The question is kindly meant. She's undoubtedly noticed that all morning I've been rifling my pockets for something that isn't there, as if I were suffering from an electronic version of phantom limb syndrome. Besides, she's already getting her own little fix, pressing the buttons on her Fitbit, calculating something or another. Her phone is just like mine, and as I pick it up, I see that her wallpaper is a handsome man, running across a finish line with his arms flung wide, evidently at the end of a road race. Of course. The husband would naturally be just as athletic as the wife. My fingers move automatically through the familiar sequence as I go to type in my password. My dog's name and my year of birth: freddy1967.

I have 119 emails.

119. How on earth could I have accumulated 119 emails since yesterday afternoon? But I guess normally I check them so frequently that they never get the chance to pile up past ten or so. I scan through the subject lines quickly, dragging my thumb across the glass. At least a dozen of them are from Ned. Ned, Ned, and more Ned. *Where are you?* asks the subject line, politely at first, and then he begins to scream his questions in

caps. *DAMN IT, WHERE ARE YOU?* And *SERIOUSLY, CHE, PICK UP THE DAMN PHO*

Pick up the damn pho. We aren't ordering Vietnamese takeout, so he must be calling me as well as emailing. I see another message, this one from Steffi, who is sitting beside me, grumbling as she calculates the numbers from the morning's walk. She's already forwarded the picture of me beside the Canterbury pilgrims, taken at 8:29 this morning. *I could send the picture to Ned,* I think. It's sort of an answer. It shows him that at least I'm still alive, but then again, an image of me standing beside some big wooden men, frowning uncertainly and clutching a walking staff, might muddy the waters even more. I know that my silence is only prolonging his worry, but maybe that's a good thing. Would it be such a crime to be unreachable, to hold my silence for just this once? I've never kept Ned guessing before. In fact, I don't think I've ever kept anyone guessing. I answer every question the minute it's asked, respond to emails and texts so fast that half the time I'm typing my response before the full message has even downloaded. People compliment me on my speed. I am known for my efficiency.

But speed and efficiency are the twin horses that have dragged me to this sad point in my life. I look around the table. Not a single woman is talking. No one has even picked up her menu. We are all checking messages, staring into the dark, slick waters of the Internet, hoping for some sort of sign.

I hand the phone back to Steffi.

"Nothing pressing?" she asks.

"Nothing that can't wait."

The menu is a folded piece of paper, no bigger than a grocery list. It reads:

> Large Cod
>
> Small Cod
>
> Cod Cakes
>
> Cod Salad

"I guess we're having cod," I say.

"We could make a musical out of it," Valerie says. "Bring it to Broadway. *The Ubiquitous Cod of County Kent.*"

Claire laughs.

Tess looks up from her own phone. "Personally, I'm having a jacket potato," she says. "They're always available at the rural inns, even though they don't bother putting them on the menu. And quiche, of course."

"What sort of quiche?" I ask, although I have a pretty good idea what the answer will be.

"Jacket potato?" Becca says. "Is that another word for a baked potato?"

As it turns out, you can get a baked potato stuffed with roast beef and cheese, which sounds simple and hearty and damn near unruinable. We order eight of them—Jersey rather surprisingly breaks rank and takes the cod—and then Valerie asks if it would be all right for us to have wine with lunch. Tess says of course, this is our vacation, we can have whatever we want. But of course there's no wine list, so Valerie disappears into a back room with the elderly waitress and reemerges a moment later with a whole bottle of—God save us—white zinfandel from California.

"Glasses for everyone," Valerie proclaims and the waitress creeps off to fetch a trayful of shot glasses. She pours a small amount of wine carefully into each one, and when the tray comes around I accept mine, because it would be rude not to.

"So all right then," says Tess, unwrapping the deck so that Jean can put the queen of diamonds back in. "Who's next?"

"I have the jack of clubs," Jersey says. Angelique, I think it is, or possibly Angelica? No, Angelique. Shit, I've forgotten already. Angelique. Angelique. The angel who has sprung a leak. Her hairline comes to a perfect peak. Angelique. I won't know her name at the end of the week.

"Brilliant," Tess says. "Can anyone beat a jack? No? Then that means Angelique is up on the afternoon segment."

"There's no telling what sort of story we're in for now," Steffi mutters under her breath as the women begin to lift their shot glasses and sip. I raise an eyebrow in question, and she whispers, "Seriously? You don't recognize her?"

I study Angelique. At some point in her life she must have submitted to the laser, for her face has been tattooed with permanent makeup—her upper eyelids are lined in black and her eyebrows are sketched into that high, exaggerated arch. Most disconcertingly of all, the shape of her lips has been traced in a dark brownish rose, but the lips themselves have not been filled in with color, which makes it almost look like she has a little spy mustache. Other than this, her face is bare. She is a sketch of a woman. A caricature you'd have done on vacation, drawn somewhere on a boardwalk or a dock, the more subtle details to be added later.

Steffi hands her phone back to me under the table and I look down to see she's googled the name Angelique Mugnaio. Of course. That's why she looked familiar. She's one of those reality TV stars on Bravo, the kind of low-wattage celebrity that's impossible to ignore, even for people who don't watch TV. She was on a show about prison wives—women married to mobsters, exploring how they pass the time while their husbands are in the big house for embezzlement, extortion, fraud, one of those things. *Godmothers,* is that what it's called? *Goodladies? The Mezzo-Sopranos?* The article says only that she parted ways with Bravo last month, but I can't imagine why. What would a woman have to do to get kicked off of a show that's nothing more than nonstop screaming and cursing and the turning over of tables? I wonder why she's here, and especially why she's alone. I didn't think people like Angelique went anywhere without a camera crew.

"What do you think of the wine?" asks Valerie.

The question is directed toward me, even though I've been discreet about what I do for a living. People get nervous if you tell them you're a wine critic. They begin to apologize about whatever they're drinking, or maybe they suddenly try to speak French. I pick the shot glass up and take a cautious sip. It's even worse than I would have imagined—like someone plunked a cherry cough drop into a cup of hot water—and I want to tell the women that true zinfandel is garnet-red and robust, not pink and weak and sweet like this crap. They do understand at least that much, don't they? But they probably don't understand that much, and most of them probably don't want to. They've lived perfectly good lives while drinking perfectly awful wines and I feel a sudden swoosh, a sense of air going through me, like wind whistling through a hollow tube. *I have a chance here,* I think. *A chance to reinvent myself in the midst of these women with all their martyred and incarcerated husbands, their white zinfandel and baked potatoes.*

I force myself to swallow the wine and nod my thanks to Valerie. She is my companion, after all.

"Che is an unusual name," Angelique is saying to me. "Were you named after the stadium?"

"It's not that kind of Shea," I say. I know what she's talking about, because I've heard that theory before. Angelique is looking at me with wide, trusting eyes. She must have been pretty, back in the days before she tried to make herself hot. There's a sweetness to her face that speaks more of homecoming queens than mobsters. God love her, as my Southern grandmother used to say. God bless her stupid little heart. "It's C-H-E. I'm named after a revolutionary. My parents were hippies."

"So what do you think of the wine, Che-who-was-named-for-a-revolutionary?" Valerie asks, a small smile playing around her lips. "It's pretty good, isn't it?"

Okay, so I really am being challenged. She saw I didn't want to drink it. Saw that I winced when I tried. Maybe she even googled me under the table while I was googling Angelique. Maybe she's seen the picture on my website, me toasting someone at a far distance, smiling broadly at an imaginary companion hovering just out of sight.

"Valerie, you must be the most easily pleased person I've

ever met," I say. "I think you must like just about everything on earth." It's the worst insult I can think to hurl at someone, but Valerie only smiles again.

"Thank you," she says. "I try very hard to."

The Tale of Angelique

"That damn cod's repeating on me," Angelique says with a burp. "I should have gone to the bathroom back at the inn."

"We can turn around," Tess says and I start to protest before I stop myself. Turning back after we're twenty minutes into the afternoon segment of our walk seems like an admission of failure, like we've broken some sort of Canterbury rule before we've even begun. And yet on the first day they turned back for me, did they not?

Angelique is already shaking her head. "I'll just find a bush," she says. "There's got to be some kind of bush on this goddamn path."

We contemplate the view, but the land we're walking through does not appear to be particularly bushy. It's another field of hops and a few minutes earlier Tess had paused at one of the piles and crushed a dying leaf in her hand. She had insisted that we all smell it in turn and then said, "When they call a beer 'hoppy,' this is what they mean." The leaf had an earthy, musty aroma I've encountered before in bars, or on the happy breath of men, but I had never known that it was precisely hops I was smelling, for I know nothing of beer, no more than Valerie knows about wine.

But now the smell of hops is with me for life. I have a decent palate, but an extraordinary nose—I like to tell people that it was my nose that led me to wine, and not my tongue. Once I have sniffed something I can never forget it, even if I try, and Ned used to tease me about having an olfactory version of a photographic memory. "Could you find me?" he'd asked, playfully lifting his arm and exposing the pit. "Could you pick me out if you were blindfolded and in a whole room full of naked, sweaty men?"

"Maybe . . . assuming that I wanted to," I'd said and he'd laughed because whenever I was flippant, he was always quick to laugh. It was one of our little brags, that we were both clever and both appreciative of the other's cleverness, but now I'm starting to see all that banter in a new light. Who did we think we were—characters in some Oscar Wilde play? Why did I never speak the truth—that of course I could have found him, no matter if he were lost among legions of men, and why did he never pull me onto his lap and tell me not to worry, that nothing could make him leave me in the first place? But we were always joking, speaking in shorthand. Even when one of us would say "I love you," the other one would say "Ditto," until we got to the point that all we would say was "Ditto." "Ditto," he would say at the airport on a Sunday afternoon, when I had pulled into a drop-off lane, him dragging his bag from the backseat and blowing me a kiss as he stepped onto the curb. "Ditto," I would call back, my gaze already fixed in the rearview mirror, already trying to figure out how to ease back into the flow of traffic.

"There we go," says Angelique, emerging from behind a

stack of hops, buttoning her jeans. "Not the Ritz, but hey, I've never been too good to take a crap outdoors."

"We could have turned back," Tess repeats faintly, but her professionalism stops her from saying what the rest of us are thinking: *So you didn't just pee, you crapped? Seriously? Right here on the Canterbury Trail behind some farmer's stack of hops?* "But now that you're feeling better, maybe you'd like to start your story."

"It isn't just my story," Angelique says with confidence. "It's everyone's story. I'm going to tell you girls a fairy tale."

Somehow I wouldn't have figured the Queen of Jersey for a fairy tale. "Once upon a time in a country far far away . . ." she begins, then stops. "Maybe this is really more of a myth," she says. "Yeah, a myth. My mother used to tell it to me when I was a little girl. This is the story of Psyche and Eros."

She pronounces "Psyche" with no accent on the *e,* so it was the same sound as if you said "I don't want to psych myself out." Tess is tolerant, tolerant enough to let some American mobster's wife take a shit right in the middle of a perfectly lovely British hops field, but even she can't stand for this. "It's 'Psyche' with an *e,*" she says. "*Psych-ee.*"

"*Psych-ee,*" Angelique repeats obediently, first to herself, and then out loud. "I guess Mama had it wrong." She doesn't seem offended at having her pronunciation publicly corrected. It's probably something that's happened to her a lot over the last few years, as she has risen from obscurity to Bravo TV fame.

"Anyways," she continues. "Once upon a time in a country far far away, a king had three daughters. The youngest one was called Psych-*ee* and she was so sweet and beautiful that all the other women in the kingdom were jealous of her. Her two sisters and even the goddess Aphrodite. In fact, Aphrodite was so jealous that she ordered her son Eros to make Psyche fall in love with the wrong man. The worst possible man. The one man on earth who would surely break her heart."

She pauses again, but this time for effect. She's aware that she has quickly captured everyone's attention, for who among us does not have an absolute wronger in her past? Who among us has not fallen under this particular curse of Aphrodite, doomed to ignore a dozen nice guys in pursuit of that one singular man who is destined to break our hearts?

"I think Mama told me this story because I was the youngest of three girls," Angelique says, which is a strange little flicker of insight for a woman so un-self-aware that she can't even detect the need to crap before it hits her in the middle of a hops field. "And because my sisters were total bitches to me growing up. You know that Aphrodite and Eros are the same people as Venus and Cupid, right? Like the razor blades and valentines?"

"Indeed," says Tess, "Aphrodite and Eros are the Greek names for the gods the Romans called Venus and Cupid." She has a way of summing things up neatly, with very little inflection in her voice to reveal her personal opinion. She probably thinks we're all hopeless. Utterly incapable of telling tales of true love and quite beyond the reach of Canterbury's salvation. I wonder if we're the most hopeless group she's ever led.

"I guess that's why Mama called them Aphrodite and Eros," Angelique says. "Because this is a serious story. Eros wasn't some silly baby with a bow and arrow. He was the most handsome of all the gods." She pops her hands in quick violent gestures, punctuating the air with her acrylic fingernails as she talks. Maybe it's an Italian thing, maybe the result of being on TV, the pressure of trying to make every minute of her day camera-worthy. Hard to say. Either way, it's distracting. I feel like I should be watching her as well as listening, as if she might stop at any moment to act a scene out. "So here's what happens. Psyche's been cursed by the goddess of love, which means that even though she's perfect, she grows up without any boyfriends. All these years pass and not a single man comes calling, not one. Her parents can't understand what's wrong, so they take her to the Oracle of Delphi, which is like a psychic and a priest all rolled up together, and he says that Psyche will have to marry a snake. A snake. A total monster who's going to devour her. That's what he says, and nobody fucks with the Oracle of Delphi."

Her voice drops to a whisper. "So the day of Psyche's wedding is also the day of her funeral. Her whole family and all the servants take her up to this high mountain where her snake husband says she must wait for him, and everybody is weeping and wailing, except for the sisters. They're secretly happy because they think the pretty little sweet one is going to finally get what she's always had coming to her. And her parents just leave her there at the top of the cliff and go home, crying the whole way. But the snake doesn't show. Psyche waits but nothing comes except the wind. It picks her up and carries her gently gently gently down to a castle at the bottom of the cliff. And once she gets to that castle, everything's great. She lives in perfect comfort and has whatever she wants. In fact, things appear with a *poof* the moment she wishes for them."

"Why do I have the feeling this story is getting ready to go sour?" Silvia asks drily.

"Not yet," Angelique says. " 'Cause see, what's happened is that when Eros came to destroy Psyche, he accidentally pricked himself on one of his own arrows and fell in love with her. That's how Mama used to say it, 'He pricked himself,' and then she would laugh, but of course I was a little girl and I didn't get why it was funny until later. Prick, get it? You see the joke?"

We nod. We see the joke.

"So it was Eros who sent the wind to rescue her and who set her up in this terrific castle as his wife," Angelique says. "But she can't know she's married to a handsome god; she has to think the prophecy has come true and her husband is a monster. And his mother, Aphrodite, can't know he's screwed up and fallen in love with a human. So their marriage must remain secret. Psyche has everything she could want, except for the knowledge of who her husband really is, and that's heavy, right? Super heavy. Eros only comes to her in bed, when it's too dark for her to see his face. And night after night they have banging sex—my mother didn't tell me that part, I figured it out later—but in the morning he's always gone and she's always lonely. I mean, what does she have to do all day, living in that castle, with only servants around her and nowhere to go?"

Here she pauses again, and shoots a sympathetic look toward Jean, who, now that I think of it, had come to an almost identical point halfway through her own story. The woman manages to get herself to paradise, and to get herself married to the perfect man. She lives in luxury—in a castle at the bottom of a windy cliff, in some gated community in Guatemala, it hardly matters which, because we've all been trained from girlhood to know that this is what we're supposed to want. But we can't stand it once we get there. Loneliness sets in . . . boredom, curiosity, impatience, some sort of profound and wordless discontent with the status quo. *There is only one female story,* I think, *and it's the original one.* We are all of us Eves, determined to break out of Eden the minute God and our husband turn their backs. *Where's the snake?* we think, as we look around our perfect little worlds, so lonely and so sickeningly bored that we would do anything, anything for some good old-fashioned trouble. *This is all very fine and good, but bring on the snake.*

"In fact, Psyche feels so lonesome there in the castle," Angelique says, "that she even asks her awful sisters to come pay her a visit. And that's how I knew I was Psyche."

She says this last line with a strange sort of casualness, flipping the dark curtain of hair away from her marked-up face, stopping halfway astride one of the rough, low fences we've been crossing all afternoon, teetering a moment, until her boots find solid ground on the other side. They have small pointed heels and small pointed toes, utterly impractical for the trail, but I've noticed that tiny women like Angelique are often masters of walking in impractical shoes, willing to go to any degree of discomfort just to be a bit taller.

"I guess you've all seen our house," she says, glancing around for confirmation. "It's the one on the series and it's got four whirlpool tubs and a chef's kitchen and Nico even called it The Castle, that's what he used to say, but once we moved in, I was just like Psyche. So desperate for company that I broke down and asked my older sisters to come for a week and visit us. They said I did it just to show off, to say, 'Nah-nah-nah, look at the size of my bathroom,' but that wasn't it. I really missed them. And I was, like, trapped. Which sounds stupid, because how can you be trapped in a castle, but that's what it felt like."

"Wealth and leisure," Jean says, "can be surprisingly hard to bear." She smiles warmly at Angelique. It's hard to imagine two women with less in common on the surface, but they have found a kinship in their stories. It's a secret, I suppose, that supremely successful women can share only with each other. God knows, none of the rest of us want to hear it. The secret that having it all isn't nearly enough. That what we've been taught is the end of the story is actually the beginning, that paradise can become just one more box to escape.

"When Nico first moved us into The Castle," Angelique is saying, "having all those servants flipped me out. Like one day, I was craving these pomegranate martinis. The kind they have at Del Frisco's, you know? They're super good, so I went down to the bar in the billiard room and I started messing around, looking for the stuff to make them, and suddenly this guy comes in out of nowhere. He was like the butler and valet and bodyguard and bartender and all that stuff rolled into one and he says, 'Oh no, ma'am'—he called me 'ma'am'—and he takes the ice tongs right out of my hands and he makes a big pink pitcher of martinis. But here's the thing: I didn't want a pitcher of martinis. I was by myself. I only wanted one. But they were good, so I drank them, and the next day when I come in from my workout it's sitting there on the bar, another pitcher of pomegranate martinis. And after that he made them every day, just in case I might want one, and it seemed mean not to drink them when he's made them just for me and the next thing you know there's a whole episode of me checking into rehab at Promises Malibu, because I've got a pomegranate martini monkey on my back." She stops, exhausted from the chore of walking and talking simultaneously, just as Tess warned that the speaker would be. "They made my life into a fucking joke. Pomegranate martinis. Did you see the bit they did on *SNL*?"

"You were speaking of Psyche?" Tess prompts. "How she couldn't bear living forever like that, never seeing her husband's true face."

"Oh yeah, Psyche," Angelique says. "That poor little bitch. She has everything, except, like you say, the knowledge of her husband's true face, and her sisters are flipped out when they see her castle. More jealous than ever. So they start working on her. Sure, this all seems great on the surface, they tell her. You've got the designer clothes and the limo, but your husband, bottom line, he's still a snake. Which is just fucking word-for-word what my sisters said about Nico. Nice bedspread, they would say. Nice car, and nice coat, but your husband—he's Mafia, and you're the only one who's too stupid to see it. So there I was, living out the story my mother told me, and I know what you're all thinking. That I really was as dumb as a rock not to understand what was happening right in front of me."

"No woman sees her own myth," Tess says.

"But I should've," Angelique says fiercely. "Because my wedding was like a funeral too, you know? When I said I was going to marry Nico, my father said, 'You're dead to me,' and my mother wore black to the wedding, fucking black, and in case there was anybody on earth that missed the point, they showed up at the church in a long limo that looked just like a hearse. Even standing there in the vestry before I went down the aisle, my father was still trying to talk me out of it. He said I was marrying a monster, just like they told the girl in the story, and once my sisters got inside the castle and saw . . . once they saw all the nice shit Nico had given me, they couldn't stand it. They convinced me to get a private investigator and have him checked out, just like Psyche."

Angelique smiles bitterly. "Oh, I know. Psyche didn't really hire a private investigator. But her sisters convinced her that she must kill the snake, that she needed to cut off his head with a knife and even though the sex was great, stupid Psyche believed them, because deep down in her heart she knew it was all too good to be true. And if there's anything that can make a girl pull a knife on a guy, it's if she knows he's acting too good to be true." We have all stopped here, just over the last and largest of the rough-hewn fences, waiting for the end of her tale, and she looks slowly around the circle, pausing on the face of each woman in turn.

"She knows she can't kill Eros in the light," Angelique says. "So she waits for him to come for her in the darkness, like he always does, and they have great sex like usual. Maybe better than ever, who knows? I bet it was better than ever, because sometimes a little danger is hot. And when it's all over and she knows he's asleep, she takes up an oil lamp and goes to where he is laying . . . lying?"

"Lying," say Tess and I in unison.

"She lifts the oil lamp," says Angelique, still mimicking the characters of her story. Exaggerating each motion, like a mime. "And for the first time she looks upon his face. You think she would have figured it out by now, after that many nights together. You would think she could tell the difference between having a man on top of her or a snake, but anyways, she takes the oil light and she goes to where Eros is sleeping and of course he isn't a snake at all, he's the god of love. Beautiful. Just a beautiful man lying there asleep on the bed before her. Her hand starts shaking. It shakes so hard that drops of hot oil spill from the lamp and fall on Eros and he wakes up. He's furious. He's given her everything, every luxury, his whole heart, and now she's gone and disobeyed his only order. She's seen him for what he really is."

"Men don't like to be seen," says Claire.

"Oh, please," says Valerie. "Are you kidding? They strut like peacocks."

"That's not the same thing as being seen," Claire says.

"No, it sure as hell isn't," says Silvia, putting her hand on her friend's shoulder. It looks like Claire is wearing cashmere, like the woman is hiking in a cashmere sweater. We're all just a tiny bit seedier today than we were back in London, except for maybe Valerie, who was such a wreck yesterday that she had no ground to lose, and Claire, who stepped out of her room this morning ready for a photo shoot in *Town & Country*. I wonder how she got her hair so smooth without a blow-dryer or flatiron, or if she's one of those women who travel so frequently that they have a whole other set of European-wired hair care appliances.

"Eros flew away in anger," Angelique says, vigorously flapping her hands. "And Psyche's left standing there with the knife, so at first she thinks she'll just kill herself on the spot. But something stops her. I don't remember what." She hesitates and looks around again, this time her eyes slipping over the rural scene, pausing on the sheep, the barns, the shabby little trailers in the distance where Tess has told us the Polish migrants live during harvest. The farms we are walking through are all part of conglomerates now, even here, even on the trail that leads to sweet Canterbury. The local kids don't hang around the county after graduation—they go to London looking for opportunity, or maybe farther still. Farmworkers from eastern Europe come in on buses to harvest most of the hops, and the apples too, and they shear the sheep. The migrants do it all, except for when Londoners travel down sometimes on Sundays, claiming they want to work the fields. Tess says it's the new thing among the pseudo-humble, eco-conscious fashionable city set: to take the train south for the day, lugging along their Wellies and a picnic basket full of pâté and pear tarts from Harrods. They play at farming for an hour or two, take lots of pictures to put up on Instagram, and return home, no doubt having brought more trouble to the Poles than help. But I'm hardly in a position to sneer. Some might say that paying to walk somewhere is ridiculous, that Americans playing pilgrim are no better than Londoners playing farmer, and I wonder at the solitary woman weaving now between the trailers, what she thinks of us as we pass. She is pregnant and her arms are full of wet laundry.

"There was a point where I thought about killing myself too," Angelique says. "Dr. Drew stopped me. You might have

seen that episode. You might have seen the whole thing, because the private investigator I let my sisters hire . . . he came
back with this shit about Nico owing a fortune to the IRS.
That's the tax man," she adds to Tess, who soberly nods. "Do
you have a tax man here?"

"Everywhere has a tax man," says Valerie.

"Did you know that if you turn someone who is delinquent
in to the IRS you get ten percent of whatever it is that person
owed to the government? So the more in arrears a person is, the
bigger the payday for the snitch." She laughs, an ugly sound.
Angelique may stumble over some words but she has no trouble
with the language of the courtroom. Terms like *delinquent* and
arrears roll right off her tongue. "My sisters sure as hell knew it.
That's the kind of fact women like them make a point of knowing. So yeah, I'm the dummy in the story. I let them talk me into
hiring an investigator and when he comes back with his dirt,
they turn around and use it to screw Nico. He goes to jail and
they go to Barbados."

"You can't blame yourself," says Jean, who's made a lifelong
career out of blaming herself.

"Do you really think that's true?" Valerie is asking Tess. She
is suddenly serious, with none of her usual silly jokes. "What
you said a minute ago? That every woman is living her own hidden myth?"

Tess shrugs and takes a sip from her water bottle. "It's a
tenet of child psychology. We recognize our story when we're
very young, which is why children can be so passionate about
fantasy play. You know, superheroes and princesses and the like.
It's why as little girls we may have demanded to hear the same

fairy tale over and over, because we somehow knew that it was our story. But as we grow older, our lives become more complex and blurred with details. We no longer see the patterns in ourselves as clearly."

"Mine was Cinderella," I say.

"And that would not have been my first guess," Valerie says softly, straight back to the snark, but I let it slide. Because the memory has suddenly come back to me, full force.

"My mother hated it, of course," I tell them. "She did everything she could to try and guide me toward a more politically correct story. She told me that Cinderella started as a Chinese legend, that it came from a culture of foot-binding, because in the end the girl with the smallest foot won the man. And after that every time I wanted to watch *Cinderella*, she made me watch this documentary about foot-binding first."

"Jesus Christ," says Silvia. "Your mother must have been a barrel of laughs."

"Actually, she was," I say. "In her own way. You all would have liked her, a lot better than you like me."

Maybe I meant it as a joke. I don't know why I ever said it, that part about nobody liking me—it just came out, but there is a brief, painful beat in which no one denies it. And then Jean says, a little too quickly, "If your parents were truly hippies, I'm surprised you were allowed to watch Disney movies at all."

"They were revolutionary hippies," I say. "Out fighting the good fight. I was left alone a lot."

We fall back into a pack and walk on for a minute, past the Polish woman who has shifted the basket of laundry to her hip, and whose face is tilted back, bathed in the soft afternoon sun.

She looks like a painting. Maybe a Vermeer. The effect is marred only by the fact that when she turns, I can see she has earbuds in, the source of her music evidently tucked in some sort of pocket. They look like the same kind Becca has pulled out a couple of times, when it's late in the walk and she's completely had enough of all these old women who just don't understand love.

"What happened next?" Claire finally asks. "With Psyche, I mean."

"She spends her whole life trying to get back what she lost," Angelique says. "And her sisters . . . after they've driven Eros away from Psyche, they actually have the gall to make a move on him themselves. They figure if it worked for her, it'll work for them, so they go up to the same cliff where she was supposed to meet her snake husband all those years ago and they jump off, thinking the same wind that carried her gently down will carry them down too. But it doesn't, so it's just splat, that's all, a great big splat at the bottom, and I wish my sisters would jump off a cliff too, but they don't. They just gloat."

"Do you still speak to them?" asks Jean.

"Fuck no, I don't speak to them. I guess you don't watch the show. My sisters are dead to me. Dead," she echoes, looking down at the ground.

"I watch the show," says Valerie, surprising everyone. "I love TV." Which may be the most shocking statement that's been made along the trail so far. Nobody says "I love TV," especially not people who love TV. I mean, everybody loves TV, we all have our guilty pleasures, those shows on the high channels that we gobble compulsively, late at night, but we don't admit it.

We say, in fact, "I don't watch much TV," even if we know damn well that we grew up on the stuff, that it's pressed into our collective DNA. That we can name every kid on *The Partridge Family* and quote whole scenes of *Will & Grace* by heart.

Angelique smiles at Valerie. She seems anxious about the possibility that people might watch her show, but then she isn't totally comfortable when people don't watch it either. For what does it mean if she's sacrificed her fortune and her family for Thursday night glory and yet here, in this lonely hops field, fifty miles north of Canterbury, we all tilt our heads and look at her quizzically? It must be some very low circle of hell, I would imagine, to have sold one's soul for fame and to still not be quite famous enough.

"I'm off the series now," she says. "And as long as Nico's in the New Jersey State Correctional Facility, I just go from one place to another, even if I don't know why. I went to the Great Wall of China, and to Iceland and Crete, and I cruised through the Panama Canal."

"Psyche was doomed to circle the world in search of her husband," says Tess. I'm not surprised she knows the details of the story. It seems the more random and obscure the fact, the more likely she is to possess it. "And now you must wander too, it would seem."

"I don't really mind," says Angelique. "I liked China. I got a lot of cheap shirts there." I have a sudden urge to hug her, to pull her black slick little head to my shoulder and let her cry it out. I bet she's wanted to cry it out for a very long time.

"How did they get him?" Becca asks. "Nico, I mean."

"I guess you don't—" Angelique stops herself. "No, you're

all classy ladies. Out of my fucking league, that much is sure. Of course most of you don't watch the show. Tell them, Valerie." She seems suddenly drained—somber, exhausted from her recitation.

"Nico came to her," Valerie says. "Up in her high white bedroom that looked just like a cloud. He put one of his hands on each of her shoulders and he looked her right in the eye and he said, 'So I guess this is adios, babe.' It was like something in a movie. South America, is that where he was going? Columbia?"

Angelique nods.

"But they nabbed him in Newark Airport," Valerie finishes. "Took him straight to jail with his passport still in his hand."

We've come to another hill, the biggest of the afternoon, and my thighs are already aching. When I look over at Silvia's watch I see that it's almost three, which means we have walked for six hours so far today, not counting the stop for lunch. Tess had said that our goal was to cover thirty kilometers on this first leg of the journey, which converts to about twenty miles, which is a lot for a group of women who are probably used to working out an hour a day, if that. And our pace has been slowed by the fact that this is country walking. Rolling hills and rugged footpaths, not the paved suburban streets we're used to, meaning that we've probably progressed more like three miles per hour than the four I'd originally predicted. But the stories have distracted me, just as Tess no doubt intended them to do. I'm only conscious of my exhaustion when no one is talking.

"Is Psyche ever reunited with Eros?" Becca finally asks. "Does she ever find him and get to apologize for having doubted him in the first place?"

"I don't know," says Angelique. "When I was a little girl and my mother told the story to me, I always fell asleep during the part where Psyche was wandering. She wandered a long way. There were a fucking lot of chapters. I've never stayed awake all the way to the end."

"Oh, come on," Steffi says sharply. "You think your fate is linked to this mythic girl and yet you expect us to believe that you never had the slightest curiosity about how her story ended?" She pulls out her phone. "I have a bar out here," she says. "Half a bar, at least. Do you want me to google Psyche? Put it all to rest right here and now?"

But Angelique is biting her pale, dark-lined lip with anxiety. It's clear she doesn't want to know what happened to Psyche. She shakes her head, somewhat violently, and walks faster, the other women trailing behind her until Steffi and I find ourselves at the end of the line.

"Do you buy all that?" Steffi hisses. "It's obvious she's put two and two together and has gotten, like, four and a half. Not the perfect answer, but close enough. It's not like she tried to tell us that two plus two equals twenty-seven or something. She's not near as stupid as she seems on TV. So why doesn't she want to know how Psyche's story ended and thus, presumably, what lurks in her own future?"

"Would you?"

"Would I what?"

"Want to know how your own story ends?"

"Of course. And so would you."

"I'm not so sure. I feel sorry for Angelique."

Steffi snorts. "Don't. No matter how much the government

seized, I guarantee you there's still plenty left, and then a book deal and maybe a spin-off show, who knows? All this traveling is just a way for her to drop from sight while her agents and managers prepare for the big comeback. Because she's a hot mess now and everybody loves a hot mess. And besides, I'd kill to know the future," Steffi adds, abruptly lengthening her stride so that I have to trot beside her just to keep up. "Anything you see coming, you can prepare for. It's a fair fight. I don't want anything to ever sneak up on me again."

"Again? If your story is about the first time something snuck up on you, it would have to have been a cheetah."

She grins like a schoolgirl. Walking fast, even now when we're scrambling to catch up with the group, doesn't seem to affect her. "You'll have to wait to find out," she says. "But not too long. I pulled a nine of clubs."

When we fall back in step with the others, they're talking about how men hide things. Bank accounts, mistresses, medical diagnoses, porn. "There's a whole school of myths," Tess is saying, "where the reality of a man must remain unknown from the woman he loves or else the truth will destroy one or both of them. These stories mostly fall along the lines of Angelique and Psyche, that the man can be himself with his wife, especially in bed, in the dark. That's where he can let his guard down. But each morning he changes back into the beast or monster or god, or whatever part of him she is forbidden to behold in this particular story. Think about it. A man who must keep his true identity hidden is the basis of so many of the superhero myths. Batman, Spider-Man, Superman, Whateverman. It says a lot about the male ego, don't you think? That they would create so many of these stories, the man with the split and half-hidden self?"

"But in the stories," says Claire, "I assume the woman always finds some way to uncover his secret?"

"Almost always," says Tess. "Otherwise there's not much of a story, is there?"

"And then, when she sees him, what does he do?"

"Sometimes he dies . . ." says Tess. "But mostly when she learns the truth, he has to leave her. Flies away like Eros. For her sake, he always says. That's a built-in part of the story. That knowing the full truth about a man places a woman in danger."

I think of Ned. The other women are doubtlessly thinking of their own men. Most of them probably found a way to remain forever in darkness and those are the ones we left, in exasperation, describing them as dead and cold or unknowable. And then there are the others, that unfortunate few who we managed to drag into the light . . . and damn if we didn't lose them too, just in a different way. The man dissolving before our very eyes in the process of feminine discovery, fading from existence even as we're still trying to analyze him. The man who disappears without a trace while we're asking our girlfriends what it all means.

"But sometimes men go away and come back," Becca says. "Come on, don't you guys ever go to the movies? That happens all the time, that the girl thinks she's lost the cute guy but he comes back, right at the very end and then the music plays. Like, what's that old movie? *Pretty Woman*?"

"Once a man is out of my life he's dead to me," Claire says.

"I don't believe in reunions and second chances and booty calls with the ex."

"Nico's in for so long he may as well be dead," Angelique says. "And I'd like to say my sisters were my stepsisters, because then it would be okay for them to be so evil, but there's no way that's true. They're blood, I just know it. We all used to have the same nose." She stops and spits, and when she lifts her chin her eyes are bright with determination. They are blue, brilliantly so when the light hits them, a beautiful shade, and I am surprised again by the prettiness that sometimes breaks through the mask. *Priscilla Presley,* I think. On the day she married Elvis. That's who Angelique looks like.

"But it was really my fault in the end, you know?" Angelique is saying. "Because me and Psyche just couldn't leave well enough alone. That's why I'm going to Canterbury. To get a high-powered priest to forgive me, and then to tell me what I have to do to make it right."

"A Canterbury priest can't tell you how to make it right," Tess says. "They're Anglican. He can't even forgive you, not really. He can offer you a blessing, but each person has to find the way to make her own story come out right."

"But that's why I'm here," Angelique says. "For a blessing and maybe, I don't know. Maybe when I get to the Cathedral and actually see it, something will pop in my head and tell me what I have to do next. That's all I'm asking. But enough . . . Enough about me. I've talked for a million miles. Who's next?"

"I am," says Silvia. "I have a ten."

"I have a ten too," says Claire, smiling at her friend. "Now that's funny, isn't it?"

"Mine is hearts," says Silvia.

"Diamonds," says Claire.

"Then Silvia will go next." says Tess. "Love before riches."

"Good. We're due for a happy story," Silvia says. "And mine is happy."

"But mine was a happy story too," Jean says. We all stare at her.

"At least it was happy for a while," Jean amends.

"And so was Psyche," says Angelique. "Happy for a while, I mean, and happy for a while is saying something. Me and Jean, you see, we made the same mistake. We just couldn't appreciate how good we had it. We worried about the little shit and we got bored and we compared ourselves to other women and that's when you start straight down the road to hell, you know. The minute you start comparing your life to someone else's."

"It's hard to know that what you're feeling is joy right while it's happening," says Jean. "You call it something else at the time and years later you think, 'Wait a minute. Maybe that was my joy and I missed it.'"

"It's the secret to life," Tess says. "If we could only learn to recognize happiness in the present moment none of us would need to walk to Canterbury."

Oh come on, I think. *There's got to be more to life than that.*

"How far are we from tonight's inn?" Valerie asks. "It seems like we should have been there by now."

"Another hour," says Tess. "Maybe a little longer. Why? Are you getting tired?"

"A little," Valerie says. "All of a sudden. I don't know why."

SIX

Our next inn is even smaller. In fact, it makes the place that we stayed in last night seem like a palace. From the layout, I'd guess that it was once a private home—and perhaps it still is, for there's no formal check-in process and we're given our room assignments by Tess. The nine of us are to share a single bathroom, located at the end of an upstairs hall, and the sequence of narrow rooms opening off both sides of that hall are remnants of an era when families had a dozen children.

"Claustrophobic," Silvia mutters as she enters hers. Directly across from Silvia's room I can see Claire through an open door, tossing what appears to be three or four dark sweaters onto her bed. More cashmere, no doubt—but I can't think why she would have brought so many seemingly identical sweaters on a five-day trip or why she would feel compelled to completely unpack at each brief stop along the trail. "I hope you're not expecting a closet," Silvia calls across the hall to Claire, her voice still aggrieved, but small rooms have never bothered me, nor have small beds, even though I'll admit it's a little disconcerting that the upstairs ceilings are so low. Walking down this long dark hall is what I've always imagined death to feel like, but the only thing that's truly unendurable is that when I finally enter my room and shut my door, I can still hear the others talking, their voices floating through the walls.

This issue of personal space is so confounding. I have the solitary nature that I'd imagine is typical of only children, but I also grew up on a commune; thirty faces around the breakfast table was the norm, with people coming and going at all hours, springing their presence upon each other without the courtesy of an invitation, or even a knock. The philosophy of the colony demanded unlatched doors and shared property, and I always vowed that when I became an adult with a home of my own the first thing I would buy was a dead bolt. But now, as I flop down on my bed, hearing Silvia bumping around on one side of me and the high, breathy voice of Jean on the other, it's clear that a lock isn't enough to protect my solitude. I want silence.

I pass Steffi on the steps, coming up as I'm coming down. "I'm going for a walk," I say, before she can ask, and her eyes immediately narrow with suspicion. We've been walking all day, so this is the last logical thing I might decide to do, besides . . . walk where? We got a good look at the town on our way in, and there isn't much to explore. It's a dreary place, a dying country village, the modest population steadily shrinking due to the fact that local farmers no longer work their own crops.

"Our stop for this evening will be a bit more rural than last night," Tess had said and a couple of us had chuckled before we realized she wasn't kidding. "And," she'd added, "I'm sorry to report that this particular village is not noted for its beauty." The one store was closed, the post office shuttered. A town hall was empty except for a notice saying Methodist services would be held on Thursday. Thursday, not Sunday, which means they probably share a pastor with churches in other villages. A sign nailed under the only streetlight informed us that if we required the services of the police, we should telephone the constable in Dartford posthaste. The only problem is, we're not in Dartford. We're at least three miles south.

Now I follow the entry road back to the town square, where I sit down on one of two oppositional benches and unlace a boot, pull out my foot, then ease off my sock. I bought these boots the morning I left the States and unpacked them in the taxi on the way to the airport, abandoning the big square box they came in right there on the cab seat. There was no time to break them in, and seven hours of walking today have wreaked havoc on my feet. The skin isn't broken anywhere, but a blister is rising on my big toe and my heel is red and puffy. I rub it, counting myself lucky things aren't worse. I have a supply of bandages and that paint-on second skin somewhere in my suitcase. Tomorrow I'll have to protect myself a little better, or I'll be completely hobbled by the time we reach Canterbury.

Or maybe these damn two-hundred-dollar boots don't really fit, I think, and then I squash the thought back down as quickly as it sprang up. It's too horrible to contemplate that I might be out here, as Steffi says, twenty-eight miles from nowhere, and my only pair of shoes doesn't fit. That would make me an American Cinderella or, more accurate, one of her unlikable stepsisters. Because I suspect Tess is right; every woman's life comes back to a fairy tale in the end. So I sit on one of the only two benches in this strange little town, my boot in my hand, and stare into space. Precisely why was Cinderella my favorite story? She's a cliché, the most predictable of princesses, and I usually steer clear of clichés, but I watched her movie so frequently as a child that even now I can close my eyes and it plays against the screen of my mind.

Maybe I had loved her simply because there hadn't been that much else to love. We only picked up the three major networks out on the farm, back in the days before cable, but we had a VCR, which was a noteworthy machine for its time. I don't remember how we came to first possess it, or why my parents, who were normally so insistent that everything we owned should reflect the homesteading values of the commune, would have ever allowed such an item in the house. Most likely my grandmother sent it, along with the stash of Disney movies, in a last-ditch attempt to assure that at least one thing in my childhood was normal.

One day I was watching *Cinderella* and my mother walked into the room. She seemed a bit surprised to see me there—she always seemed surprised to see me, even if I was exactly where she'd left me. If I were to be unkind, I would say that my mother frequently failed to remember she even had a daughter, but it's truer to say that she had trouble remembering all kinds of things. Diana was like a baby playing peekaboo who forgets the face the minute it disappears behind the hands, and who is thus amazed and delighted each time it reappears.

"Your mother is easily distracted," my father used to say, whenever we would be walking through the woods or down a city street and would suddenly realize that she was no longer with us. She had invariably been pulled from her intended path by what Daddy called "one of Diana's bright shiny things"—a book in a store window, a piece of twisted driftwood, the elegantly exotic face of a Mongolian refugee, the bones of a rabbit. She probably had what they now call adult ADD, for she would say "Che?" whenever she saw me, always with that lift of a question, as if finding me there on the couch watching TV each afternoon was a lovely little miracle.

On this particular day she was with the religious leader of the commune, a man named David, although he pronounced it *Da-veed*. I can't remember exactly what sort of pagan he was— Druid, most likely. They were popular at the time. It must have been the mid-seventies, which would have made me eight, nine, maybe ten. Conventional Christianity was beginning to fail, and churches were combining or closing, even out in the sticks where the commune was located. All I can remember about David's particular brand of preaching is that he once spontaneously began to channel a message from somebody's dead brother in the middle of the love offering and that he had a pet axiom with which he closed every service: "Religion," he would intone, "is nothing more than the study of other people's experiences with God. But true spirituality is the opportunity to have your own experience with God."

It was the sort of statement that would cause all of the women in the fellowship to swoon, and half the men as well. My father was not among them. He had limited patience with the Davids of the world and despite all this talk of share and share alike, no one was ever quite allowed to forget that it was my daddy's family who left him the farm where we all lived. That his name was the one on the deed. He had rebelled once, fifteen years earlier, and now he was stuck with the lees of that rebellion, all these little flecks of sediment sinking all around him to the bottom of his half-empty glass. He disappeared a lot—hiking, fishing, inventing, reading—and so I was largely left to my mother's machinations, as I imagine most girls of my generation were. I think of Becca, and her daddy going off the bridge. It was a brutal shock, no doubt, but only in the swiftness of the departure. All daddies go off the bridge to some degree.

My own father died in the woods, the blood vessels of his brain betraying him in the middle of one of his long, lonely walks. Rather surprisingly—for he was a young man, younger than I am now—he had left a will of sorts and instructions for his funeral. He did not pull a Diana and ask for his remains to be scattered. Instead, he was buried in the most conventional manner possible, lying placidly in a box at the feet of his own father, vaguely eulogized by a Presbyterian minister whom he had never met. His one request was that the box be pine, a simple unadorned affair, but of course the local mortuary didn't stock that type of coffin, so the funeral had to be delayed a week while an ostentatiously plain pine box was special ordered, at great expense, from the Amish. There's a clue in all that somewhere, but I can't think what.

And, before you can even suggest it, I know . . . I know. All signs point to the possibility that my mother and David were having an affair. There was certainly enough gossip in the commune hinting as much, and God knows Diana was the type. Braless, feckless, with a morality that could best be described as "flexible," and she was always dashing about with one man and then another. More than once, bags were packed late at night and she and I were loaded into someone's car. There were men who claimed they would save us from the commune and there were men who furthermore wanted to save us from the men who were saving us.

And yet, when push came to shove, I don't think Diana would have ever had the guts to actually leave my father. He was the stable one. The rock that everything else grew around, and she simultaneously relied upon and resented that stability. The other men? They may have been nothing more than the way she tested him, for my mother was an indiscriminate flirt, a woman who pumped out rounds of sexuality shotgun-style, with the bullets of her charm hitting all sorts of innocent bystanders, leaving complete strangers wounded and shell-shocked in her wake. She would smile suggestively at the random man paying for gas at the next island, at our elderly family dentist, the fathers of my friends, and then, as I grew older, even my friends themselves. It was all surface. She needed to be perceived as sexy far more than she needed the actual sex.

Or so I suspect. But maybe I'm wrong. Maybe none of us knows anything about anybody else, especially our parents. The covers of some books must remain closed. But I can say that, physical affair or not, this minor-league holy man named David was Diana's latest conquest and he was the one who first tried to ruin Cinderella for me. He sat down on my grandmother's brocade couch that afternoon, the one with the lumpy afghan stretched over it in an attempt to hide the fact that once upon a time my family had been rich, and started telling me how in China they bound the girls' feet. They began this cruel ritual, he said, when the children in question were not much older than I was at the time. Just as they approached puberty, at that point in life when young women are at their most malleable, when the forces brought to bear upon them have the most lasting and damaging effects.

"How would it feel to have your feet bound?" David asked, and he dug under the blanket and extracted my left foot, pulled it out and shook it at me to prove his point. It was an unanswerable question, but he didn't care. A lifetime in the pulpit had made him accustomed to asking questions that would go unanswered. "How would you like it if you couldn't even walk?"

I watched *Cinderella* over his shoulder. We were just getting to my favorite part, near the end. The ball is over, the magic has receded. Cinderella has been locked in a high turret and it seems all is lost. But when the Grand Duke comes to the house looking for the owner of the glass slipper, the animals free her from her cell and she rushes down the stairs at just the last minute. Her stepsisters have already tried and failed to cram their own feet into the slipper. Their large, puffy, inappropriate feet, with their cartoon toes poking out in every direction. And when the Grand Duke pulls out the glass slipper for Cinderella to try, the evil stepmother trips him and the glass shatters and it's all disaster until Cinderella says, in that impossibly sweet voice of hers, "But you see . . . I have the other slipper."

It was the best movie moment ever, or at least that's what I thought as a child and even now, so many years later, I can't think of any subsequent scenes that have pleased me more. The Duke slides the slipper on, it fits perfectly, and soon the whole world becomes a montage of confetti, wedding bells, and joy-fully leaping mice.

And it was just at this point in the story that David sat down on the couch, wrested my foot from beneath the afghan, and went into his long speech about the little girls in China. How painful it was to submit to the binding chair, the infec-tions, the broken bones, the agony, the premature deaths, all done in the pursuit of some warped idea of female beauty. And our Western minds, he added, were just as warped as the East-ern girls' feet. He gestured contemptuously toward the televi-sion screen with my foot. The idea of Cinderella may have come from China, but once it reached Europe it became darker still. In the old fairy tales, before that repulsively cheerful Walt Disney cleaned them up, the stepsisters would cut off parts of their own feet in their doomed attempts to cram them into the shoe. That's where the idea of the glass slipper had first come in, a transparent way to prove that Cinderella was the one true princess. That her foot really fit and she had not mutilated her-self in her greedy desire to marry the Prince.

My mother was enchanted by David's story. She was possi-bly the only person on earth who would have been enchanted by such a bloody tale, but then she was always collecting evi-dence of the ways women had suffered throughout history under the fist of male oppression. And she was not about to let the fact that David's story was actually a tribute to self-mutilation slow her down at all.

"So you see, Che," she said, perching on the armrest beside him, "this is a lesson for you. If the shoe doesn't fit, don't wear it." And then she and David had both laughed long and loud, as if this were a fantastically witty thing to say, and he had offered to loan her some series of videos on the worldwide plight of women so that she could, in his words, "head me off at the pass." I wasn't sure what pass he was talking about, where I was going from or to, and I didn't want to hear tales of bound feet or amputated toes, warnings about what could happen to a girl if she chooses the wrong prince or the wrong shoe. The fairy tale was coming to its close. The little mice were wearing their tiny palace uniforms and waving at the departing carriage, and there it was, the happy ending, hovering just over the holy man's shoulder.

"All girls go through their romantic phases," my mother said, frowning at the television screen, at Cinderella and the Prince leaning in for their first and final kiss. "But they grow out of them soon enough, don't they?"

Now I look down at my own foot, puffy and swollen too, and wonder how in the hell I'm going to get back to the inn. Probably I'll have to put the boot back on without lacing it and limp my way up the street. I wasn't being totally honest when I said they are my only shoes. I do have a pair of those bedroom socks that are almost slippers somewhere in my bag, thrown in at the last minute. I can wear them down to supper. I can't imagine the dress code in the pub will be very strict and I'm determined to join the women tonight. To talk and to agree and sympathize, to graciously drink whatever wine they pour, and for once in my life to not be so strange.

Out of the corner of my eye I can see Valerie approaching the square, coming from the opposite direction of the inn. Odd. She complained of being tired and yet she must have also opted to take an additional lap of the town. The sun is setting behind her and I have to squint to even make out her form. Just as I do, she pauses, and looks around and sees that these two benches are the only place to sit. Despite all this brave self-talk about being charming at dinner, I dread her approach. I'm not ready to be charming quite yet. If she joins me, she will offer me her phone or ask me why I have one of my boots off or make *tsk-tsk*-ing noises at the wounds on my foot.

But she does none of these things. She merely nods and sits down on the bench across from mine.

Now I'm the one who feels obligated to say something. Greet her at least, maybe begin to gossip about the two stories we've heard today. Speculate as to what they might indicate about the women who told them, or perhaps we could talk about ourselves. There's probably an ocean of things Valerie and I could discuss, a million words we could spew out into this empty village square.

She says nothing. We look in opposite directions, Valerie away from the sun and me into it.

A minute passes. Maybe two. This is why you should never sit still. If you sit still, you might think, and if you think you might . . . what? Remember your parents, and your childhood, and every stupid thing you've ever lost? If you start to think, who knows, you might start to feel and there's no telling where that winding road might lead. This is why we must have our books, and phones, and earbuds, and lovers, even if they're the wrong people, even if they seem to be taking us to places where we don't want to be. Because otherwise we'll end up just like this: sitting on a bench in the middle of nowhere, starting that ugly cry. You know, the kind where you snort. I try to wipe the tears . . . unobtrusively at first, but then they pour.

Okay, now she's definitely going to ask me what's wrong, I think. *Nothing opens the door to feminine confession like tears—we'll run across a bathroom to ask a weeping stranger if everything is okay, and when she does ask what's wrong, what am I supposed to tell her? That I'm crying over* Cinderella *or my father's coffin, or the fact that they bind the feet of little girls in China? Of all the women who could have found me like this, why does it have to be her?*

But she doesn't even look at me. The silence stretches between us, grows ever more awkward, until finally I slide my foot in my boot and limp up the street, like some absurd actor in a spaghetti western. It hurts, but as I progress I find myself walking faster and faster, tripping over my shoelaces, dragging them across the mossy cobblestones, clenching my toes in an effort to keep the boots on. By the time I am back at the inn, I am almost running to get away from Valerie and the empty silence of that square.

SEVEN

W e don't want to break the rules, but we're breaking the rules," Silvia says, with a bark of a laugh. It's the next morning and we are barely twenty steps into our walk, the village still sleeping over our shoulder. "We've talked it over. Claire is going first."

"I know that Tess told us hearts should go before diamonds," Claire says. The sun hits her perfectly composed blonde hair like light bouncing off a helmet, and the cashmere turtleneck of the day is a color that looks black at first but on deeper study reveals itself to be a muted slate gray. "And I'm sure she's right. But in this case it really shouldn't matter which of us goes first, because our stories are so similar."

"Similar?" says Silvia. "I should think they're quite the opposite."

I should think they're quite the opposite? Well, shit, let's all have crumpets and tea. Silvia must be one of those people who's cursed to go through life picking up the accents and speech patterns of anyone she meets. I shouldn't judge, for I'm a bit that way myself. Put me in a cab with a Pakistani driver and I exit it singing, "And thank you too, kind sir." I try to fight the tendency—I'm always afraid it will seem like I'm mocking the other person—but it's a struggle. Just two days in the British countryside and I'm already adding those little upticks of questions to the ends of my sentences. "Lovely morning, isn't it?" I said to the girl who was serving breakfast at the inn, automatically cushioning my definitive American statements with the soft cotton of British consensus-making.

"But opposites are similar, at least in the heart," Claire is saying. "Haven't you ever noticed that? When Silvia and I were talking over breakfast this morning, we realized our stories covered the same theme. Faithfulness. What it is and how it changes over time."

"These stories are all too complicated," Becca says. She tends to be congested and phlegmy in the morning, I've noticed, and her voice is just on the edge of a whine.

"Love is complicated," her mother tells her. "Life is complicated."

"No, it isn't," Becca says, with the confidence of the young and untested. "Or at least it doesn't have to be. Is it really that hard to tell a plain and simple love story?"

Crickets.

"You can tell a simple love story when it's your turn," I finally say. "Bring out the unicorns and rainbows and make it as sweet as you want."

"I didn't say sweet," Becca says, and her pitch goes even higher, cutting the morning air. She's wearing the most bizarre combination of colors today—a cherry hoodie, brown pants, neon-green socks. It isn't just the casual mismatching of a girl who dressed in haste. It takes effort to look this bad. What we are witnessing is an orchestrated bedlam. A deliberate and conscious assault on the retina. "Sweet sucks. I mean happy. Sexy. Do any of you even remember sexy?"

"But my story is quite sexy," Claire says. She says it smoothly, her answer damping down Becca's rudeness, smothering it completely, like a thick towel over a grease fire, and Jean smiles at her in gratitude. I feel for Jean. Having Becca for a daughter must be like living with one of those low-rent boyfriends every woman dates at some point in her life—the kind where you enter every social event with a stone in your chest, just waiting for that inevitable moment when he makes a stupid joke or insults your hostess or says something about politics. "But it is rather complicated, and thus you may not like it, Becca dear. I wouldn't have liked it when I was your age."

"Don't equivocate," says Silvia. "Don't apologize or explain. Just leap right into the middle of the action. The way you always do."

Claire laughs. "I've been married four times, as you all know, and I live with a younger man now. But this story isn't about him. This story goes all the way back to my third husband. I was just shy of forty years old when it happened. You know, forty. That dangerous, dangerous age. That year in which everything you've built to that point suddenly cracks and turns to dust in your hands. Are any of you close to forty?"

She glances at me, which is flattering, because I'm actually pretty far past it. Up until last week I would have said "safely past it." If I had to guess anyone else in the group was looking down the barrel of this particular gun, it would be Valerie. And possibly Steffi, although no, she's more likely still somewhere in the middle of that long nap known as a woman's thirties, along with Angelique. Tess is younger, and of course Becca is younger yet, while Claire, Silvia, and Jean are all in their late fifties or better. I stop and try to sequence us in my mind. Silvia, Claire, Jean, Che, Valerie, Steffi, Angelique, Tess, and Becca—that's how I would line us up if I had to, with me more or less in the middle of the pack, just as I always seem to be. But I could be wrong. So many factors come into play in how well a woman wears her age—money, nationality, weight, posture, Botox, luck.

"As a matter of fact I turned forty just last week," Valerie says.

"Did you?" Claire says. "Happy birthday, and get ready for your whole life to fall to shit, if it hasn't already. I'd just turned forty in the story I'm about to tell you, and I felt safe at the beginning of it, so safe that I couldn't imagine how everything was about to—heavens, what is that?"

Tess's gaze follows Claire's pointing finger to the path ahead. "It's an apple orchard. Surely you have them in the States."

"No, of course I've seen an orchard," Claire says, pausing and pushing up her oversize sunglasses to the top of her head. "It just surprised me. We've been walking in the land of beer for so long and now, boom, we turn the corner and here we are in the land of apples. That's wonderful."

The orchard before us is enormous, with rows upon rows of neatly planted trees, and a number of the branches are still heavy with fruit. This surprises me. I would have guessed the time for harvest was long past, but it's warm today . . . the fifties rising into the sixties if you measure temperature the American way, which all of us do. When Tess had cheerfully announced "We'll be hitting seventeen by afternoon," back over breakfast, at first we had thought she was talking miles, which was bad enough, but then we'd realized she was talking temperature and we really winced. Seventeen sounds so damn cold. But now we've been walking no more than thirty minutes and most of us have already taken off our coats. They dangle from the tops of our backpacks or are tied around our waists, and we will give them to Tim when we stop for lunch. One of the advantages of having the van meet us at whatever pub Tess chooses is that we can change socks and bandages, and remove our outerwear as the temperature rises.

"Well, turning forty is just like this," Claire says. "A shift in the climate, the tiniest movement of the sun within the clouds, a bend in the road, and suddenly, just like magic, the whole world looks different." She lowers her glasses, takes one of those deep cleansing breaths like they teach you in yoga, and we all begin to walk.

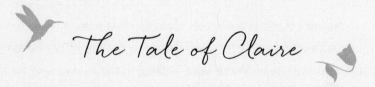

The Tale of Claire

"When a woman has moved as often as I have she becomes expert in the art of packing and unpacking," Claire begins, once we've all settled into our pace. "My third husband's name was Adam, which would probably be a better name for a first husband, but there you have it. He was a college professor with what seemed like a hundred boxes of books, and books are the worst things to move, any professional will tell you that. Adam was hopeless at helping. He would begin to unpack a box and then he'd just stop and pull out a particular volume and start to explain all about it. The story, if it was a novel, or how he'd come to own the book, if it was nonfiction, and thus he suspected the topic would be over my head. Almost everything was over my head, at least according to Adam. We were just a few months in but I was already beginning to have my doubts about him."

"You looked scared in those wedding pictures," Silvia says.

"I look scared in all my wedding pictures," Claire says. "Show me a bride who doesn't look scared and I'll show you a bride who's drunk. But anyway, Adam was no help at unpacking, and in fact he was making things worse. So after the first morning of enduring his lectures, I told him to just forget it, to go back to campus, and that I would handle the rest. I was very nearly at the end when I found the box with the videotape. Yes, a videotape, and that was the first clue. Even at the time, VHS was going out of fashion. Almost everyone had switched to DVDs by then, so I asked myself, 'Whatever is this?' and then I saw that bit of masking tape and that single word: *Edith*."

"Edith?" Becca says, with a crinkle of her nose. "No one's named Edith anymore, not even people your age."

"Exactly," says Claire. She appears to be expert at not being insulted, able to divert a barbed arrow just before it hits, moving so deftly that even the shooter forgets she's taken the shot. I suppose it's the legacy of having been married so many times. "Edith was Adam's wife before me. And just as you say, Becca, it's such a plain name, such an old-fashioned name . . ." She shrugs. "But it suited her. The two of them had been married for almost twenty years and she was the mother of his children. The proper faculty-wife sort, all about charity and committees and dinner parties. I know the type to a T, because all four of my husbands were married to the exact same woman just before they married me." She laughs. She laughs automatically, just the way the close-cropped man back at the bar claimed that Americans smile, and yet the sound is clear and melodic. A bell, not a bellow, and I envy her yet again.

"For this is my destiny," Claire says, "to follow in sequence behind the Ediths of the world, and I knew without thinking that I was holding a tape of their wedding. It chafed me. Adam and I had been married in Lake Tahoe, in one of those five-minute ceremonies, and he had been quite insistent that it would be just the two of us. No one else there, not even his children. He tried to present it as madcap and romantic, but it felt like we were sneaking off. Like he was ashamed of me."

"That's the only one of your weddings I missed," Silvia said.

"I sent you a picture."

"It's on my refrigerator with a magnet."

"Still?"

Silvia nods. "I never take anything off my refrigerator. It's my personal time capsule. That's how I know you look scared in the picture. But there's a nice view of Lake Tahoe in the background."

"Tahoe's perfectly grand," says Claire. "The problem wasn't Tahoe."

"If Edith had been his wife that long ago, I'm surprised he even had a tape of their wedding," Steffi says. "People didn't use videographers back then, did they? At least not like they do today." A valid point, and I guess it's not surprising she would have been the one to do the math and find the first flaw in Claire's narrative. She's always counting something.

"Excellent," Claire says. "Good for you, Steffi. You're far more clever than I was. I just assumed that the tape I was holding in my hands was twenty years old, but in truth it was no more than two or three. But that didn't strike me at the time, and besides, I'm getting ahead of myself. The point is I was so sure that I'd found a video of Adam's first wedding that no other possibility crossed my mind. We didn't have a VHS player in the house and so I stuck it back in a drawer and told myself I'd look at it later."

"And then you forgot about it," Valerie says. It's an odd guess as to what might have happened next, for if Claire had forgotten about the tape, she wouldn't have chosen this for her story. That's what we should have told Becca, that of course we were going to tell complicated stories. Because if there isn't a complication, there isn't a story.

"Oh, I should have forgotten about it," Claire says, with another tinkly little laugh. "That would have been the smart thing to do. But my problem is, I'm incapable of forgetting anything. It probably explains why I've been married so many times. I've always thought the greatest skill a wife can possess is the ability to judiciously forget certain things, to just delete them right out of her brain at will. Because that's what we've been talking about this whole time, haven't we? The difficulties women have in understanding men . . . how we never really see them, really know them, even after years of love and marriage? But there's a whole other category of problems: those that come when you've seen too much. Trust me, when you're talking marriage, seeing too much is far more dangerous than seeing too little."

We digest this as we walk, along with a few of the apples. For almost all of us have pulled one, at some point, off a tree. The branches were so heavy, it would have seemed ungracious not to. Only Steffi demurred, muttering something about pesticides.

"I was taking care of a friend's cat while she was out of town," Claire goes on, tossing her half-eaten apple to the side as she walks, "and the cat was really unhappy being alone. When I was in her house one day, feeding him, I saw she had a VCR and I remembered the tape. I thought, *Why not bring it over and watch it here? I can snuggle up and visit with the poor lonely kitty and watch the tape and I'll see what Adam was like at his first wedding.* When we were married he'd said he was an atheist and he wasn't going to go through that silly charade again . . . yet I knew he had gone through the charade for Edith, that he'd been willing to put on the tux and say the vows for her. So I was prepared to curl up on that couch and have myself a complete pity party."

"Okay, the truth," Silvia says. "That was my house and my cat, wasn't it? You've never told me this story."

While her best friend is as perfectly groomed as ever, even now, just a day deeper into the trail, Silvia has already taken to brushing her hair straight back, flat to her head, so that she looks like a swimmer emerging from a pool. I had this science project once, way back in fourth grade or something, that measured the speed at which various things decompose. It was the perfect project for a kid raised on a commune, where everyone was obsessed with composting, because all I had to do was go outside the kitchen and start digging things up. But the more organic the substance, the faster it fell apart, that was the take-away of my little experiment, and this basic truth comes back to me now. If we were to be hit with a sudden rockslide, Silvia would dematerialize at once, while future archaeologists would probably find Claire pretty much intact.

"I've never told anyone this story," says Claire, and, that fact in itself makes her different from Jean and Angelique, both of whom told well-practiced tales, the sort they had obviously re-peated many times. I'm a little surprised that there's anything about Claire that Silvia doesn't know—they speak in that sort of shorthand only best friends use.

"I'll confess. It was your couch, your television, your cat, and your house where all these atrocities took place," Claire goes on. "I was probably eating your ice cream out of your bowl as well. But I went over the next afternoon, got myself all set up on the couch, popped in the tape, and got an eyeful of . . . who can guess?"

"Porn," say Angelique and Valerie, almost in unison.

"Yes, porn," says Claire. "Homemade porn. What else?"

I'm ashamed to admit the thought had never occurred to me.

"Your husband with his first wife?" says Becca. "Oh my God. That is without a doubt the grossest thing I've ever heard in my whole life."

"My first impulse was to agree with you," says Claire. "Imagine me lying back on the couch in that empty house, pil-lows propped up all around me, the cat on my lap, the ice cream bowl on the table, expecting to see candles and roses and bridesmaids in pastel dresses. Then the first image is upon me full-blown, like some sort of horrible hallucination—Edith, totally naked, lying back on a bed and smiling, looking straight ahead while he's still adjusting the camera, and I'm struggling to my feet, knocking the ice cream one way and the poor cat the other and then Adam appeared on the screen. Or at least his body appeared, not his face, because the camera was focused on the bed, but of course I knew it was him, of course I recognized . . . Well, I just froze. I couldn't believe it."

"Because he was younger and hotter in the video?" Becca asks. Despite the fact that she claims to be grossed out, her tone is slightly hopeful. She's still looking for a love story. If not one of ours, then at least somebody's.

"But that's just the problem, he wasn't younger," Claire says. "Or at least not by much. It wasn't as if they'd made this sex tape in the early days of their marriage. That would have been easier to take. What I was watching clearly had been made within the last few years. It was a last-ditch attempt to save the marriage, I suppose, and it happened before I met him, but either way there was the Edith I knew from the kids' graduations and birthday parties, the woman I thought of as 'plain Edith' with the permanent circles under her eyes and the thick waist. But the way they were . . . performing, it was obvious they had taped themselves before."

"Seriously," says Becca, now truly horrified. "Even though they were old and ugly? Why would anyone want to take a picture of that?"

"I never said they were ugly," Claire says. "And they must

have been just over forty, an age that seems quite young to me now. But yes, in a way, you're right. They certainly didn't look like your typical porn stars, they looked just like themselves. And there was Adam, naked on the screen before me, and he was . . ." She stops and traces her lower lip thoughtfully with a fingertip, as if debating precisely what to say next.

"It must have been horrible," Jean says softly. "Seeing your husband having sex with another woman."

"Or was it exciting?" says Angelique. "Or exciting and horrible, a little bit of both?"

"Was he the same with her?" Valerie asks. "As he was with you?"

"No," says Claire sharply, whirling around to look at Valerie. "Thank you, because it's a simple thought and yet somehow I couldn't find a way to say it. That's exactly the issue. Adam was a different man with her. He was loud and rather violent."

"Violent?" asks Jean. "Surely you don't mean violent?"

"No, 'violent' is the wrong word," says Claire. "Completely wrong. It's just that on the tape he moved in a more . . . uninhibited fashion, there was something more animal or maybe you'd even say . . ."

"He was more passionate with her than he'd ever been with you," Tess says. She's either back to her trick of summing everyone up, putting the stories into neat little boxes before we've half-finished telling them, or she's terrified to think what sort of explanation we all might collectively come up with if she doesn't step in to supply a suitable one. So she gives us a word like "passionate," which is nice and soft and polite and thus sounds like the exact opposite of what it's supposed to mean.

"Passionate," Claire says slowly. "Yes, I suppose that's it, and she was . . ."

A pause. A long pause. Uninterrupted. No one among us has the slightest theory about what naked Edith might have looked like on that bed, not even Tess.

"She was what?" Valerie finally asks.

"She was much better than I was. Better than I ever was. Better than I am now."

"Edith?" says Silvia, in complete disbelief. Evidently she's met the woman at some point. "You're telling me that Edith Morrison, the Queen of the Faculty Teas, Miss I-Won't-Vaccinate-My-Children-Because-I-Read-Some-Report-About-Autism, the woman who's worn the same pair of black pants for ten straight years because she claims they still have plenty of wear in them . . . You're telling me that woman was good in bed?"

"No," says Claire. "I'm telling you that she was spectacular. What's that line from 'Pinball Wizard'? *At my usual table, she could beat my best.* And she could—no comparison, hands down, slam dunk. Edith Morrison was a goddess of sex."

We walk on, munching our apples, each of us likely contemplating the irony. That the plain, cautious, stalwart first wife was sexier than the thin, pretty, elegant second wife. The possibility raises a rash of questions, none of them comforting. For if the sex was so good in the first marriage, why did it fail? And exactly what did Claire mean by saying Edith was spectacular? The word implies trampolines and whips and choirs of angels—something beyond ordinary coupling, something that could reach right through the television screen and shake a woman to her core. And this time the man is literally faceless. Off the bridge, in the shadows, out of focus . . . why do we have so much trouble seeing the men in our stories? If we continue in this vein much longer, soon we won't even be bothering to name them. But Adam—intellectual, arrogant Adam—what could he have been thinking? When he swapped Edith for Claire, did he realize that even though he may have been rising in the eyes of the world, that from a bedroom sense he was stepping down? Because I believe Claire when she says that she knew at a glance that Adam's sexual connection with Edith was stronger than the one he had with her. That's the sort of thing women just know.

"Did you watch the whole tape?" Steffi asks.

"Several times. It was sixteen minutes long, I remember that most specifically. Sixteen minutes for me to realize that everything I'd ever thought about my husband was wrong." Claire sighs. "And I watched it the next day too, and the next. Every day I was supposed to feed Silvia's cat. I became quite obsessed, I suppose. I turned up the volume, in case they were saying things I was missing. They weren't. I studied it from every angle. I played it in slow motion. I even ran the tape in reverse, can you imagine? As it turns out, sex is one of the few things in life that looks exactly the same backwards as forwards. There's no difference at all."

"Did you tell him you'd watched it?" Angelique asks.

"Of course not. How could I do that? We didn't have a VCR player so there's no way I could have claimed to have seen it by accident. I tried to go on as if nothing had happened and the next week, there was a banquet at the high school. Adam and Edith's middle son Graham was getting a basketball award. So we were all there. I wore a pink dress, I remember, a sleeveless Dior with a matching coat. It was the best thing I owned—a gift from my first husband, come to think of it—and probably far too extravagant for a sports banquet in a high school cafeteria. What am I saying? Of course it was completely wrong. But it was my favorite dress and I put it on like a suit of armor. Because I knew I'd see Edith, sitting there at the same table, wearing her good black pants, and she looked exactly the same as she always had, and she was friendly enough. You know, I don't think she ever resented me at all. I never got that feeling. We ate the chicken and green beans and afterward they called the boys up, gave out the awards, and made the speeches. We clapped and took pictures and that was that. A perfectly pleasant evening with the extended family, everyone acting appropriately and keeping the attention on Graham, just as it should be. But all the time I kept staring at Edith. I couldn't seem to stop myself, even though there certainly was no flirtation between her and Adam. No crackling sexual electricity. They were polite and all about the children, just as they had always been. But everything had changed."

"Changed like how?" Becca asks. She's dropped her attitude now. The question is sincere.

"I'm not sure if I can explain it," Claire says. "All my life I've never been the smartest or the most talented. I was never the best at anything. Except for attracting men. That was my singular God-given gift. And I had never envied another woman before the moment that I saw that videotape. I suppose it had never occurred to me that a man might find another woman more desirable—and I know that makes me sound like a dreadful person, but why tell these stories if we aren't going to be honest about them? What would be the point?"

"There would be no point," says Silvia.

"We aren't sharing these stories to entertain each other," says Tess. She's walking at the rear of the pack for once, because here in this apple orchard the path is clear enough and it is Jean who has somewhat improbably emerged as the morning's leader. Jean who is walking fast, who must be almost out of earshot, chopping the air with her arms and pulling the rest of us into her pace. Tess's statement is odd. If we aren't telling these stories to entertain each other, why are we telling them? My head swims for a moment in a temporary vertigo. I get these attacks at times, especially when I'm driving, when I look up and around and for a minute I don't know where I am, what road this is, or even what city. Perhaps it's nothing more than what Claire said, the confusion that comes upon a woman in her forties. Because it's one thing to not know where you're going, but it's a whole other thing to forget where you've just been. It's terrifying. I could accept uncertainty about the road ahead—everyone feels that at some time or another—but this is something else. A more complete kind of disorientation.

"Tess is right," Valerie is saying. "The stories aren't meant to be a distraction, or a way to pass the time. They're our confessions."

"Mom," Becca calls up to the head of the pack, "slow down. You're leaving us."

"What do you mean by 'confessions'?" Steffi snaps. "I wasn't aware I had anything to confess."

"Then why are you walking to Canterbury?" Valerie says, in

an irritatingly calm tone of voice. No inflection at all, just a series of words. She sounds like a therapist.

"The Cathedral is one of the great wonders of the world," says Steffi, "and when I studied it in school I always promised myself that someday—"

"And that may be why you're going to see Canterbury," Valerie says, "but it doesn't explain why you've turned it into a pilgrimage. Walking the whole trail from top to bottom, that's a pretty grand gesture, isn't it? We all must have some sort of reason."

"Trains run between London and Canterbury on the hour," I hear myself say. Who told me that? Oh yeah, the closely cropped man at the George in London. This is the second time I've thought of him within an hour, and an idea bobs up from the confusion in my head. Could he have been the one who took my phone? But why would he do a thing like that? I was in the pub for quite a while after I said goodbye to him, sitting with the other Broads Abroad. If he'd seen I'd left my phone on the bar, he would have just brought it over to the table. I'm being crazy paranoid now. Making up stories out of nothing. Some busboy stole my phone. There was no cosmic message behind its disappearance. Nothing more than a random crime.

"Right," says Valerie, shaking her finger at me. "Che is exactly right. Trains do run from London to Canterbury, hour after hour, all day long. But trains are for tourists, aren't they? And we have declared ourselves to be pilgrims."

"Mom," says Becca, her voice shrill. "Seriously, slow down. Are you trying to leave me right here in this field?"

Mom.

Mom . . . Shit, I'd forgotten all about her. My hand goes automatically to my backpack, straining to reach for the familiar shape. But the ashes are crammed down into their appropriate place, a side pocket. She's fine. She's been there all along, right where she should be, zipped up in her little bag. I look over my shoulder at Tess, who is still at the rear of the pack. She doesn't seem to have noticed that we're disintegrating as a group. Walking too far apart, almost shouting back and forth to each other, and there is discord, palpable discord among us for the first time since leaving London. I wait for her to play her usual professorial card, to break in with some calming tidbit about Chaucer or the growing of apples or the legend of how some particular little burg got its queer name. But Tess seems as spacey today as the rest of us, far from her usual self, and it falls to Angelique to get us back on point.

"So you never told Adam?" she asks. "He never knew you found the tape?"

Claire shakes her head. The sun is hitting her squarely in the face now, and for just a passing instant she shows her age. "What was I going to say? It wasn't as if he'd done anything wrong. He and Edith had been married at the time they'd made the tape and if part of their deal was that they liked to film themselves and watch it back, then who was I to judge? Besides, Adam wouldn't have liked the fact that I'd watched the tape, I'm sure of that. He was very particular about how people viewed him. He had a sort of formality that he always said came with the job. He wouldn't have liked to hear that anyone had seen his homemade porn."

"Not even his new wife?" Angelique asks.

"Especially not his new wife."

"So . . ." says Angelique, surprisingly persistent, or maybe she's just thinking that this sort of problem is more on her home turf than anyone else's. "Did you see it as a challenge? Try to do some new stuff to surprise him in bed?"

Claire smiles. "Is that what you would have done?"

Angelique nods. "I would have stolen all of Edith's best moves."

"That probably explains why you've only been married once and I've had four unsuccessful runs at it. You're a trouper, Angelique. Good for you. You hang in there, and I admire that. Because I did the exact opposite, I'm afraid. Began avoiding him in bed altogether. First one excuse and then the next, until not only was I failing to live up to the image of Edith, I wasn't even being a good version of Claire anymore."

"What happened to the tape?" asks Steffi.

"On the day my dear friend was at last due back from her trip," Claire says, inclining her head toward Silvia, "I knew I had to destroy it. I couldn't leave it in her house and I didn't want to take it back to mine. But I didn't think it would be right to just toss it in a Dumpster. It might have been found. You're always hearing of people pulling things out of Dumpsters. We lived in a small college town, remember, where everyone knew everyone, and Adam had his reputation on campus to consider. Edith did too, I suppose. So I watched them one last time and I went out in Silvia's driveway and I put the tape down on the concrete and I ran over it in my Jeep Cherokee. Several times, back and forth."

"You really wanted to grind it away," Steffi says, with a twist of her mouth.

"But I couldn't," says Claire. "The case broke and went flat but the tape itself was still intact, hanging out the sides. So I went back into Silvia's house and got a pair of scissors and I cut it up, into a hundred pieces, none of them any bigger than a postage stamp, and I threw some of them in one trash bin and others in another until pieces of that tape were scattered all over town. I just kept driving from one mall to the next, putting a handful of celluloid into every Dumpster I found. And all the time I was thinking to myself, *No one must ever know this tape existed."*

"You were that determined to protect his reputation?" asks Jean. She has slowed down and looked back at us at last, but her face is flushed. That unhealthy mottled sort of flush that I've come to associate with her. *My first impression of you was so wrong,* I think, watching her blot perspiration from her forehead with the cuff of her chambray shirt. *I thought you were Princess Grace, the serene royal highness of some minor kingdom, but as it turns out, I was only fooled by your hair. Once the bun comes loose, there's nothing serene about you.*

"That's what I told myself at the time," Claire says. "That it was all for Adam. But in retrospect, I was only trying to protect my own reputation." She says it flatly, without embellishment. They're so different from each other, Jean and Claire, one of them spinning a tale meant to inspire envy, the other delivering a story so honest it makes the roots of your teeth ache. Despite her sweaters and hair and jewelry and figure and obvious wealth, it hits me that this is what I really should admire about

Claire. Her willingness to turn the garment of her life inside out, exposing all the frayed seams and hasty alterations. It's her flaws that make her likable. I need to remember this.

"I was the second wife, the trophy wife," Claire goes on. "It was my job to be the bombshell, and I'd failed miserably. Here I'd managed to get myself married to an incredibly sexy man and . . . I hadn't even noticed. So my first step was to destroy the evidence, and my second step was to avoid Adam."

"That marriage didn't last long," Silvia says quietly. "Not quite two years, was it?" She hasn't spoken much in the last mile or two and I suspect Claire's story has shocked her more than anyone. It's one thing to learn that you don't really know your husband or your lover. That's sort of a given, really. And I think most women would admit that they don't understand their mothers or their daughters all that well either. But it's a real kick in the gut to consider the possibility that maybe you don't know your best friend.

"No, that was the shortest marriage of all four of them," Claire says. "Not two years, soup to nuts, just as Silvia says. It was easy to leave Adam. I'm good at leaving men. Can pack and unpack in an instant, remember? But the irony is, I've never quite managed to leave Edith. The image of her on that bed still plays in my head and no matter how many times I try, I can't destroy it. It's like by cutting her up and spreading her over town I made her stronger. Maybe she's one of those sci-fi characters who turn into everything after they're dead. Who was that?"

"Obi-Wan Kenobi," I say.

"Exactly," says Claire. "Edith was the Obi-Wan Kenobi of sex. I struck her down and she became more powerful."

"Did you ever see her again, after your divorce?" Steffi asks. "The real her, I mean."

"Never," says Claire. "Well, hold on, that's not quite true. In fact, what am I saying? I ran into her in a bookstore not that long ago. It had been years, of course, and there was another husband since Adam, and I was with my new man, Jeremy. He's thirty years younger, so it's all very racy and forbidden. Started out as our pool boy, and I hope that doesn't make it sound as if I'm stereotyping him or just using him to shock people."

"I'm pretty sure Jeremy's using you to shock people too," Silvia says, running a grimy hand through her hair. Now that we've warmed up enough to pull off our jackets, I can see she's wearing a shirt that's oversize, not in that deliberately oversize, faux-jacket Chico's-catalog sort of way, but as if it's simply too large for her frame. It's a man's cast-aside oxford, the work shirt of a husband who no longer works, with the sleeves badly rolled up and the neck gaping. Silvia's one of the three pilgrims among us who is still married—and happily, evidently. Otherwise why would she bring her husband's shirt on vacation?

"No doubt you're right," Claire says. "But Jeremy and I ran smack into Edith in the cookbook section of that bookstore and the years . . . the years have not been kind to Edith, and there wasn't that much to work with from the start. I recognized her at once, but the funny thing is, when I first approached her I'm not sure she even knew who I was. I introduced Jeremy and later, when I told him, 'That woman and I were married to the same man,' he was the one who was shocked. He said all the right things, that I'm a thousand times prettier and sexier and more desirable. But while he's whispering this in my ear, Edith was paying for her books and leaving. When she got to the door I thought that surely she would turn and look back at me. Get one more eyeful of the woman who replaced her. But she didn't. She just walked out. I was nothing to her, and she changed my life."

"Changed your life?" Silvia says. "That's a strong way to put it."

"Maybe so, but it's accurate. Because you know, when I married Adam I was pretty much on track. I'd been divorced a couple of times, but a lot of people have been divorced a couple of times. And I'd had a few beaus in college . . . but a lot of people have had a few beaus in college. I wasn't significant in the way I am now."

"Significant?" Silvia asks. "What the hell does that mean?"

"Other women call me a slut, darling," Claire says, her bell-like laugh echoing through the orchard. "Maybe not in front of you, because you're fiercely loyal, but that's what they say about me behind our backs, and I'll admit they have a point. I have been with a lot of men and they weren't always the right men, or even the close-to-right men. It adds up to more than all the rest of you combined, I'm sure. Don't misunderstand. I'm not apologizing for my past, or making excuses, but it does have something to do with Edith. She rattled me. So for the past twenty years I've moved from man to man, and I wait, each time, for him to tell me that I'm the prettiest and the sexiest and their praise, you know, it's like a tiny pill. I take it and I feel better for a while, but the next day I need another tiny pill. Turning sixty has slowed me, I'll admit it, but not as much as you younger girls might guess."

God, I think. *Is that what Diana was doing all those years, with all those men in all those cars? Simply self-medicating?*

"You haven't had more men than all of us put together," says Silvia. "You're just exaggerating, like you always do."

"You said this was going to be a happy story," wails Becca. She needs to put the phrase on a T-shirt.

"Did I?" says Claire. "I thought I said it was going to be a sexy story. Isn't that what I said?"

"I think you said happy," says Angelique, her face illustrating what the rest of us are likely thinking—that Claire's story was neither particularly happy nor sexy. But it certainly was different, I'll give her that.

"Oh God," says Becca. "This is all so depressing. Nothing anyone has said so far has made me want to get old."

"Who do you think is winning?" Steffi asks.

"Winning?" says Becca in confusion. Steffi's question was thrown out to all of us but Becca seems to have assumed it was directed just at her.

"Winning the story competition so far?" Steffi clarifies, slowing her pace. "For the free dinner in Canterbury?"

"Oh dear," says Jean. "What's this?"

We have come to a little stream. It is perhaps ten steps wide at its narrowest point and it would seem we will have to cross it one at a time. Tess gamely wades in to show us the least treacherous route. She steps from one shallow to another but as she nears the other side, the water grows deeper, rising almost to the top of her boots. We all stand on the bank, watching and thinking.

"See?" she says. "You need to use a bit of ginger, but it's quite crossable."

"I'd forgotten we even had a bet," Claire says to Steffi.

"Me too," says Silvia. "And the three stories so far have all been totally different. There's no way to compare them."

"The easiest way to lose a competition," Steffi says, "is to forget that you're in a competition."

"Eleven," says Valerie.

"Eleven?" Tess echoes. She has climbed to the top of the bank on the other side and now is pointing to the shallow places in the stream, trying to show Jean where to step. Tess's boots, I note, are wet almost to the top but the waterline stops short of her pants. She crosses streams competently, just as she does everything else.

"That's how many men I've slept with," Valerie says. "Claire threw a gauntlet down, didn't she? I'm not afraid to meet the challenge. Eleven."

"Only six for me," Angelique says. "That's not many, is it? When you consider where I come from? I bet most girls in my high school had done six guys before they got out of tenth grade."

"Only the one," says Jean, then she makes a little yelp as water sloshes over the top of her boot and into her sock.

"Come on, Mom," says Becca. "You don't have to lie for my sake. I don't care if you've been with other men since Daddy. Of course you have. It would be downright sick if you hadn't."

"One," Jean repeats grimly, and Tess extends a hand to help her to the bank. She is splattered up to the knee on her left side and when she gets on dry land she finds a mossy place to sit down and unzip her backpack. We all carry extra socks on the advice of the Broads Abroad website and today I suspect we'll all use them.

"Well then it's one for me too," Becca says. She says it defiantly, staring down her mother, who isn't even looking back.

"Do you have a boyfriend now?" asks Angelique. She has ventured in next, choosing a different route across the stream. Despite the fact that she watched Jean carefully, trying to learn from her mistakes, Angelique doesn't seem to be making any better progress. In fact, she's only halfway across and her right boot is already splattered, with an ugly ribbon of algae fluttering from the suede fringe. "You've never mentioned anyone."

"There's someone," says Becca. "Mom doesn't like him. Mom doesn't think he's good enough for me. Surprise, surprise."

"I thought you said your story was about faithfulness," Jean says to Claire, pointedly ignoring Becca. She has a muddy boot in one of her hands, those hands with their perfectly shaped fingernails, painted the exact color of her skin. Her socks are abandoned on the riverbank, crusted with mud.

"It's about how I lost my faithfulness," says Claire, her voice as pleasant as if she were discussing the weather. "It's the story of how I slipped from being a respectable if somewhat roadworn wife and became the village tart. And all because I was trying to live up to the image of a woman on a videotape. That's funny, isn't it?"

"Hilarious," says Jean drily, shaking out one of her muddy socks.

"You're not the village tart," says Silvia. "Honestly, Claire, you say the most outlandish things. And besides, I think I'm going to bring up the average all by myself. My number of lovers, believe it or not, is seventeen." She says this with pride, and her total is indeed higher than I would have guessed. I know that finding men willing to sleep with you has virtually nothing to do with your level of beauty. Men will sleep with anyone, even a woman who looks like one of Chaucer's pilgrims. He described them all so cruelly—gap-toothed, pockmarked, humpbacked, and covered in boils. But a woman could have all of the above and more and still get laid. It's the one advantage of our sex, I suppose—that and early admission into lifeboats. But it's still strange to contemplate a universe in which a woman who looks like Silvia would have had more lovers than a woman who looks like Jean. Seventeen times more, to be exact.

"I was single for a very long time, you know," Silvia is saying, smiling as if she were lost in memory. "Between husbands one and two, that is." She's one of those women who is less attractive when she smiles, her face folding up on itself like origami, her eyes nearly lost in the pillows of skin.

"Look at me," Jean says. "I'm a mess."

"We're all going to be a mess before this is over," says Claire, with the confidence of someone who's never been a mess in her whole life.

"Maybe," says Jean. "But I didn't want to be the first mess."

I've spent a lot of time comparing how the older women are holding up on the trail, so now that we're stalled here on the bank, I take a moment to consider the others. I suppose it's fair to say that Valerie, who wears no makeup and makes little effort with herself, looks pretty much like she did back in London. Steffi has gone from city polish to country athlete with prac-

ticed aplomb, her hair in a twisted braid and her face shiny with
moisturizer. She's by far the best equipped of us, and with her
high-tech jacket and Patagonia boots she looks ready to scale a
glacier, not merely stroll the English countryside. The youngest
three women seem completely unchanged—Angelique because
her face is tattooed on, Tess because she knows how to prepare
for these walks, and Becca through the sheer resilience of
youth.

I wonder where I am in the mix, if the others are thinking
that the trail has made me better or worse. Probably worse. I
glanced at the small round mirror in the bathroom briefly this
morning and then looked away. There was no need to linger—I
brought nothing with me but Crest and Secret and besides, my
little vanities seem to be failing me these days. Makeup slides
from my face and my hair seeks out preordained patterns and
my clothes are all knits and neutrals and virtually interchange-
able. I have the look of a serious woman, but it suddenly hits
me, standing here at this little stream watching Angelique pick
her way across, that perhaps I should buy something that is a
color. Any color. Angelique is wearing an oversize beret, the kind
that sags like a Rasta's. It's turquoise, with a woven gold band
and some sort of little tassel dangling from the side. The hat
strikes me, here in the sunlight, as an amazing thing to behold.

"Your turn, Tess," says Angelique. She has made it through
the creek less muddy than Jean, but still muddy, and she stands
on the bank pointing out spots to Becca, who's going next, but
not paying the slightest attention to Angelique's well-meaning
advice. "How many guys have you done?"

"As leader of the group and judge, I fear I must withdraw

from the contest," says Tess. "Or at least I'm going to use my title as an excuse to withdraw. I'm very sorry about this little rill. I didn't realize it would be so swollen."

"What's a rill?" asks Becca, nimbly overstepping the worst part of the puddle, moving from one slippery rock to another.

"Only one for me as well," says Steffi. "I hit the bull's-eye with my first shot."

"Jesus," says Angelique. "Such a bunch of goody-goody girls we are. Is everybody lying?"

"I'm not," says Steffi, teetering a moment before finding her balance. "And it's only been one despite the innumerable opportunities I was offered in med school and during my residency. You know all those doctor shows on TV where everyone's always hooking up in the linen supply room? Having sex on the gurneys in the ER? All of that is kinda partly true, even if most of the interns don't look like John Stamos and Patrick Dempsey."

"There," says Becca, ignoring Tess's outstretched hand and springing to the bank in one fluid motion. She rubs her feet resolutely on the velvety carpet of moss, wiping off the small flecks of mud. "That's the way to go."

"I'm not sure I can hit all those rocks," Valerie says cheerfully. "I don't have your stride length. Aw hell, why try?" And then she plunges directly into the creek, sinking past her ankles with the first step and causing Tess to release an involuntary cry of dismay. There's a loud sucking sound as Valerie struggles to pull her leg free, and in the next step she sinks worse. *She's going to be ruined beyond redemption,* I think. *Her boots, the socks, the legs of her jeans. She can wash them out when we get to the next inn, but denim doesn't dry fast, so what's she planning to do tomorrow?* Valerie is a weird bird, no doubt about that. It's like she doesn't even try to do things the easy way.

When I look up, Becca and Steffi are both staring at me rather pointedly.

"Oh, okay," I say. "My turn. I may win this whole thing for Team NotClaire. I've tried to run the tally before, but I always lose count at thirty."

"Thirty?" says Becca. "You lose count at thirty? How old were you the first time you gave it up?"

"It's always the ones you least suspect," Silvia quietly observes, which I suppose could be taken as an insult, or maybe even a double insult, when you stop to break it down.

"I was well into college before I lost my virginity, so that's no excuse," I say, looking down at the water and trying to figure out how to make that critical first step. Where is Sir Walter Raleigh when you need him? I'd accept his cape now. I'd smirk and giggle and flirt and give him ten pounds without question, because even after all this time spent watching the others, I still have no idea how to get across this ridiculous creek. "I just had a couple of years in there where the numbers really rolled."

"Well, there you have it," says Silvia. "I've been keeping track. We stood at thirty-seven before Che, who completely manned up for the team, just as she says. So if we go with an estimate of thirty for her, that's a grand total of sixty-seven and there's no way you can top that, no matter how distraught you were about the Edith situation." She has followed Valerie into the stream and is moving well, stepping steadily from one spot to another, forging her own route and confirming my suspicion that she's an outdoor girl at heart. Strange that she would be the one to keep a running track of the total in her head, but she still seems peeved at Claire for telling a story she'd never heard, especially one like this. She wants numerical proof that her best friend isn't really the village tart.

"The Edith situation . . ." Valerie says, scrambling to the bank at last. She is covered in mud and I can't even think how she's going to get herself cleaned up enough to enter a pub for lunch. "I like it. It's a good name for all the women we compare ourselves to, all those tapes we run in our head that tell us someone else out there is better than us." Then she looks at me when she turns, with that annoying slight smirk on her face, and I'm sure I'm looking back at her with the exact same expression I pulled when she ordered the white zinfandel. I'm critiquing her creek-crossing performance in my mind, but it's easy to mock the muddiness of others when you're still standing on the bank. When you haven't even started the process yourself. Who knows how many times you might slip before your own journey is done? I've looked up and down along the rill and there is a tree with a low-hanging branch not far away. *I'll just mosey downstream and hold on to that*, I think. *Use it to stabilize myself, at least for the first few steps.* But there will still come a point where I have to let go, halfway through, and then . . . who knows? With my luck the branch would snap back and hit me in the face and knock me into the stream ass-first. I have the feeling a couple of the women would totally enjoy seeing that.

"Sixty-seven men," Silvia is saying, as she reaches the other side of the stream, stepping up near Steffi, who is wiping nonexistent mud from her boots. "It's an admirable number of conquests for a group of gentle pilgrims. So you see, darling, your number isn't so shocking after all."

But Claire is following the same path across the stream that Becca took and, despite the fact that she's more than forty years older than the girl, she's doing an admirable job of jumping from stone to stone. We watch as she avoids every trap and takes Tess's hand, pulling herself up without the slightest splash on her pale-gray boots.

"Still winning," she says softly, as her feet hit the moss.

EIGHT

That night, for the first time in forever, I am aroused.

It takes me a moment to realize it. I toss and turn in the bed. Count my breaths, picture waves breaking on a beach, prop a pillow under my knees. All my standard tricks to go back to sleep, but none of them work. And even when I finally sit up and admit that something is happening within me, I don't call it arousal. I give it every other name I can think of—insomnia, indigestion, anxiety, ennui. Even homesickness for Freddy.

I went to sleep easily enough. I always miss my phone, of course, but for the first time since we started the trail, I didn't need to read a chapter from my thriller to wind down. We've upgraded from the evening before. This time our inn is located in the village square of a sweet little town—everything your fantasy of the English countryside might be. Roses in the window boxes, sleeping setters by the fireplace, that sort of thing. The pub had been packed at dinner and it had taken some shuffling to move enough tables and chairs to seat a party of nine. Two other groups of Americans were staying there too: a family with teenagers, and three elderly sisters—named Mary, Margaret, and Martha or something like that—who were traveling by Bentley with a private guide. We had chatted back and forth among our tables as we ate, and they had been intrigued with the idea that our group was walking to Canterbury.

It had been Steffi who'd first announced our collective mission. When one of the old ladies asked what had brought us all together, Steffi had leaned back in her chair and rather proudly said, "We're pilgrims, on the trail to Canterbury Cathedral."

Interesting. She'd been reluctant to claim the title during our walk this afternoon, but suddenly she couldn't wait to call herself a pilgrim. I suppose that's why she's doing this. Not to confess her failings or receive a blessing—she's walking to Canterbury simply so that she can tell people that she did it. The faces of the other Americans had indeed lit up as she spoke. *Why yes,* their expressions seemed to say. *That's what we should be doing too. Undertaking a grand quest, embarking upon something definitive and purposeful instead of just mucking around the countryside with a private driver. We need a trip we can eulogize to our friends when we return.* Canterbury may not be the ultimate destination, but it's the ultimate brag.

Still, it had been a pleasant evening, the most relaxed and generous we've shared so far. The pub had a decent wine list and Tess ordered a couple bottles for the table, saying it was on the company. My foot had held up better through the day's hike than I'd feared, but now some of the others were complaining about blisters and hot spots too, probably the result of the last hour's walk in wet shoes following our slog through the stream. As we finished our coffee and pudding, we all seemed to grow tired at the same time, and we had gone upstairs early, about half past eight.

Steffi offered me her phone just before she went into her room. She's offered it to me each time we've reached a place with wi-fi, and I know she means well. But I'm on a roll now and I don't want to lose my momentum. Two and a half days without checking messages is a personal record for me, and besides, I still don't have the foggiest idea of what I should say to Ned. You're thinking that I'm playing a cruel game with him, making him worry just to even the score, but I swear I'm not. It's just that I've been seized with a sort of uncertainty that began in the bar back in London and seems to have grown incrementally with every step of the trip. When I know what to do, then I'll do it.

And it isn't as if I've left Ned utterly dangling. He's an attorney, after all. If he's worried enough to investigate, he should be able to ascertain that I've put a hold on my mail, boarded Freddy, left notice of my absence with the condo manager, and bought a ticket from Philly to Heathrow. I can't say exactly how he might discover any of these things, but I have no doubt that a lawyer knows a thousand ways to get the dirt on people.

I was in my nightgown and turning back the bed by 8:45. Face washed, teeth brushed, feet slathered in Vaseline and encased in thick, fuzzy socks. And I think I dozed immediately, but my room's located just above the pub and it's hard to tune out all the noises from below. The sounds of laughing and drinking, doors slamming, the drone of the telly turned to a rugby game, the shouts of celebration or disgust when one team or another scores. Noises like this always seem to seep up through the floorboards and into your sleep and I think I must have been dreaming about the pub, or specifically about one of the men I had seen there, when I startled awake.

So here I am. Here I lie, doing all my breathing and pillow-plumping tricks, frantically trying to jump back on the sleep train before it passes me entirely. But instead I seem to be caught in that worst-case scenario—when you've had an hour or two of sleep and it's recharged you enough that you know you'll be up for a while. If I were at home, I could work. But I'm not at home, and there is no work. Besides, something else is wrong with me. Something I can't yet name.

I pull on my jeans and sweatshirt, then ease down the steep, narrow staircase and back to the pub. It feels a little strange to be walking around in public wearing just my thick, fuzzy socks, but I can't face putting those boots back on a second before I have to. It's not like I'll ever see any of these people again. Let them laugh and point.

But they don't. They don't look at me at all. The pub is still fairly busy, and I squeeze into a seat at the end of the bar, in that undesirable spot directly in front of the cash register, and order a glass of the okay cabernet we'd had with dinner. *That would be a good name for it*, I think, *a good label. "I'll have a glass of the Okay Cabernet."* The man I was dreaming of is still here, and that's an odd thing, isn't it? He's playing darts and he's the only one in the pub who's bothered to notice me, in that way that even a blind man can sense the glance of a woman across a crowded room. I contemplate calling out, "You're the man of my dreams, you know." I don't remember the details of the dream itself, only that he was there and that he was carrying some sort of camera.

A camera. Yes, the man was taking pictures of me, that's right.

I watch him throw the dart. Lightly, with a low, long arc. It's an effortless and artful movement, probably the result of innumerable evenings of practice. It lands in what appears to be the center of the board, although it's hard to tell at this angle, and he turns and looks at me openly now, not a sideways flicker of interest but a full-frontal stare, making sure I've noted his prowess. I smile and raise my glass.

No, he wasn't taking pictures of me. That's not it. Not quite.

But he had been taking pictures of something. Something naughty and forbidden. Because when I had tried to look through the camera lens he had pulled it back and laughed roughly. A pirate's laugh. And he had said, "That's not for the likes of you to know."

Not for the likes of you to know. That's what woke me up, his voice and the fleeting image of a man crouched behind a camera, a notion so clearly lifted from Claire's story. She'd said she was obsessed with the videotape of her husband and his first wife, and I wonder if I would be the same. If I had the chance, would I watch Ned and . . . what's her name? Now, that's strange too. According to the rules of romance, I'm supposed to hate this woman. I'm supposed to tell everyone I meet how she ruined my life—or at least that she changed my life, and for a woman like me there's not much difference between being ruined and being changed. They gallop like the same horse. But less than a week after learning of her existence, I've already gone and forgotten her name.

It started with an *R*, I believe. Rebecca? No, that's the full name of our Becca. Her mother has slipped and called her that a couple of times. Rhonda? Robin? Rachel? Rachel. That doesn't sound quite right, but it will have to do.

So . . . if I were offered the chance to see a movie of Ned and Rachel in bed, would I take it?

I know what the answer is supposed to be. I'm supposed to say "Of course not," for curiosity leads to comparison and comparison leads to disaster. If we've learned anything from The Tale of Claire, it's that. And yet if I were watching the two of them now, making the beast with two backs right here in front of me and God and everyone in this quintessentially British pub, I think some part of me would know that whatever Ned was with Rachel was not my Ned. He would be some darker, wilder version of Ned. The half of the moon you never see.

And if I'm going to continue along this stream of honesty, I must add that the thought of Ned and Rachel on this scarred wooden floor doesn't make me jealous, it makes me . . . something else. I'm not quite ready yet to use the word *aroused,* but I am distracted by the image. Distracted enough that I don't notice that the man has left his darts and approached the bar. He is standing beside me, one hand on the back of my chair and the other waving a pound note at the barmaid, and he says, "So I see you've managed to lose your friends, but haven't you, love?"

I look at him blankly.

"We get a lot of Americans coming through here," he says. "Mostly girls, but always in groups. Hard to cut a bird out when she's flying with a whole flock of them, isn't it?"

"We're walking to Canterbury," I tell him.

He nods impatiently, as if to say, "Of course you are." Apparently that's been the source of this pub's trade for a thousand years, its prime location halfway between London and Canterbury.

"What's your route tomorrow?" he asks, probably more out of habit than out of any particular curiosity. He is shorter than I generally like men to be, probably no more than an inch taller than I would be if I slid off this stool and looked him eye to eye. No taller than Michael. His hands are thick and rough—something about him suggests a truck driver, or maybe a deliveryman, someone who lifts and carries things all day long. But his face is animated, the eyebrows shooting up and down as he talks, the mouth mobile and expressive. He's easy. The sort of man where you see it all, right there on the surface.

"I'm not sure where we're going next," I say, surprising myself with the answer. But it's true. At each previous stop, whether for lunch or dinner, someone in the group, usually Steffi, has peppered Tess with questions about the road ahead. How many hours we'll walk, how many miles we'll tally, the names of the towns we'll pass through. But tonight no one thought to ask.

"I'm not sure what you call a group of pilgrims walking," I say to the man, who's just standing there and smiling, fiddling with the dart in his hand. I'm stalling for time, trying to figure out if he's attractive. I think he is, in a way that's Definitely Not

My Usual Type, but that's a good thing too, isn't it—like taking an occasional swig of white zinfandel? He has that sort of testosterone-fueled self-confidence that I'm unaccustomed to, and my mind flashes back to a vineyard tour I took last summer in Sonoma. They had let me drive the truck, a big trembling truck loaded with grapes, and the road had been rutted and all of us wine writers on the tour had been "helping with the harvest," just like the rich Londoners come out on Sundays to "help with the hops." The real vineyard workers must have resented the hell out of us, but it had been fun to drive that big trembling truck.

I wouldn't mind driving a truck again.

"Everybody knows a group of geese is a gaggle," I babble on, and now he's the one whose expression is growing vague. "But some of the group names for animals, especially birds, are very clever. A group of larks is an exaltation. An unkindness of ravens, that's another good one. A murder of crows. A mustering of storks. Have you ever heard any of these? I've always found this sort of thing fascinating. And a group of hummingbirds is called a charm. Isn't that one especially wonderful?"

He scrapes his palm with the point of the dart. It's like I'm speaking a foreign language.

"A flamboyance of flamingos?" I try. "A parliament of owls?"

I don't know why I keep trying to talk to men. It rarely goes well. And this poor guy is now standing here before me with his mouth literally hanging open. No, we're not each other's type at all. He's nothing like the man back in London with the closely cropped gray hair, another person whose name I can't remember, or maybe I never knew it. But that man and I had spoken of serious things. I had told him about my mother dying and Ned leaving. This conversation will not be anything like that.

Instead, he pulls over a bar stool, and we begin to talk of nothing. Or maybe I should say he begins to talk of nothing and I begin to drink harder. He says he has a part interest in this pub, that he's sort of a silent partner, and he tells me stories of the people who have passed through. He offers to buy me a beer, even though I am clearly drinking wine. "You'd like a pint, wouldn't you now?" he says, and I feel myself nodding before I even understand the question. So I end up with a beer sitting on my left side and the glass of wine on my right.

He says all the usual stuff, the stuff I guess he feels he has to say. How he noticed me right from the start within the group, how I'm the looker of the table. It's not true and even if it were, the fact that he feels he has to talk like this makes me like him a little less. I've got a knee-jerk suspicion of flattery. Always have. Another thing that goes back to Diana, who would savor a compliment the same way I savor a good Bordeaux, rolling it around on her tongue, sniffing at it a little, her eyes closed and her expression expectant. Since I started thinking about this yesterday I've been doing a little inventory in my head, and if memory serves, she left my father three times for men who claimed to see things in her that he did not. Her flatterers always managed to fail her within days, maybe even hours, of her leave-taking. She always returned to the commune in the end, walking up the steps without explanation, dropping her satchel on the rocking chair beside the door. Her experiences with these temporary men never seemed to leave her either sadder or wiser, and there are times when I feel that my entire childhood was spent held hostage to a succession of trifling strangers who happened to tell my mother she was beautiful.

Strangers like this trifling man sitting beside me now, scratching some figure in the bar with his dart. An S, it looks like. Maybe he's trying to spell my name.

"Don't tell me I'm pretty," I say, not because I don't believe I am. Women who are always saying they're ugly or fat or stupid annoy me. They're the biggest egoists of all, just trying to turn one compliment into twenty. So don't get the idea that I'm self-effacing. I don't play dumb or let people cut me off in traffic or dig around in my pants for handfuls of fat to shake at my girlfriends, wailing, "Can you believe this?" I do not deny that on occasion I can be clever, witty, talented, good in bed, and yes, even attractive, but I've never trusted the men who point any of this out. Because I've known since childhood that flattery is the first shot fired in the battle of the sexes, and I can remember, all too clearly, listening to a newcomer at the commune telling Diana how special she was, seeing her eyes close, and knowing that soon enough I would be in the backseat of another car.

"All right then," says the man with the dart. "You can be pretty and I can shut up about it and we can both have another drink. Because the whole world gets prettier, doesn't it, love, when you take yourself just one more drink?"

And, fueled by this burst of philosophy, ten thirty becomes eleven and then eleven thirty and still we are sitting thigh-to-thigh until there are three empty beer glasses on my left side and two wineglasses on my right, and at some point he says, part command and part entreaty, "Come with me to the smoking garden."

Come with me to the smoking garden. Just the invitation every girl hopes to hear. But I am quite drunk by this time and so I slip down from my stool, wobbling as my furry socks hit the wooden floor. We walk hand in hand from the bar, our departure apparently fascinating to the clumps of locals who still linger there. Heads turn, and one of the men at the dartboard snickers, but I ignore it. I've gone into that zone. I couldn't be deterred if this snickering man tried to tackle me. We go down the hall and through the kitchen, where a boy is washing dishes, out the back, the screen door slamming behind us, and into the smoking garden.

It's dark. Only two dim lights, one over the door and another farther away, flickering uncertainly in the parking lot. I'm cold. I don't have my jacket. But it doesn't matter, for there is little preamble. He wraps his arms around me and kisses me. It's good. Better than good. Quite a bit better, but wait . . . how can it be this good? For this kiss to be this good goes against every law of logic. I hardly know this man. He knows me even less. We have never seen each other before. We will never see each other again. But I guess that's why it's good, this kiss that comes with no past and no promises.

"Do you want to go somewhere?" he says. He speaks roughly, just as he did in my dream.

I'm woozy, both from the kiss and from my slow-dawning realization that somehow I've managed to get not just drunk, but capital-D Drunk, drunker than I've been in decades. Far worse than the tipsy afternoon back at the George and what is this country doing to me, making me slip and stagger, lose my equilibrium just a bit more with every step I take? I dig my fuzzy toes into the cold, wet bricks of the courtyard and try to focus. He says he wants to go somewhere, but where? It would seem as if we're already at the only place in town there is to go, but he isn't asking me out on a date, of course he isn't. It must be close to midnight by now. Most of the village is sleeping. Upstairs the pilgrims are too. What he wants is for me to get in his car with him, to drive down a dark road. Park in some field and have quick, anonymous sex.

Which is insane, of course. It's irresponsible. Raw. Risky. And probably exactly what I need.

The man standing before me is nothing if not confident. He takes my silence for consent. "I'll get my car," he says and then, with another little deal-sealing kiss, a drag of his salty tongue across my lower lip, he disappears through the arch of a trellis gate. It's the sort of thing that in the spring is undoubtedly covered in climbing roses, just that sentimental and sweet. But it isn't spring now, it's autumn. This is the season in which things fall off of other things, the time of letting go. The trellis before me is swathed in brambles, their tangled brown thorns barely visible in the watery light.

This is a fine mess. I'm probably about to be raped and killed and I don't even have a phone to call the constable in Dartford. I step toward the gate, maybe just to look out into the parking lot, to reassure myself that this is all real, that there really is a man going to get a car, and suddenly a bright, hot pain rips through the sole of my foot.

I've stepped in glass. Someone's broken beer bottle. This

courtyard is undoubtedly full of nothing but ashes, thorns, and shattered glass, and I stand on one foot and lift up the other, wincing as I move, weaving on my singular drunken leg. I can feel blood seeping through my sock and shards from the bottle are probably embedded in my foot and I've really screwed it up this time. For a second I think I might puke or faint, but I stave off both impulses and finally put the ball of my foot down—the worst of the damage is in my heel—and tiptoe back toward the screen door. Back through the kitchen, down the hall, and into the pub, where my rapid return from the smoking garden, solo and half-hopping on one foot no less, brings the entire assembly to silence.

Valerie is there. She is sitting at the bar, sipping a cup of tea. She says, "My God, what happened to you?"

"I don't even know where to begin," I say. I climb awkwardly onto the stool beside her and show her my foot. She curses at the sight of the blood. We ease off the sock while one barmaid dips me up a towelful of ice and the other goes to find the pub's first aid kit.

"What were you doing outside in your socks?" Valerie says, bending low over my foot, flicking away the bits of glass. She doesn't appear to be squeamish, which is lucky.

"Kissing some local. He's gone to get his car. He thinks I'm going off in a hops field to have sex with him."

"Why on earth does he think that?"

"Because I sort of told him that I would."

"That would be our own Randolph Robbie," says the bar-maid, back with a rusted white box that holds bandages, alcohol, and iodine. From the look of the kit, it's seen a lot of use. "He likes the ladies."

"Can you go out back and tell him to just go on home, that I've cut my foot?" I say, crazy to the end. Still trying to explain myself, even to a rapist in a smoking garden.

"Oh, not to worry, love," she assures me. "He's used to the girls not showing up where they say they'll be." She bends down too, holding out a clean napkin in which Valerie can place the pieces of glass. The shards seem to be coming out large and whole, another stroke of undeserved luck. "A thousand birds have given Randy Boy the slip in a thousand ways. He'll just toddle off home and wank off like he usually does."

"He said he owns this bar."

"Did he now?" She produces another towel, this one bearing the faded face of the Princess of Wales, and holds it carefully below while Valerie pours alcohol over the heel of my foot. It stings like the end of the world, and tears come to my eyes, but I struggle to not make a sound. She's being very nice—they all are, considering it must be closing time and here I am bleeding all over their bar. "Hear that, Lucy? Randy Boy Robbie will be paying our wages from now on. Seems he's the new boss."

The other barmaid snorts. *Randy Boy Robbie*, I think. *Perfect. Claire may be the village tart, but I've just gotten the kiss of a lifetime from the village idiot.*

"How much do I owe you?" I ask. "Since he's not the bar owner I'm assuming these drinks aren't on the house?"

"Let's see. Three pints and two wines comes to . . . twelve pounds."

"Really? That doesn't sound like much."

"We aren't in London now, are we?"

"Can I charge it to my room? I'm staying here, with the—" but she is already shaking her head. All our meals and lodging are included in the tour price and I guess it gets complicated when we start trying to charge extras willy-nilly. Valerie is already reaching for her purse. It's slung over the back of her bar stool, a Coach bag. I've never seen her with a pocketbook and not a backpack and a Coach bag is approximately the last thing in the world I would've imagined she'd carry. She wrinkles her nose.

"It was a gift," she says.

"A nice gift," I say.

"Yeah?" She lifts the bag to the bar and studies it. "I suppose you're right. But my mother . . . she's always giving me these pricey, elegant things that I don't want. She doesn't understand me."

"Nobody's mother understands them. I owe you about fourteen dollars. Or fifteen. Maybe sixteen. All things considered, I think I need to leave a pretty big tip."

"Don't worry about it," Valerie says. "We can settle up later." She doesn't say anything about my willingness to take off with Randy Boy, or about today's confession that I'd been with thirty men. Funny thing is, before that very moment, I'd never thought of thirty as a lot. In fact, you could argue that thirty men over the course of thirty years adds up to a pretty sexless life, but from the expressions on everyone's faces it had been clear that they were adjusting their opinions of me on the spot. Good thing I left it at thirty and claimed to have lost count there, because I actually think the total may be closer to forty.

"The thing is, I can't even remember the last time I felt this drunk," I say, babbling a bit, as if Valerie is judging me, even though I know she's probably the last one of the group who truly would.

"Seriously. If I'm at one of the big festivals, I can do wine tastings from nine in the morning to midnight without getting the slightest bit buzzed. But you're being a good girl, I see. Having tea."

She makes another slight grimace, just like she did with the Coach bag. "It's peppermint. They say it helps with nausea."

"You don't feel well?"

"Maybe I'm just not used to good wine." She stretches. "Maybe drinking anything over ten dollars a bottle makes me feel kind of sick, just like carrying a Coach bag. But I do think I can sleep now. What about you? Do you need help up the stairs?"

"I'm okay," I say. "The cut sobered me up." And then I realize she's talking about my foot. The wound didn't seem to be too broad, just deep. A puncture, a stab, a single stigmata-like circle of blood, but the barmaid has cushioned my heel with a square of gauze and crisscrossed the gauze with Band-Aids. She's done a damn fine job, actually. I should be able to walk on it tomorrow.

The stairwell sways like a hammock, but I make it up and to my room. Flip the dead bolt and sit down on the bed. Ball up the ruined socks and toss them toward the wastebasket, missing. And I stare at the door. *There's such a thin panel between me and the world*, I think. *Plywood. Parcel board. Any stranger could break it down at any minute.* And I wonder why we feel safe at some times—like speeding down the highway, for example—when we're actually probably in a fair amount of danger and why at other times when we're actually very safe, our hearts begin to pound and the world feels sharp-edged and treacherous. It took a broken beer bottle to save me from myself tonight, and all of this is so unlike me, so—

A noise. It's coming from outside, just beneath my window.

I hop over and look down. It's Randy Boy, of course, and how the hell did he know which room was mine? He's yelling up, like a drunken, slack-jawed Romeo, or no, maybe he's more of a Stanley screaming for his Stella, because he's calling out my name, over and over. He's going to wake everyone up. All the other women in the group. Everybody in town.

When he sees my face at the window, he stops. Tilts his chin to one side and says, "Did you forget me, love?"

I probably never will. "I'm not coming down," I hiss.

"Then I'll come up. Don't you know I've scrambled up this chimney a dozen times before."

Somehow I don't doubt that in the least. "I've hurt myself," I say.

"And I know how to make you better," he says. He spreads his arms out and begins to twirl in slow motion with his head thrown back. He looks like a child trying to catch snowflakes on his tongue.

"No," I say. "I'm not coming down and you're not coming up. I cut my foot. It's over. They told me you'd just go home and wonk off." Or was it wank off? Something like that. Either way, he needs to go home.

"What?" he says, stopping midtwirl, brow furrowed. "They told you what?"

Wrong. Wrong thing to say. I don't want to make him mad. Don't want to set off another round of him yelling my name into the darkness. I try a new tactic.

"You've played me for a fool, you have," I say. "Leading me to think you owned this pub and now the barmaid tells me that's a lie."

He shakes his head. "She's a bitter one, that Lorrie. Or was it Lucy? Doesn't matter, they're both of them dead bitter."

"Maybe so, but are they liars?"

There is silence from the darkness below. He has no comeback to that.

"I only went with you because I thought you were a man of property," I tell him. "I thought you had some standing in the community, could give me a home and a proper future. But you lied and now it's over between us."

He nods slowly. It's the sort of rejection he can understand and accept.

"On your way then, Che de Milan," he says softly. "On your way then to Canterbury with your gaggle of pilgrims."

"Goodbye," I say, closing the window, surprised to note that I feel a small but sharp pang of regret. For this all meant something, this strange confluence of events tonight, even if I don't know what it is yet. Tonight I may have felt crazy, but at least I felt something, and that part was nice. Besides, what am I to make of all these men, each sending me on my way in turn? "I wish you the best," one says. "Fare thee well," says another, or "So it's off with you, I take it?" or "On your way then, Che de

Milan." There are so many ways a man can tell a woman good-bye, and it seems like in the past week I've heard them all.

"How did you used to handle it, Mom?" I say out loud to my backpack in the corner, to the bag of ashes tucked inside. "How did you run so many men without it ever getting out of hand?"

But she keeps her counsel on the matter, just as she did when she was alive.

I crawl back into bed for the second time tonight. Maybe I'm having some sort of psychological breakdown, some delayed PTSD from Ned's letter. Because I had been minutes away from getting into a car with a man I didn't know. Driving into the darkness, down an empty road. Letting him unfold me across his seat, taking his body into mine, throwing back my head and baying up at the milky moon. Put it that way and it sounds like madness, but then again, Claire had been married and still found herself sleeping with a man she didn't know. Maybe they're all just different levels of the same madness. The only thing I know for sure is that I must fall asleep soon or to-morrow will be a nightmare. I cut off the light and roll over. Try to make a comfortable nest out of the stiff quilts and thin pil-lows. Exhale loudly and slowly, just like the meditation tapes say to do.

Renee. It comes to me unbidden, but that's her name. That's the girl Ned left me for. Well, God bless her, she has him now. Actually I guess she has her own personal Ned, but she doesn't have my Ned, because just like I thought at the bar, that's impossible. It's like that saying "No man can step into the same river twice." Who said that? Confucius? No, I think it was someone else, someone Greek. But it's true, so I guess it's also true that no two women can step into the same Ned twice, and Jesus, I think, I'm either still drunker than I thought I was, or I'm getting really deep. Because I am suddenly consumed with the notion that it's impossible to lose anything, at least at the core. That whatever we think is lost or dead has really just moved on and taken another shape.

Ned is a new person now, I think. *And you know something? At least for this moment, that is absolutely fucking fine with me.*

I roll over in bed. The mattress sags in the middle, sinks me into a soft groove, and my heel throbs like a heartbeat and I'm tired, very tired. The sounds from below are more muted now. The thud of a car door beneath my window—one of the last men standing is finally leaving the pub. God bless you, stranger from the bar. Safe travels home. God bless Renee and Randy Boy and Valerie and Lorrie and Lucy, the bitter barmaids, and Allen in the Guatemalan water—or was it Honduras where he went off the bridge? It hardly matters. God bless all the men who fell into all the water, wherever they were, and Nico in prison and Tess, who must have seen and heard so much on these walks but who tucks it all inside her shirt pocket, who bends her head and folds her hands just like a nun, and bless the charms of hummingbirds with their small wings fluttering across the world and God bless Diana above me in heaven and in her baggie down below, and God bless me. I think I might need the blessing of God. I think I might need it more than anyone. Because something else has occurred to me tonight, out in the smoking garden, in that world of ashes and beer and thorns and glass. Another thing that you're probably way ahead of me on, another obvious sign that the ever-so-discriminating

Che de Milan has somehow managed to miss. Another illustration of Tess's point that while it's easy to analyze the stories of others, it's nearly impossible to grasp the meaning of our own.

When my mother told me that it's never too late for healing, she hadn't been talking about herself.

NINE

I can't believe none of you heard him," I'm saying to the others the next morning, as we walk down the country road leading to the trailhead for the day. "He was right under my window, yelling my name."

"Like *Romeo and Juliet*," Becca says. "It's my favorite Shakespeare play."

An unlikely choice for a girl who claims to be in search of a happy love story, but then again, Becca's still in high school. *Romeo and Juliet* is probably the only Shakespeare she's ever read and it's designed to appeal to teenagers, this idea that the star-crossed lovers could have been eternally happy if only their stupid parents had managed to get their shit together.

"*Romeo and Juliet* crossed my mind too," I tell her. "But then I thought he was more like Stanley out of *A Streetcar Named Desire*. Randy's a little too rough around the edges to play Romeo."

I've decided I may as well confess the whole thing. If I don't, Valerie might bring it up, and who knows how bad her version of the story will be, me making out with a stranger in my sock feet and bleeding everywhere and not having any money. Which is all true enough, so my only hope is to beat her to the punch and when I finish describing my adventures of the previous evening, everyone laughs. It's sympathetic laughter, the inclusive kind.

I should go around all day long confessing my mistakes, I think. List them in alphabetical order, like the capitals of the states. Or maybe in chronological order, and then in ascending and descending degrees of severity. Add in accents and hand gestures as I talk, show them what it looked like when I hopped through the bar or Randy threw the dart. It's a piece of vital information from another lifetime that I keep having to relearn—that when you tell people exactly how and when you screwed up, it only makes them like you better. All the accomplishments in the world won't earn you as many friends as one embarrassing story, and I remember how I once overheard two baristas in a coffee shop, standing behind the bar steaming their milk and scooping their foam. And one of the girls had said to the other, "What'd you do last night?" and the second one answered, "The wrong thing." They'd laughed, just as the women on the trail are laughing now, in that true camaraderie that only exists among the fallen. The sort of friendship that can only arise from the ashes of failure.

"He may have been dumb," I say. "But he was a hell of a kisser." And at this Claire and Valerie erupt in fresh gales of giggles, which echo throughout the group. Everyone is in high spirits this morning. The sun is bright, the air is fresh, the temperature feels more like October than November, and we have just passed a marker that Tess said indicates we're more than halfway to Canterbury. The combination of a night in a comfortable inn with ample showers, a breakfast of eggs and sausage in our stomachs, and the story of my midnight tryst has cheered us all up.

"What made you go down to the pub in the first place?" Angelique asks.

"I woke up from a really strange dream. I think Claire's story made me horny."

At this more laughter, and a couple wails of protest, because I think we all know that Claire's story wasn't supposed to make a person horny.

"It's sick to get off on something like that," Becca says, but for once she's giggling too.

"Don't let them make you feel bad, Che," says Claire. "I never told you what I was doing while I was watching that videotape."

Now the loudest chorus of denial yet arises, with Steffi yelling, "TMI!" Becca saying, "That's gross," and Silvia moaning, "Oh God, my poor cat." We walk a bit more without speaking, but every single one of us is smiling.

"We have an option today," Tess says. "A ten-kilometer route that takes an extra loop around some stables or a more direct seven-kilometer route. Thoughts?"

"The ten," says Steffi. "I want to see it all."

"Me too," I say. It comes out automatically, even though what we're talking about seeing is a stable and even though I'm a bit worried about how my feet are going to hold up now that I have both a blistered toe and a punctured heel.

"If we walk farther will we have to walk faster?" asks Valerie.

"A bit," says Tess.

"Then I'm not sure we'll see more," she says.

"Of course we will. The faster you walk, the more ground you cover and the more you see," says Steffi. Slowly, in a tone of voice most people save for toddlers. "That's how it works."

"I'm not sure I agree," Valerie says, and then Jean and Silvia chime in too. Even Claire. It's okay to slow down, they all murmur. Take a breath now and then. We don't have to circle every stable in Kent trying to prove something. Sometimes we walk too fast.

Steffi looks at me and I shrug, as if to say it's not worth the fight. And it isn't. Ten miles don't necessarily take you any farther than seven. Thirty men don't necessarily teach you more than one. The closer we get to Canterbury, the more it's beginning to dawn on me that whatever answer I've been seeking, it isn't numerical. I still don't know what success in life is, exactly, but I can almost hear Diana's voice in my ear, whispering one of her fortune-cookie sayings. *If you can count it, it doesn't count.*

"Are you up-to-date on your tetanus shots?" Steffi asks, and it takes me a beat to figure out what she's talking about. The puncture on my heel. Of course a doctor would wonder about it. I nod.

"I tour vineyards for a living," I say. "I keep up-to-date on all that stuff."

"Your parents had a vineyard, didn't you say?" Valerie asks. "It's kind of sweet you went into the same work."

"They had an orchard."

"Same thing, more or less," she says. "Isn't it?"

Is it? Damn. She has a point. A very obvious point. Apples

to grapes, that's about as far as I've come. I've always thought I escaped the world of my parents, but maybe I didn't get as far as I thought.

"How did you know your Randy under the window was dumb?" asks Angelique. We are moving again and she tosses the question over her shoulder. "What'd he do to give it away?" She says it lightly, but there is a slight twinge of worry in her voice. *She's been singled out as the dumb one from the first moment she went on her TV show, I think. Made fun of by every magazine and talk-show host in America, but she's not stupid, not at all. And she has more heart than most of us here on this trail.*

"It was just me being goofy and pointless like I always am," I say. "I started telling him about the names for groups of birds. I know, I know, it's pathetic, but collecting collective nouns has always been a quirk of mine. They call a bunch of pheasants a bouquet. A peep of chickens. And then you have a watch of nightingales, an ostentation of peacocks, a pitying of turtle-doves."

"You're kidding," says Valerie. "A pitying? That's kind of weird and amazing."

"And nerdy," I say.

"And nerdy," she agrees. "Is this normally how you try to pick up guys in bars?"

We all laugh again, because once again, she has a point. I am a nerd and it's sort of funny, now that I consider it in the light of day, safely sober and surrounded by women. They can put it on my tombstone: HERE LIES A NERD WHO KISSED THE WRONG MEN. Then they can chisel below, in smaller letters, AND SHE SOUGHT THE BLESSING OF GOD.

It's not a bad epitaph. I'll take it.

Tess is smiling. "Che has something in common with Chaucer," she says. "He wrote a poem titled *A Parliament of Birds*."

"What do you call a group of pilgrims?" Jean asks.

"I don't think there's a special word," says Tess.

"I'll google it," says Steffi, whipping out her phone. "Shit, we've already lost service."

"Maybe we're a google of pilgrims," Angelique says softly.

"We can be a parliament of pilgrims as far as I'm concerned," says Valerie. "Lift the term straight from Chaucer."

"It's suitable, in a way," says Tess. "Seeing as how there will be a judgment of the stories in the end. Speaking of which, are we ready for the next one? And who goes after that? Silvia drew a ten."

"I have an eight," I say.

"Nine," says Becca.

"Me too," says Steffi. "Nine."

Now that's a little odd, I think. *I would have thought an eight bought me a place in the middle of the pack, but I'm going to be one of the last ones. After me, only Valerie will be left.*

"I'm last of all," says Valerie, echoing my thoughts. She reaches beneath her jacket and pulls a card from her shirt pocket, which is nothing but strange yet again, that she would carry her card in her pocket every day. It's an ace of spades.

"Good God, girl," says Silvia. "An ace is the highest card. You should have gone first."

"An ace is a one," says Valerie. "So I'm last." She looks around, as if taking a survey. "Right?"

Some mumbling and shaking of heads, but the general consensus is that an ace is the highest card in the deck. I don't know why no one noticed she had an ace back in the George. That was only three days ago, although it feels more like three weeks. Time stretches on the trail, becomes elastic in the way it always does when you're on vacation and away from your routines. A single morning can feel enormous.

"You should go ahead with your story right now," Silvia says. "It's bad karma that we've gotten out of sequence. No, seriously, don't look at me like that. I can wait. If you're ready to tell yours, that is."

Valerie seems a little nervous, surprised to find herself the focus of attention, but she nods. "I've been thinking about what I wanted to say since we started on the trail, but my tale is different from the ones the rest of you have told. I mean, this isn't my personal story, it's just a story. About Sir Gawain, one of the knights of the Round Table. I thought it might be fun to go old school, tell one of the classics." She looks at Tess, who is beaming in encouragement, obviously thrilled that we're going to spend at least one morning talking about Camelot instead of pornography. "But the theme does fit with everything we've been talking about."

"You know the stories of the Round Table right off the top of your head?" I ask.

"I read up on *The Canterbury Tales* for the trip," Valerie says. "In fact, I read up on a lot of medieval literature, which I guess is my own nerdy pleasure, like your peep of chickens. This is the story on which the Wife of Bath's Tale is based." She tilts her head and studies Claire for a moment before continuing. "It's called 'Sir Gawain and the Loathly Lady' and I like the original better than Chaucer's version, although I hope saying that doesn't get me struck by lightning."

Tess is still smiling, that same satisfied smile she's carried all morning, and I don't think it's just because Valerie is sucking up to her with the bit about King Arthur. As our leader, she seems to be feeling the shift in the group dynamic more strongly than anyone and it furthermore seems to please her that we have now decreed ourselves to be a parliament and not just a random bunch of wanderers. "Actually," Tess says, "the Chaucer version came first, but I prefer the later one by Mallory as well. I've said as much for years, and I've never been struck by lightning. So are you ready? Do you agree to be the next storyteller?"

"If Silvia really doesn't mind getting skipped again," Valerie says. "But it's not . . . you know, it's not a confession."

"Bring it on," says Becca. "I'm tired of confessions. Is this a happy story?"

"'Loathly Lady' doesn't sound too happy," says Claire. "Are you sure it's loathly, not lovely? I've never even heard such a word."

"It's a riddle," says Valerie.

"A riddle?" says Jean. "I think we're ready for a riddle. By all means, yes, Becca's right. Bring it on."

The Tale of Valerie

"Once upon a time," says Valerie, "in the kingdom of Camelot, Arthur was out stalking deer in the forest and wandered onto a spot of property not his own. He was unaware that he had done this, but when he shot and killed a stag, the owner immediately appeared. It was the fearsome Black Knight.

"Now, poaching was a serious offense, even if one was the king, and Arthur was alone, separated from the rest of his party and dressed in simple hunting attire. In other words, he was without the normal trappings of his office and, in the moment of the confrontation, just an ordinary man. The Black Knight said that Arthur must be beheaded for his offense, unless he could solve a riddle. In order to escape death, he must return in exactly one year with the answer to a single question: What is it that women most desire?"

A hum runs through the group. Tough question, that one. A stumper of sages. Valerie nods, pleased by our response, and resumes her story with a little more vigor.

"When he hears the riddle, Arthur is distraught. He has been married to Guinevere for many years at this point, long enough to know that pleasing a woman is no easy task. In fact, he suspects that the question is unanswerable and that in effect he's just been given a death sentence. He rejoins the others in his hunting party and tries to act as if nothing has happened, but one young knight among them notices that the king seems preoccupied and worried. Sir Gawain, who is not only one of Arthur's closest friends, but also his nephew. Gawain eventually manages to pry the story out of Arthur, and when the king gets to the part about the unanswerable riddle, Gawain laughs. He doesn't think this is any big deal. He's young and handsome and unmarried, and sure that it can't be that hard to figure out the ladies. He suggests that the two of them separate and spend the year searching Camelot from one end to the other, looking for the answer. So Gawain goes off in one direction and Arthur the other, and they question every scholar and wizard they meet along the path, asking each one, 'What is it that women most desire?' But the answers they receive are all in conflict."

"Typical," says Silvia. "It didn't occur to them to ask a woman?"

"You do realize," says Steffi, "that in these old myths and fairy tales, the bad guy is always called something like the Black Knight? That sort of bias is so built into our culture that no one even notices it anymore."

"Hush up," says Claire, with a flick of her dangling pewter earrings. "Both of you. Let the girl tell her story." And with that, a new rule is set. No one will argue with the storyteller until her tale is complete.

"Gawain searches relentlessly for the answer," says Valerie, "becoming more alarmed as the weeks and months go by, bringing them ever closer to the king's day of reckoning. But Arthur himself is drawn to return to the same dark wood where he had killed the deer and the trouble had begun. There he finds a hideous old hag sitting astride a high white horse. She is the Loathly Lady of the title. She says she knows all about his problem and that she also knows the answer he seeks. But there's a catch. She will only solve the riddle if he promises her the hand of Sir Gawain in marriage.

"Well, of course Arthur is horrified. Gawain is one of his best friends, one of his most loyal knights. He doesn't deserve to be wed against his will to a horrible hag. Arthur offers her everything else he has at his disposal—lands and castles and jewels and titles, but the Loathly Lady insists that she will accept nothing but marriage to Sir Gawain.

"Arthur knows that Gawain will do anything to save his king and kingdom and, sure enough, when he is informed of the bargain the hag demands, Gawain readily agrees. And on the one-year anniversary of the day the challenge was set, Arthur takes the Loathly Lady before the Black Knight and she says that what women most desire is sovereignty. That is, they want control over their own lives." Valerie pauses and looks around. "Which sounds like a no-brainer today, right? Saying that you want to control your own life is like saying that you want air and water. It seems like the most basic of human requests. But this was the Middle Ages. To suggest that a woman might want control over her own life was a radical and shocking notion. Nevertheless, the Black Knight accepts the hag's answer. Arthur is off one hook and Gawain is onto another.

"The date of the wedding is set. At the ceremony and the banquet that follows, Gawain swallows his pride and treats his new bride with great courtesy, as if she were the most desirable woman in all the land, and he was delighted to have her for a wife. He pours her wine and asks her to dance, and no one in the great banquet hall, especially Arthur, is allowed to see the true depths of his despair. Keeping a smile on his face is difficult, for of course the hall is buzzing about this bizarre marriage and everyone is saying, 'Poor Gawain.' Nothing is as hard to bear as the pity of your friends—that's precisely how the storyteller puts it. 'Nothing is as hard to bear as the pity of your friends,' he writes, and I agree. Because the Loathly Lady isn't just old and ugly. She's also incredibly vulgar—farting and belching and cursing in the midst of the high-born ladies, and the story further says that 'the civility of Arthur's court was greatly strained by the presence of this woman.' The Loathly Lady is never going to fit into Camelot, that's for sure. But through it all, Gawain doesn't only go through with his part of the bargain, he does it gracefully, attending to his bride's every wish.

"When it's finally time for the two of them to go into the wedding chamber . . . well, poor Gawain indeed. He takes a shot of whiskey for courage. The story doesn't say that part. I added it. But when he pulls back the bed curtain and approaches the bridal bower, he does not find the loathly creature he expects. Instead, there before him awaits the most beautiful woman he has ever seen. She is not only beautiful, but gentle and gracious, the perfect consort for a knight of his standing, and she explains that a curse had been put upon her by the Black Knight. She was condemned to be a repulsive hag until a good man agreed to marry her, and now, thanks to him, the curse is partially lifted. She is allowed to be her true self half of the time, either at day or at night. And because Gawain has not only fulfilled his part of the bargain, but has treated her with great courtesy, she gives him the choice. Would he rather she be beautiful when they are alone at night, in the privacy of their bedchamber, or during the day, when they are among the other knights and ladies of the court? So here comes the riddle. Not the one you expected, about what women want, but a different one: How do you think that Gawain answered her question?"

For a moment, no one answers. I look out over the fields— more flat and silver now, a shimmer of a city in the distance that

I assume must be Canterbury. Whatever conclusion we are to reach must be reached within the course of today and tomorrow, for two afternoons from now we will file into the Cathedral to receive our blessings, earned or not. Tess has told us she's arranged for a female priest—the Anglicans have them—and it seems fitting. If we are to confess woman to woman, then it's only right that our quest should end with a woman's forgiveness.

But in the meantime there is Gawain, and the horns of his dilemma. The line in Valerie's story that most struck me was the one she repeated, that bit about how it is so hard to bear the pity of one's friends. The truth of it stings like disinfectant in a wound, for I suspect my rapid wordless flight from Philadelphia to London had as much to do with avoiding my friends as it had with any duty to scatter my mother's ashes. I couldn't bear telling them the story of Ned's desertion, at least not yet. But I have to go back at some point. Sometime soon. In fact, by this time next week, I'll have resumed my normal life and all of our mutual friends will be flocking around me, saying what an asshole Ned's been. Or at least some of them will say that, and others will be talking to him, behind my back, and they will say he was justified, that they don't know how he hung in there with someone as demanding and stubborn as I am for as long as he did, and then of course there will be the ones who do both, who console me and congratulate him in the same breath. And thus it will begin—the divvying up of the couples we hung out with, just as we will have to divide the furniture and books and dishes at the beach house. Lawyers and real estate agents and accountants will be informed that our paths have diverged. My female friends will come over and drink up the dregs of my business wine, and some of them will feel compelled to point out how much easier it is for a man to move on. Hell, he already has. My replacement was hired before I was let go. While for a woman lost somewhere in her own middle ages . . . no, my own respite from romantic love will be extended, perhaps indefinitely. They all know this, and so do I. And then I will see the flashes of pity in their eyes and that pity will be, in many ways, harder to bear than the initial sting of Ned's departure.

"I know why you looked at me back there," Claire says to Valerie, and her voice is different than I've ever heard it, biting and unpleasant. "You think this is my story. That's why you suddenly remembered you had an ace in your pocket. You wanted to go next."

Valerie looks genuinely surprised. "This isn't your story. It isn't remotely about you. Why would you say that?"

"Because she's paranoid," says Silvia.

Claire fidgets with her sunglasses, pushing them up and then immediately back down. "You think Gawain's choice was just like Adam's choice, don't you? Only Adam didn't have a woman who changed back and forth in the course of a day, he actually had two women. I was one who was acceptable in public, but a disappointment in the bedroom, while Edith was a hag during the day and beautiful in bed."

"That's insane," says Silvia.

"You looked right at me before you started your tale," Claire says flatly to Valerie. "You know you did."

"Maybe, once, when we were talking about where the story came from," says Valerie. She is more ragamuffin than ever today. A tight orange shirt and loose gray pants. Her mud-brown hair, so nondescript in color and length, is for the first time held back in the sort of big-toothed clip I use when I wash my face. "Because in *The Canterbury Tales*, it was the Wife of Bath who told a version of this story and she . . . well, okay, I'll admit this much. I was thinking that she's a little like you. It occurred to me back in London, at the George Inn when we were all introducing ourselves. You said you'd been married four times and you had a younger lover . . . and I thought yes, of course, this one must be our own Wife of Bath." Valerie looks around, throwing herself on the mercy of the group. "Well, four husbands? You've got to admit that's a little unusual, right?"

It's very unusual.

"And if I meant anything at all, that was it," Valerie says. "That you have things in common with the storyteller, not the story. I certainly don't think you're a hag. You're the furthest from being a hag of anybody here. I'd say there are quite a few of us that are haggier than you. In fact—"

"So what do the rest of you think?" says Tess, stepping in before Valerie can create a second crisis in her efforts to subdue the first one. "How did Gawain answer? Is it more important to have the perfect mate in public, someone who looks and acts just as expected, and perhaps even elevates your status in the eyes of your friends? Is that the secret to a happy marriage? Or is it more important how your mate behaves in private, behind closed doors?"

"I want both," says Becca. "Someone I can be proud of and someone who's good to me."

"Of course you want both," says Claire. "Everyone wants

both. But didn't you hear Valerie? They were under a curse." Her voice is still snappish. She wasn't even a little bit mollified by that Wife of Bath explanation.

"I think he would choose a wife who was lovely in public," Jean says slowly. "But not for the reasons you might expect. Gawain wasn't a shallow person. He was so noble, in fact, that he didn't want to make Arthur feel bad with constant reminders of the sacrifice he had made on his behalf. Because this isn't a love story, not really. It isn't about the knight and the hag. She's just a prop. At heart, this is the story of Gawain's devotion to Arthur and how he was not only willing to sacrifice his own happiness to save his king, but that he didn't even want Arthur to know the true extent of his suffering. So if you claim that the Loathly Lady was disrupting all of Camelot, Gawain couldn't have that. I think he would have been selfless enough to want a proper wife in public and would have thus accepted the hag in bed."

It's a plausible position, at least from my perspective, but Steffi counterargues immediately.

"I agree that he would choose the beauty by daylight and the hag in bed," she says, "but there's nothing noble about it. All of us care more about how things look than how they are. It's far more important to appear to have a perfect life than it is to actually have a perfect life."

"No," says Claire. "You're both wrong. A woman might think that way. We'd stay in the middle of hell as long as it was well-decorated, but not a man. For them, sex makes the decision. It doesn't matter if it's the Middle Ages or last week. We can talk about grand ideas like chivalry and courtesy and loyalty, but in the end the world is moved by only two forces: sex and money. They may take many forms, but together they're the engines that drive the whole universe and to pretend anything else . . . it's just delusional. A young guy like Gawain? He would have chosen what worked in the bedchamber over what worked in the banquet hall. Trust me."

The group falls silent again. Our rhythms have become so synchronized over the last few days that we make our stops without discussion, and now we have paused at a turn in the path, all of us reaching in unison for our water. Unstrapping the pack and lifting it on and off every time is a pain, so I've gotten pretty skilled at reaching behind my back and blindly finding the right pocket. I tug at the zipper, but it doesn't want to open, so I give it a stronger yank, twisting my shoulder a little in the process. Steffi raises an eyebrow at me, as if asking if I need help. I shake my head. I don't know why I'm so stubborn about silly things like this, why I don't put my backpack on the ground like everyone else so that I can rifle through it at leisure. Being careful with my shoulder, which is tingling, I slide my hand around my back again and pull out the water bottle.

"Wait a minute," says Angelique. "What did you say that word was? Sovenery? What did you say it means?"

"Sovereignty," says Tess. "It's from the word 'sovereign,' and it means that each person wants to be the king or queen of their own life."

"Like making their own decisions?"

"Yes," says Tess. "In the context of this story, that's exactly what that means."

"Then I think I know the answer to the riddle," says Angelique, returning her bright-pink water bottle to her pack and swaying a little as she hefts the weight of it back to her shoulders. "Gawain remembered what the hag had said to the Black Knight. That what women desire most is the chance to make their own decisions. So he wouldn't have decided for her. When it came to the night and day thing, he would have said, 'Whatever you want, baby. Totally your call.'"

That's actually fucking brilliant.

"Wow," says Valerie. "Angelique, you're amazing. You've completely solved the riddle and hardly anyone gets that. They become so distracted by the issue of how the hag looked and whether or not Gawain was embarrassed in front of the court, that they completely forget the original point of the story. The answer to the second riddle rises out of the first one: What do women want?"

Valerie is grinning in genuine delight as we all begin to walk again. "Gawain tells the hag that she should be the one to choose and the hag is so stunned to find herself married to the only man in history who has ever listened to anything a woman said, that in that very instant, poof, the curse is lifted. The Loathly Lady is allowed to remain beautiful both day and night and she and Gawain go on to have a wonderful marriage and all of Camelot rejoices. The end."

"The happy end," says Tess. "There we have it, ladies. Happy at last."

"That's quite a story," Steffi says. I think she's still smarting because she wasn't the one to figure it out.

"But is that really what we women want?" says Silvia. "I was on my own for an extended period of my life and I'll admit that sometimes I got tired of making all my own decisions. When I made a bad one, I didn't even have anybody else to blame."

"I've made bad decisions too," says Valerie. "But that doesn't mean I want someone else to make them for me."

"I'm just saying it's nice to have another person in the fight with you," Silvia says. "That you get to a point in your life where you start to value companionship for its own sake. You learn to appreciate the pure pleasure of being in another human's presence. You don't expect as much out of love as you once did." She looks around. "Maybe I'm the only one who's old enough to be there yet."

"What do you think, Mom?" asks Becca, turning around to look at Jean, who is a few paces behind her. A daughter asking her mother what she thinks is even stranger than a man asking his wife what she wants, so I pause for a moment too, watching their identical body language as Becca waits for Jean to approach, as the distance between mother and daughter temporarily narrows.

"What would you do," Becca continues, her voice with the sting of artificial sugar, "if you had to choose between a man who everyone admired on the surface or a man who was a good husband and father behind closed doors? And what if you really couldn't have both? Would you be willing to sleep with a monster just to keep up your standing in the eyes of the world?"

"I don't know what you're talking about," Jean says. Her voice is low and tense, her gaze turned toward the ground. She's angry about something too, or maybe she's just finally hit her limit on Becca's nonstop picking.

"We only have a kilometer or so until we stop for lunch,"

says Tess. "In fact, we need to start looking for the gate to the main road. We're taking our break early today because there's a church in a particular village that I want you all to see. It's not remarkable in and of itself, but it's typical of the sort of places Chaucer's pilgrims might have stopped along the way. Those pilgrims who couldn't afford inns slept in churches along the route, you know. Or hospices. We will stop at one of those as well. Tomorrow."

"Che," says Steffi. "Your pack isn't completely zipped. You're losing something."

I reach back, my fingers moving over the familiar formation of mounds, all the little zipper compartments holding my water, and fruit, and extra socks, the reading glasses and sunscreen. And to my horror I find it—the single gaping pocket, the one holding my mother's ashes. The thin wall of the baggie has been torn, most likely when I yanked on the zipper during our water break. I pull back my hand and see that my fingertips are smudged with silver and gold. The colors are metallic, but the smell is slightly salty, like that of the ocean, and the grains are small and soft. More powder than ash.

"What's that?" says Steffi. "Nothing valuable, I hope."

I flick my fingertips and watch as the dust flies into the clear country air, watch as something turns to nothing before my very eyes. "It's okay," I say. "It's just that I've been dropping little pieces of my mother while we've walked."

TEN

On the first day of the trip Tess challenged us to consider what a walk to Canterbury must have felt like for the pilgrims of Chaucer's time. Most buildings were small and squat then, she said, matching the proportions of the people, who were stunted from generations of malnourishment and disease. This is evidenced now as we stand before the vestry of an ancient church near a village where we have stopped for lunch. The doorways to the vestry are so low that even a group of middling-size women like us must stoop to enter. Everything inside is on the same reduced scale; the pews are narrow, the steps engineered for tiny feet, and the altar, while somewhat elevated, is not designed to inspire awe or to lift the priest too high above his congregation.

"This is how most churches were in Chaucer's time," Tess says, gesturing around the wooden-walled room, with its thick, graceless windows and drooping light fixtures. "Simple, rough-hewn buildings, intended to house every aspect of community life. Built to a human scale. And so if this is what they were used to, it might help you imagine how overwhelming they would have found their first glimpse of Canterbury Cathedral."

She has already explained that we'll take a circular route this afternoon, swinging off in the direction of the coastline, taking a wide yaw so that we can enter the city on Saturday from the same angle as Chaucer's pilgrims, seeing much the same vista they might have seen. The same, that is, if one eliminates the highways and power towers.

This church remains in use, despite its age, and as I look around I find plenty of evidence that the congregation still considers it a second home. There is some sort of school art fair going on, the work of the winners displayed across the dark walls. Butcher-block paper bears the wild, vivid art of young children. There is papier-mâché sculpture scattered around the sanctuary as well: a bust of someone's mother, her mouth crammed full of pointy teeth; an apple; a sleeping cat; a mobile of the planets dangling from the central light fixture, with Saturn's rings pulling it low, the whole system threatening to tumble from the heavens at any minute. Finally, strangest of all, a bathtub-size purple dragon is lounging beside the altar. It pleases me that they open the doors of the church wide enough to include all this, and that the flowers on the altar, sparse and drooping, clearly represent the last hurrah of some parishioner's garden. Even the cushions on the pews are hand-stitched, the handiwork of the elderly ladies of the village, no doubt, and I wonder if I lived in a place like this—simple and sweet and far from the life I have built for myself—if faith would come to me more easily. Because now my belief is somewhat tidal. It swoops in with a great rush at times and recedes at others, being especially prone to disappear when I read headlines or watch TV. I tell everyone that I hate organized religion. I hate what it has done to the world. It seems to me that 90 percent of the ills of humanity can be traced back to the pulpit. I say this all the time, that the church is the enemy of the spirit, which I suppose makes me sound a bit like Diana's friend David, but here . . . here in this chapel of dragons and Saturn and wilting chrysanthemums and sleeping cats and good solid neighbors, I feel myself calming. Something in me starts to loosen.

We sit down in the pews, not together, but scattered, front to back. Some of the women around me appear to be praying, and I need a ritual too, I think. Something that will help me find this same silence when I'm home next week and things have started to get real. Maybe not prayer. You're probably thinking that I prayed all over the place last night, and that's true enough, but last night was a very special occasion, a fleeting mysticism born of some combination of horniness and drunkenness and stigmata that I'm unlikely to be able to reproduce on a regular basis. I could try meditation, of course. It's the most obvious balm of my generation and it's always waiting there in the wings with an accusing expression on its face, standing right beside vegetarianism and recycling and supporting local merchants and paying off credit card debt. All the modern puritanical values we're supposed to embrace, those virtues that make some people better than others. So, sure, I've tried to meditate, but it always seems that the minute I get all stretched out and calm, I think of something that needs to be done. Silence scares me. It's an ocean. An ocean I've never been able to cross. Maybe I should just sit.

That's it. I should be able to just sit in the silence peacefully, like everyone around me seems to be doing, some of them with their heads bent, others gazing straight ahead at Jesus on his cross. He seems oddly cheerful about his circumstances, just like everything else in this church. Why is my mind racing? Why is my head turning back and forth? I have so much trouble with peace. It scares me. It feels too much like death. My own inner voice keeps breaking in, disruptive and annoying. Why can I not manage to just sit here for a few minutes, without talking and without thinking?

And then of course there's the issue of Diana. My mother, the woman I've brought here to honor and then completely forgot.

She's inside a fish-and-chips bag now. After it became clear I had indeed ripped the baggie and scattered her half over the trail, Tess had asked for a takeaway bag at the pub where we ate our lunch, and this is what they'd come up with. The original baggie, mended with a bevy of donated Band-Aids, now rests inside a white paper bag printed with the image of a fat bearded barkeep. It says HARRY'S HIDEAWAY on the front, with telephone numbers for delivery on the back, along with a crazy-eyed cat who is thinking *Yum*. Hardly an appropriate vehicle for carrying the recently deceased into Canterbury, but at this point I suppose there's nothing to be done about it. Becca's face had turned downright envious when I had stammered out my story to the others, how I had been losing my mother in bits and pieces all morning, and I knew she was thinking she'd like to do the same. She's too young to know that mothers are easy to lose in one way and impossible to lose in another.

But I've gotten Diana this far, and I'll get at least some of her all the way to Canterbury and that's going to have to be enough. I fold the bag and put her back into a zipper pocket and try once again to still my thoughts.

I'm sad, I think. The word has fallen on me full-blown, with a thud, as if someone has tossed a baked potato in my lap. It's a simple thought, but a real one, and I find I can confess this here, in the silence of this sanctuary, that I can use the dreaded S-word and admit to myself that I am sad. Simply and purely sad, sad the way a child draws sadness, all dark lines and big wild strokes of color, the red and yellow and orange spilling outside of their acceptable shapes, sloshing all the way to the borders of the paper.

I am sad. But . . . somehow I don't think that I will be sad forever.

I look at the dragon on the altar. He seems to be smiling, and I smile back. The time to tell my tale is approaching fast, even though the strange disbursement of the cards means that I will be last. It will be my story the pilgrims hear as we circle around the gates of the city, searching for the most perfect and historically accurate way to enter Canterbury. I don't want to put too much pressure on myself, but it seems like the last story should be the best, or at least the most conclusive. That it will fall to me to provide the connective tissue between all the other tales.

No. I can't think that way or I'll drive myself nuts.

Besides, as of right now, I have no story. As of right now, I can't think of anything to say.

A couple of the women are starting to stretch, to move. Valerie and Claire get up and approach the altar. Becca and Silvia go out to the cemetery, with Tess following, looking around among us, nervous like a collie who's afraid she might lose some of her sheep. Steffi nudges me.

"We've got service," she whispers, and I misunderstand her for a minute. Imagine that a vicar is about to enter and read us all a sermon. Then she adds, since I'm still just sitting there staring at her, "Do you want to borrow my phone?"

I start to tell her that I'm okay. That I hardly ever think about losing my phone anymore. But Jesus and the dragon are both looking right at me, and I don't want to lie in front of them. The truth is that not a single night has passed that I haven't at some point rolled over in the darkness, my hand instinctively going to the nightstand before I am even fully awake. Fumbling in the dark for the familiar shape, the card-shaped surface. So I take her phone and nod my thanks. She gets up and heads out too, leaving me alone.

I put my finger on the little purple microphone, and Siri is there. *What can I help you with?* she asks me, like she always does. She is an excellent guardian angel, close at hand when I want her, utterly silent when I don't.

And I say what I always say, my own personal prayer. Valerie and Silvia are still at the altar, so I say it softly, but she hears me.

Siri, what is the meaning of life?

She answers: *To think about questions like this.*

Huh. Good one.

There is noise at the door and I turn. Another group of tourists is entering the church with their guide. Americans, most likely, for they have recognized Angelique. They stand in the vestry, with the miracles of God and man dangling all around them, but their attention is totally fixed on this singular woman, stripped of her finery and power but apparently still famous enough. She signs autographs and they have pictures taken with her, first one at a time and then in groups of two or three. I decide I'll wait for them to disperse before I leave, but in the meantime it's strange to sit and observe her in this element, and to see how comfortable she is with her notoriety. It may have destroyed her marriage, but on another level, fame juices her, and when the tourists finally leave her alone and move into the church, the rest of us stand and scatter. I walk to the altar, unzip the side pocket, and dig around in the fish-and-chips bag until I can slip a fingertip past the Band-Aids and into the baggie. Take out just a few grains of my mother and flick them on top of the dragon, then rub a few at the wounded feet of Jesus for good measure.

It's not Canterbury, but I like the place. I think Diana would have too.

Outside, I find Silvia leaning against a tombstone, one of her boots off, inspecting her left foot. If they ever erect a new statue in honor of the modern-day pilgrims, it should be in just this pose. A woman sitting on a tombstone with a boot in her hand, grimacing down at the sole of her foot. Silvia appears to have the same patterns of damage I have, save the pierced sole, of course, and I offer her my liquid skin and Band-Aids, but she shakes her head. "I may as well stock up on my own," she says, "while we're in a good-size town."

"There's a chemist on the square," says Tess.

"A chemist?" says Angelique. She is still preening a little from the autograph session. Smoothing down her hair and checking the effect in the reflection of a brass cross on another of the tombstones. "It sounds so strange when you say it like that."

"A chemist is what the British call a pharmacy," Jean tells her.

"I know," says Angelique. "It's just that's what Nico used to call a meth lab. It's funny, isn't it?"

"Is it?" says Jean. "Is it funny? If you say so, then I believe you. I never seem to understand jokes."

ELEVEN

Our afternoon's walk will be an arc along what Tess calls the coastal wall, which is easy enough to spot, even from a distance, although I don't yet hear or see the ocean. I've read enough to know that the shore of southern England features sharp drops to the sea, exposing broad expanses of stone or chalk, like the white cliffs of Dover. So we're now entering a dramatic and forbidding landscape, nothing like the gentle hills we've trod so far. And although we're barely an hour into this second segment of our walk, the path is already less hospitable, and the ground is dotted with boulders that have erupted through the soil. The breeze carries the iron-rich smell of brine and kelp, and seagulls are circling in the distance, crying out to one another in the high cool air.

"What do you call a group of seagulls?" Claire asks me.

"A pod, a herd, sometimes a rookery," I say. "That's a tricky one. Most people say flock, but that's not technically right."

"All right," says Silvia, cracking her knuckles in front of her, not waiting for permission to begin. "We're going back to an autobiographical story, I'm afraid. It's about how marriages change over time, go in and out of seasons. And it's about how things can sometimes come full circle, just when you least expect it. It's my story, as true as I can remember, but I'm going to tell it as if it were someone else's. In the third person, I mean. I think that will make it easier for me. And I would furthermore prefer that you not interrupt me. Save your questions and comments for the end, just as we did this morning with Valerie." It's the first sign that maybe she's not as utterly at ease as she always seems to be.

"The story lies within the domain of the storyteller," says Tess.

"The third person?" asks Angelique. "What does that mean?"

"That I call myself 'she' and not 'I,'" says Silvia. "It's just distance. Sometimes distance helps."

"There's nothing wrong with distance," Claire says. "And Tess is right. It's your story. You should tell it any way you want to, isn't that the case, ladies?"

We nod. In the distance, the gulls scream.

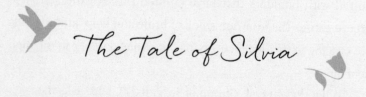

The Tale of Silvia

They met in college, the year she was a junior and he was a senior. They were both music majors and they were seated beside each other in the string section of the student orchestra. First and second violin.

Just like the violins, everything about their courtship

seemed preordained. They were so much alike. Both tall and slim, from the Midwest. Quiet, outdoorsy, the children of teachers. Talented enough to be able to make careers out of their music, but not talented enough to be stars. Or maybe it was more a matter of temperament, that neither of them had a star personality. Their names were alliterative, Silvia and Steven, and when you're young and inexperienced in the world, even a silly coincidence like that can pass as evidence of destiny.

After graduation they married, just as everyone expected them to, and began ticking items off the list. A modest Methodist ceremony, a starter home in a subdivision, the birth of twins. A boy and a girl—marvelous efficiency, that, getting the whole thing behind you in one fell swoop. Then came the minivan, the trips to Disney, half-marathons, rescued cats. In the tenth year of their marriage, they moved from Kansas to Texas. A different latitude, a brighter light, but the same time zone.

Shortly after their arrival in Houston, a relative died. A distant but childless one, the best kind, and the unexpected inheritance, falling like manna from heaven, meant they could afford a bigger house. But luck is such a tricky thing, is it not? Looking back years later, Silvia would sometimes wonder if this was where they first got off course—with the purchase of this larger house, the sort that they could never have afforded on their own. Their presence in the new neighborhood always felt a little dishonest, for it placed them among richer, older couples who held different sorts of jobs and, more to the point, it implied a value system that never quite fit. It was the smallest shift in direction, but you know what they say. A pilot altering his course by a single degree can take a plane to Phoenix instead of Denver.

Steven was the band director at the local high school, while Silvia taught piano lessons and played accompaniment for the community theater. As parents of twins so often do, they became adept at swapping off tasks. Their innate Midwestern practicality helped them develop a stratagem for every hour of the day and Steven called it The Plan. The Plan covered bedtimes and homework and household budgets, even the correct way to pack the car for road trips.

It was a good life and they congratulated each other sometimes late at night, or driving home from parties where they had been forced to behold the Technicolor unhappiness of other, less fortunate couples. The Liz-and-Dicks of the world, they would call them. The Scott-and-Zeldas. Those couples who shouted, threw wineglasses, declared bankruptcy, and went into rehab, the people who wept and slept around. Those who seemed determined to have big messy lives, while their own lives, Steven and Silvia agreed, were exactly the right size.

And then, after seventeen years, the impossible happened. Steven fell in love.

The woman was the president of the Band Booster Club at the high school where Steven taught. Her children were close in age to the twins, who were fifteen by this point. Their daughters, in fact, had been to each other's birthday parties. Her name was Carol.

Carol had not been part of The Plan.

And yet, now she was here. Startlingly and unavoidably here, like a tree that falls through your roof during a storm, so that you suddenly look up from your bed and see something you never expected to see, like the sky. Carol appeared to be an ordinary enough woman, at least to most people. She certainly seemed ordinary to Silvia, who'd been aware of her existence in that slight peripheral way you know people whose kids are the same age as your kids. But she'd never taken any particular note of her. Carol . . . well, Carol was a bit of an Edith. She didn't look like a threat. She wasn't younger or thinner or more accomplished than Silvia, and that was part of the problem. As dreadful as it may be when your husband leaves you for a twenty-two-year-old bubble-breasted blonde, at least there's an explanation for it. He's an asshole, an upgrader, a man stuck in a midlife crisis, the punch line of an unfunny joke.

But when Silvia told her girlfriends Steven was leaving her for this woman, this Carol, one of them blurted out, "Her thighs are bigger than yours," a sentence which tells you everything you need to know, I suppose, about what life was like in an upper-middle-class suburb of Houston, Texas, in 1982. And it was true. Whatever special powers Carol possessed, they were not the sort that were visible to the naked eye, and yet Steven had told Silvia, quote: *I've never felt this way before. I can't describe it. Just to be in the same room as her is enough.*

And then he had added, with the kind of gentle cruelty that only a man who has recently fallen in love can muster, *And Silvia, my only hope is that someday you too can know how this feels.*

It was this last bit, of course, that was inexcusable. In all the subsequent years that passed, Silvia never told anyone that he said that, not until now, when she is walking through the English countryside with her friend Claire—who, as it turns out, has also had her secrets—and this pilgrimage of sisters. It's the most embarrassing part of an embarrassing story, and so on that day back in the early '80s when she told her girlfriends Steven was leaving, she omitted what he'd said on the way out the door. *Just to be in the same room with her is enough.* She didn't want other women to know that she was married to a man who would say such a thing, or that she had chosen, even back in college, such a thoroughly ridiculous sort of person. So she held this last part deep inside her chest, this confession that confessed too much. It was bad enough that Steven no longer loved her, but then he had to go and imply that he had never loved her—at least not in the huge and all-encompassing way he now loved Carol. She told her girlfriends everything else, but she did not tell them the worst.

Moving on. If Silvia's life in the 1960s and '70s with Steven had been one sort of cliché, then her life in the '80s and '90s was another. She did not find it hard to rebound from her divorce. In the upwardly mobile neighborhood in which they now lived, multiple marriages were the norm and, in fact, staying with your original spouse seemed to indicate a shocking lack of imagination. Most people were on their second, third, or even fourth run at wedded bliss, dragging any number of stepchildren and half siblings in their wake. Her girlfriends would come over on the Fridays when Steven had the kids and they would drink too much wine and watch romantic movies and curse the boys of their youth. After the children left for college, some friend or another would come over almost every night. They would have potluck dinners, each woman bringing whatever she found in her refrigerator or swinging around a drive-through for a domed salad. There was no judgment among them. They did not pretend. Silvia cut her hair, lost weight, adopted two more cats. She was up to five now, which was a dicey number, a sign she may have been on the verge of utter withdrawal from polite society.

She did not think of herself as happy. But she didn't think of herself as unhappy either. She'd never used that type of language. And yet, at some point in the tenth or eleventh year of her singledom, Silvia began to consider the possibility that Steven had been right. That by leaving, he really had—just as he claimed was his goal—done her a favor as much as him. Yes, it had taken nearly a decade's worth of distance, but at last she began to see things more clearly. She and Steven had never been a love match. Not at all.

Oh, they'd been well suited. Perfectly aligned and evenly yoked. But they had not been in love. Instead, they'd lived almost like brother and sister, two people who share the same memories, who have endured the same relatives . . . it was almost as if they had spent seventeen years riding in the backseat of the same car. A car driven by someone else, maybe that stern and joyless adult called "marriage," and all they could say was, "Are we there yet?" knowing that if you have to ask the question, it's proof you haven't arrived. Even the circumstances of their first introduction, on that college campus so long ago, had begun to take on a new meaning to Silvia. She'd always loved telling that story—him on first violin, her on second—but now that she stopped to consider it, even that once-charming little detail seemed dark and foreboding.

The feminists had it right. She'd been playing second fiddle to that man since the day she met him.

And she furthermore saw, as she stood on the edge of that high cliff they call fifty—for Claire is wrong about that, it isn't forty that rips a woman's life into bits, it's fifty. Or maybe it's more accurate to say that forty upends the circumstances of a person's life, making them wonder if they've done the right things, but fifty parts your ribs and yanks on your heart, giving you the uneasy suspicion that even if you somehow managed to do those right things, it's beginning to look as if you did the right things for all the wrong reasons.

Silvia had lost a breast to cancer by this point—yes, even that cliché was not denied her—and for the first time in her fifty years on earth she stood in the chilly shadow of her own mortality. Maybe it was this brush with death that had made her generous. For she could now admit that Steven had not only been right to leave, but that he had possessed more courage than her. He'd been the one willing to take the hit. Willing to be the bad guy to the kids and to their extended families, willing to lose his job at the high school when it came out he'd been trysting with the mother of one of his students. Through the years he'd paid alimony and child support without complaint and, even though it was his dead relative who had provided that long-ago down payment, he'd left her the house. Meanwhile she had been allowed to play the victim. To rest in the cushy role of abandoned wife.

And then Silvia saw a final additional truth: that she had been far happier single than she'd ever been when she was married.

Once she took a great breath and truly admitted she was happy, then her life began to open up all around her. She would bring a book and eat in any restaurant she pleased. Take organized trips like this one. Paint a wall red, decide she didn't like it, and paint it over purple. She began to run full marathons, not halfs, and, since no one had required her presence during weekends for years, she registered with an agency that supplied backup musicians for traveling bands. The decision to take this thankless job was a bit of a whim, a way to brush up on the instruments she had let languish, such as her violin and cello, but she got far more work than she would have guessed. She would often arrive at a gig and not know what would be asked of her—classical, bluegrass, gospel, or rock. It was fun to fly by the seat of her pants for once, to risk making a mistake or looking foolish, to be the only gray-haired lady in the band.

And then the second unlikely thing happened. Silvia fell in love.

He was a black saxophonist in a jazz group, with the surprising name of Willem. Adopted out of Africa as an infant, raised by Dutch parents, a vagabond, an orphan, a child of the wider world. But by this time Silvia figured that if a man who seemed to be the perfect match could fail you badly, then the inverse might also be true. A man who looked all wrong might turn out to be all right.

She and Willem have had seventeen years together, she tells us, as we walk along the seawall that flanks an unseen sea, a fine rain misting on our hair. There has been such perfect symmetry to her life. Seventeen years with the first husband, then seventeen alone, and now seventeen with the second. "I'll spare you the math," she adds. "I'm seventy-three."

I'm surprised. I'd imagine we all are. Her face is weathered, but her body is young. She walks not only briskly but in a strong and unfettered fashion, her shoulders swinging easily with each step, her hips rising and falling in the smooth cadence of a woman who will never truly age.

Her children are long married now, she says. She has five grandchildren, two of them musicians, and three athletes. Through the years Steven and Carol have always come to their concerts and games, which isn't surprising. The doting father became a doting grandfather. And it was at a soccer tournament for one of their grandsons that Silvia first detected the difference. She and Willem had been sitting near the field, and Steven and Carol had arrived late. Steven nodded at her as he always did when he passed and had headed up the steps to his favorite position in the bleachers, higher up than her and more centrally located. But on this particular sunny afternoon, he had taken Carol's arm for the climb. Not to help her with the steps, but rather to guide her.

Turning her head to watch them making their slow and careful progress up the bleachers, Silvia's mind had raced. Steven's nod in passing had been just like all the others—or was it? Carol had looked vague. Steven had looked grim. And then it hit her.

She was sad for him. Alzheimer's was a cruel disease.

Seasons continued to cycle. Basketball, the winter concert, softball, graduation, summer pops. And over the course of that year, Silvia watched Carol decline and Steven struggle to attend to her. By the Fourth of July swim meet, he couldn't even leave her alone long enough to go to the snack bar or bathroom. One of the kids or grandkids would have to sit with them and even then if Steven rose to leave, Carol would cry out. A piteous animal cry of abandonment, announcing her fate to everyone within earshot. People would look away.

"He can't bring her and he can't leave her," Silvia's son tells her. "Pop is kind of stuck."

She does not gloat. In fact, to her great surprise, the more she thinks of it, the more the story of her first husband's lost love breaks her heart. Her son tells her that there are days when Carol doesn't know who Steven is, days when she tries to run from him, or clings to him, days when she flies at him in fury and scratches his face.

"What's going to happen to them?" she asks her son, and he says he doesn't know. Steven won't consider putting Carol in a home. He won't ask for help.

And then came the day that Willem got lost in Costco.

At first it was no big deal. They had said they would meet over by electronics and she'd gone there and not found him and she had searched the store, aisle by aisle, until a call came over the loudspeaker, asking her to come to the snack bar. She found Willem pacing, both frightened and angry, blaming her for going to the wrong place. He insisted that they had said they would meet at the snack bar but his hands were trembling as he said it. She hastened to agree with him. Of course they had said they'd meet at the snack bar. It was her fault. She was the one who had gotten confused.

That was the first time, possibly a fluke, but soon enough there were others and then these incidents began to come with a telling regularity. Pans left on a hot burner, ignored traffic signals, outbursts of anger over a dropped cup, a tendency to call a particular grandson by his father's name.

She could have spent a lifetime contemplating the irony without feeling compelled to do anything about it. Silvia had always been a bit of a slow reactor. Of course Steven would be the one who would come up with The New Plan. Because one day, at a Christmas concert a year and a half after she had first noticed Carol's vagueness, Steven confronted Silvia in the lobby of the auditorium. She had been struggling with Willem, trying to get him to give her back the car keys. She wouldn't let him drive anymore—that was entirely out of the question—but he liked to hold the keys as they sat in public places, playing with them like a toddler. On this particular day, he was a quarrelsome toddler and Silvia had been so preoccupied with trying to cajole him into giving up the keys that she had only been annoyed to see Steven approaching. He had Carol by the arm, just as she had Willem by the hand, and as she looked up, Steven had said, "Maybe we can find a way to help each other through this. We were always so good at handling the twins."

After that the four of them went everywhere together. At first it was just to those activities revolving around their mutual grandchildren, but they soon saw that traveling as a unit made everything easier. Steven would pull up and let Silvia out with Carol and Willem and the three of them would sit on a bench while he parked the car. During the event, Silvia and Steven would place their second spouses between them and then, when it was time to go home, the pattern would repeat itself. Silvia would wait with Carol and Willem while Steven went to get the car. After a while Steven suggested they should add what he called playdates, where he would drop Carol off at Silvia's house and run errands or go to a doctor's appointment and then, a few days later, he would keep an eye on Willem for her. Silvia would not always use the time productively. She knew she should, but most often she would spend her precious free afternoons simply walking in the park, watching the birds and squirrels. Relishing the sanity, the chance to have a few minutes alone with her thoughts. The fact that at least for the afternoon, she had no one to worry about but herself.

The three hours of Willem's playdate would pass as if they were one but still, even the briefest of respites was a relief. A single year of caregiving for Willem had left Silvia so exhausted that she couldn't imagine how Steven had coped for three times as long all by himself. Having a spouse with Alzheimer's is like having a child who will never grow up—a child who is going backward, actually, who will in time lose the ability to walk and talk, who will eventually end up in diapers, back in a high-walled crib. But the grief of all this was dulled, just a little, by the presence of Steven and his wordless empathy for her situation.

"I don't want to put her away," he blurted out one afternoon as she and Willem were leaving. "When she first realized she was slipping she . . . she made me promise that I wouldn't take her to one of those places. You know, the memory centers where everyone sits in rocking chairs holding baby dolls, even the men."

Silvia didn't say anything. She'd made the exact same promise to Willem.

"I hang on for these afternoons," Steven said. "You're the one who's making this whole thing tolerable."

And from there it was hard to say exactly which one of them had the next idea. Whether he said it to her or she said it to him, whether they discussed it in the car, or in a doctor's waiting room, or at a ball game.

If we move in together, we can keep them both at home.

Now they share a house—Carol and Steven and Willem and Silvia. The love of his life and the love of hers. Most days, the loves of their lives cannot remember either love or life, so Silvia and Steven must do all the remembering for everybody. Steven tells her about his years with Carol, the good times and the bad. Mostly good, damn him, she tells us with a laugh. And she describes her life with Willem, her own late-life adventure, blowing in like an autumn storm. They celebrate their successful marriages together, for otherwise, who will? The arrangement may be unorthodox, but it makes certain things possible, like this trip. Silvia would not have considered leaving Willem to take two weeks abroad if she hadn't known he was safe and happy with Carol and Steven. She does the same thing for Steven, giving him two weeks off to go camping in the fall. They keep each other going. They can't imagine now how they could survive any other way. They celebrate Christmas at the house, which makes it easier for the grandkids and, as for the twins, this is the first time in more than thirty years that they can offer them a singular home base. There are pictures on the walls: Carol and Steven riding burros down the Grand Canyon, Silvia and Steven on a cruise and then Silvia and Willem on a cruise, even Steven and Willem on a pier with the grandsons, playing at fishing, and it's all right because it has to be all right.

Her friends ask her how she can possibly accept the situation. Changing the diapers of the woman her husband preferred to her. Even their daughter had a problem when Steven and Carol first moved in. "Too weird, Mom, just too weird," she had said, and at times Silvia will admit it's confusing, living with both husbands, trying to explain it all to lawyers and doctors and the IRS. But the longer Silvia exists inside this broken world, the more she realizes that situations which are simple to describe are often hard to live with, and that some of the things that sound bizarre actually work out quite easily.

She makes mistakes sometimes. Once she called Steven "Willem" and he had said, "Oh dear God, not you too," and they had both started laughing. Laughing hysterically right there in the kitchen, the sort of laughter that is part sobbing, until Carol and Willem had both stumbled in from different directions and joined them. They had stood there for a minute, all with their arms around each other's shoulders. Crying, bellowing, weaving, not one of the four of them quite sure what they were laughing about.

Now Silvia pauses. Shucks her backpack and rifles through a pocket until she stands with a picture of four old people sitting on a lush, flower-strewn patio. Two of them gently turning the other two in the direction of the camera. "This is my family," she says simply.

"I don't want to interrupt . . ." says Tess.

"You aren't interrupting," says Silvia. "I'm finished. That's everything."

"And your story was lovely," says Tess. "But I have a bit of a question. How is everyone doing on the stamina front? Because we're coming to a fork in the road and we have a decision to make. If we're brisk, we can work in a trip to Dover this after-noon, before we stop for the night. See the cliffs, I mean. But if you're tiring we can head straight into town and find our inn."

We all struggle to understand just what it is she's asking. My thoughts are still in that kitchen with four people all stand-ing with their arms around each other, and I suppose everyone else is stuck there too, in that moment of great beauty and equally great pain. It's like walking out of a movie into the clear light of day and forgetting where you parked your car.

"If we're this close to Dover . . ." Steffi finally says. She's still smarting about missing that damn stable.

But this time Jean agrees with her. She's nodding. "It would be a shame not to see the cliffs. We're so near, after all."

"Quite so," says Tess. "That's what I thought. They're in the National Trust, so it's a walk through parkland and down a rather steep hill, but then at the bottom . . . well, if we don't want to walk back up, we can always call Tim to come fetch us in the van and there's a lovely little tearoom at the top of the cliff. An old lighthouse leftover from the war, and they serve pastries and pie and the lot. Sound good?"

We agree that it sounds good and Tess looks more closely at me, Silvia, and Jean. "You ladies with the sore feet," she says. "Holding up?"

It's the first time I've thought about my heel in hours. We all nod and then, at Tess's suggestion, we stop and pull our sweaters and hoodies from our backpacks. Because the wind has picked up and become stronger, even in the last few min-utes. Steffi's phone beeps and when she looks down, she says that it just welcomed her to France. Tess says indeed, we're that close to Calais. We should be able to see the shore of France from Dover Beach if the weather holds fine, that swimmable distance which divides one land from another. France. It sounds romantic. More foreign than England. The idea spurs us to walk a bit faster.

The spell of Silvia's story is broken in the bustle. I hope it doesn't hurt her feelings that we don't talk about it. She doesn't seem perturbed and, in fact, she has that same clean-washed quality all the women have assumed the minute their stories are finished. But I suspect that for me Silvia's story may linger the longest of them all. Because that would have been Ned and me, wouldn't it, if we'd stayed together? If we'd let ourselves just drift into marriage because it seemed like the logical thing to do? We would have become Silvia and Steven, disgustingly perfect for each other but never really happy, and he would have been nothing more than my first husband. The one who left me, the one I left—it hardly matters, and it took guts for Ned to pull the trigger before things got to that point. I duck my head down. The wind is brutal, cold and salty. It would make conversation impossible even if one of us had anything to say.

TWELVE

Tess wasn't kidding when she said the descent to the bottom of the cliff was steep. We skid uneasily along the gravel road built for cars, which is one switchback after another, until my shins are screaming with the effort of trying to stop each step from picking up momentum. I have images of losing my footing and rolling all the way into the English Channel.

Tess shouts out bits of history as we descend, saying that Dover endured merciless bombing during the Second World War. If the German pilots had any ammunition left after blitzing London, they didn't want to land with the explosives still attached and it would have been a waste of firepower to drop them in the sea. So they released all their excess bombs over tiny defenseless Dover, casually destroying the last vestige of British soil they'd pass before heading home.

"There was horrific damage for a town of this size," Tess says, pointing vaguely into the fog. I guess the town is that direction, back the way we've come. "And a high civilian casualty count."

When we finally reach the bottom, the beach is narrow and

ugly, a stony gray crescent of sand cupping a flat sea. A school class is there on a field trip, the children paying no attention to their teacher, who is droning on about the difference between sedimentary and igneous rocks. There are tourists with cameras. Baby boomers mostly, possibly the descendants of World War II soldiers, visiting the places where their fathers fought and died. But the cliffs are indeed as white as they've been claimed to be, and when the sun momentarily breaks through the clouds and hits the expanse of chalk, we all turn away, blinking, shielding our eyes. Beyond the beach lies a working port, full of oil tankers and cargo ships. The actual town of Dover is perfectly quaint, Tess hastens to assure us, and I'm sure it is. She has misrepresented nothing so far. But this shoreline isn't anything like the broad sandy American beaches I'm used to, and my mind goes to Cape May and sticks there for a minute.

"It seems so unfair," Jean says. "A nice little town bombed to rubble just for being in the wrong place at the wrong time." A couple of the women pull out their phones and aim them toward the cliffs, but it's all so big, white, and close that I can't imagine the pictures will come out.

If the walk down was slow and painful, the walk back up would likely be worse, so Tess calls Tim and he appears within minutes with the van. It carries us back to the top of the cliff, the tires shrieking in protest with every hairpin turn. The lighthouse perched there is old but whitewashed so that it's nearly as blinding as the chalk of Dover. We climb out of the van and run through the mist, entering through an arched red door that looks like it could have come from a book of fairy tales. The café inside is small and round, and so overheated that I pull my scarf off immediately.

The room holds a half dozen tables of elderly women in sweater sets. They all look exactly like Angela Lansbury . . . except, that is, for the ones who look exactly like Maggie Smith. The waitress is well-cast too, blonde and buxom and rosy-cheeked, and without asking what we want, she brings us a three-tiered tray crammed with clever little desserts. Tess goes through the descriptions, quoting names like "syllabub" and "trifle" and "fool." This is the first time we have stopped for dessert in the afternoon—I suppose this is "tea"?—and everyone seems to like the idea. We eat too much, chat and linger, aware that the van waits to carry us to the next inn. Not one of us is straining to get back on the trail. The time for proving things has passed. "I hope you don't feel like we blew your story off," Valerie is saying to Silvia. "It was a good story. Maybe the most hopeful one we've had so far."

"Thank you for saying that," Silvia says. "So many people seem to think my situation is sad and that pisses me off. Nothing is worse than being perfectly happy and having people always telling you to hang in there because things are bound to get better. Besides," she adds, boldly reaching for the last pastry on the tray, "we need to pick up the storytelling pace a bit, don't we?"

"Indeed, for I'm afraid we must tell all three of the remaining stories tomorrow," Tess says, wiping a bit of clotted cream from her lower lip. "Steffi, Becca, and Che. I'm sorry if that makes you feel mashed together but I want to keep the very last morning free for our walk into Canterbury. There are quite a few tidbits about Chaucer and the Cathedral that I always share with groups as we enter the city, and of course Saturday night we shall have our grand meal at my favorite restaurant in town. It's called Deeson's, and it's quite posh. No more pub grub for the likes of us, as I suspect a few of you will be happy to hear."

By this she probably means Steffi, who bemoans the lack of fresh produce at every stop, who is appalled by the pub menus that so cheerfully announce they are about to serve us "tinned tomatoes" and "mushy peas." Steffi, who makes a great show of taking her multivitamin every morning, holding it up and saying, "Usually this is a precaution, but on this trip, it's a necessity." As if six days off her usual regime of broccoli and quinoa might cause a woman to succumb to scurvy. Steffi, who has fretted her way through every meal since we became companions, always interrogating the poor waitress on how everything is prepared. The answer is always baked, boiled, or fried, so I don't know why she bothers asking. And she never fails to point out the irony that for a land so green, in fact the greenest place she's ever been, the British never seem to manage to get anything green on their dinner plates.

But, on the other hand, Tess could just as easily be talking of me and my own affectations, my stupid insistence that we should let each wine breathe before tasting it, even those that are clearly dead on arrival. Or she might be talking about Becca, who is chafing after so much time spent in the company of her elders, who bolts from the table the minute she swallows her last bite, disappearing God knows where, and never deigning to take pudding or chamomile with the rest of us. We three people who have yet to tell our stories . . . we are all of us pains in the ass, each in her own way. The cards have chosen us to go last, and it's rather fitting, but I wonder if the other women dread tomorrow, when we'll come charging at them like the three storytellers of the apocalypse.

And here's the kicker: I still don't know what I'm going to say. I could tell one of the stories of my mother, I suppose. I know the other women are wondering about her. Today when I dropped the ashes on the trail and panicked, enough of the truth came out that everyone now knows why I've come to Canterbury. It was just enough information to intrigue them, I could tell, but yet . . . Shoot. I should have sprinkled her on Dover too. She would have liked it, its defiant ugliness, that poor put-upon little beach with the smell of oil and tar. Maybe there's still time for me to slip away from the others and toss a bit of her over the cliff.

But anyway, now that they know why I joined the group at the last minute, they're clearly curious about the woman causing such bother and it's not like there aren't a hundred good stories starring Diana de Milan. She was a storied creature—she once danced with Elvis Presley, back in college, when he was making a tour of campuses to promote one of his musicals. She hitchhiked the length of Route 66, burned her bra in front of the White House, wrote a book with an entire chapter on how a woman might find her own clitoris, took an immersion course and claimed to have learned serviceable Russian in a single weekend. Grew pears in bottle trees and played the drums and could hold her breath underwater for two straight minutes and being her daughter was exhausting. More exhausting than navi-

gating the cliffs of Dover, and, come to think of it, m
bombed on a regular basis too. She was a master c
after trouble, pulling herself from the dust and reinventing her
life time and time again. I should have paid more attention to
how she did it. But it never once occurred to me that I could
have learned something from Diana, not until after she was
dead. And now it's too late to ask her anything.

TESS SAYS the lighthouse café has one bathroom with a single toilet, which we know from past experience means a twen-
ty-minute departure ceremony. So I decide to take advantage of
the fact that women pee slowly to slip into the little gift shop.
It's an alcove, really, in what must have once been the lighthouse
keeper's pantry. They have pretty bits of pottery, which cards
inform me is made by a local artisan. I pick up a small curved
dish, shaped like a slender leaf but light blue in color, hefting it
in my hand. It's the sort of thing Ned would like. Understated,
solid, well-crafted. We could use it for soap in the guest bath at
the beach cottage or for olive oil in the kitchen.

We were both judicious in stores, slow to spend our money,
and Ned had once laughed and said that nothing made us so
proud as to shop all day and then return home empty-handed.
Yet he would have found beauty in this little bowl, I'm sure of it.
If he were still my boyfriend, I would take it home to him as a
souvenir. I picture it in his hand, his long, slim fingers curled
around its delicate oval shape . . . and it's strange, isn't it, that I
have automatically wondered if Ned would like the bowl but I
haven't wondered if I like it? I think I do. And even though he's

gone and I'm alone, the world still has soap and olive oil, does it not? I might need places to put them. I hand a wispy ten-pound note to the girl behind the register, wave away the mysterious British change, and look over at the bathroom. We are moving even more slowly than I predicted. Jean, Becca, and Steffi are still waiting outside the door.

It's a chance to have a few minutes unobserved and I zip my new dish into my backpack, put on my coat and hat, and slip out the door without anyone seeming to notice. For Diana needs to be here too. Who knows, a bit of her might even blow across the channel, find her way to France, another place she always intended to visit. Stranger things have happened, and once I'd gotten used to the idea that she'd been falling out along the trail while I walked, it had seemed exactly right. The broken zipper was maybe one of those preordained kinds of accidents. An incinerated human body creates a lot of ash. I can afford to scatter some of her willy-nilly along the way and still have plenty left for Canterbury.

A broad lawn leads to the cliff. The fog, far heavier from this vantage point, swallows my view of France, and the wind is so strong here on the point that it threatens to pull the breath from my body. I don't go close to the edge. It feels as if I could be swept right over, plunging down Psyche-like onto the rocks, and there has been enough drama on this trip already. I pull off my gloves and my fingertips almost immediately go numb in the cold. I dig into the fish-and-chips bag, ripping one of the Band-Aids and getting a proper pinch of Diana this time. Toss the ashes into the air and say, "Fly away to France," but the instant that I do, another gust of wind hits and she blows back, right at my face, a few grains of her going in my mouth just as I say "France."

Of course. What else? I cough her up and turn back toward the van, where Tim is sitting patiently in the driver's seat watching me, probably wondering if I'm about to attempt suicide. I bet Dover gets its fair share of them, with the setting so gloomy and the history so bleak. But I'm anything but suicidal. I'm whatever the opposite of suicidal must be. *Hello, cruel world.* That's my new motto. *Move over, make a space, because maybe I want to come along with you after all.* I spit out the rest of Diana and head back to the van.

OUR INN for that evening is located in the village of Dover proper and, unlike the others, it isn't an old house that has been converted into a B&B, but rather a series of small cottages. The women seem charmed by the notion that each of us will have her own tiny house. But the check-in process takes forever, with the desk clerk gathering us all around what appears to be the inn's only map, and tracing the route to the various rooms, saying, "And then you are here," over and over.

She is making it seem horribly complicated, more complicated than nine tiny houses should be. I take my large brass key and step out into the cobblestone courtyard, running into Tim in the process of delivering the bags. His life must feel like a bloody treadmill. He asks me which cottage is mine—I doubt I've heard his voice more than three or four times all week—and I tell him "Eden," then begin weaving my way among the buildings. They are laid out in a rambling manner, evidently each one turned to take advantage of some particular view, should the sun ever manage to shine on Dover. Claire's cottage is the first one I pass and through the broad, low window I can see that Tim has already brought her at least the first of her bags. She could never be accused of traveling light, that one, but she waves me in.

The name on her door is "Churchill," so the cottages must be named after prime ministers, not utopias. I sit down in the room's only chair, white wicker with a nautical-print cushion, and watch her move clothes from her suitcase to the drawers of her bedside table.

"You do that every night?" I ask, although I know she does. It makes no sense to me.

"Just one of my little tics," she says, with her high, pealing laugh. "I can't rest until I feel properly settled, and for me being properly settled means not living out of bags." She frowns down at the black cashmere turtleneck in her hands and says softly to herself, "This one's past its prime." And then, to my horror, she tosses it toward the wastebasket beside the bed.

"You're throwing it away?"

"It has a pull."

I guess my astonishment shows on my face because she says, quickly, "Unless you'd like it, of course."

I go over to the wastebasket and pick up the sweater, pull it to my face, and feel the enviable softness of the wool. I don't have a long history with cashmere but I know enough to know this isn't the ninety-nine-dollar outlet-sale kind. It's the real stuff, the sweater equivalent of a fine Bordeaux. A whiff of Claire still clings to the wool, a perfume I have smelled before but cannot quite name. Pulling another woman's clothing from the trash is not like me; I've never shopped in consignment stores or even swapped shoes back and forth with my friends. But the casualness with which Claire has disposed of this sweater is shocking. It feels somehow morally wrong, and it strikes me that Claire is the sort of woman who throws away more in a single year than most of us dispossess in the course of a lifetime. A tiny flaw and she tosses something aside, be it a sweater or an apple or a man, and I cannot decide if this easy disregard is the source of her power or the source of her wounding.

"So you've lost your mother," she says. She is folding other sweaters as she speaks, sweaters identical to the one she threw away.

"I'm trying to. I think today I made some progress."

"How long ago?"

I have to stop and think. "About a month."

She murmurs that she is sorry and meanwhile I rub the sweater against my cheek again, wondering if it would be odd if I put it on right here in front of her. And then she asks a question that surprises me.

"What did she teach you? Your mother, I mean. Girls always learn something from their mothers, even when they try not to."

Funny. Exactly what I wondered back in the lighthouse café, but I didn't have an answer then and I don't have one now. *She taught me to despise what is easy and close at hand,* I think. *She taught me to always be on the lookout for something better, something finer just around the next bend.* But that isn't quite right. It's unfair to both me and Diana and so I stall, turn the question back to Claire. "What did you learn from your mother?"

The question doesn't give her pause. She's obviously thought about this before, but she pops a stack of sweaters into a bureau and checks her reflection in the mirror before answering. The ends of her medium-length white-blonde hair are perfectly tucked under, a remarkable fact considering that we have walked the entire afternoon in rain and the rest of us arrived in Dover either frizzy or limp. But she runs a brush through it anyway and says, "That the most important thing a woman could be was beautiful."

"Not to be rich?" The question comes out a little rudely, which isn't how I meant it, but she obviously is rich, this woman who tosses aside cashmere like candy wrappers. She's traded up with every husband, that much at least is clear, until she got to the level where she was no longer for sale at any price. The level where she could become the shopper. Could afford to pick herself out a shiny young pool boy.

"In my mother's world, if a woman was beautiful, then being rich would automatically follow," Claire says, sitting down on the bed so that we are facing each other, sitting almost knee to knee. "A girl's job was to be pretty and if she did her job well, then she would deserve a man who had done his job well, and his job was making money. So by that logic, any pretty girl would ultimately become rich. It sounds terribly old-fashioned, I know."

"Do you mind if I put on this sweater?"

"Of course not," she says, and her mouth is smiling even though her eyes look sad. Through the window I can see Tim going by with my bag.

I pull the turtleneck over my head and take a minute to absorb it all in—the softness, the scent of money. And then it occurs to me, all of a sudden. "My mother taught me that it is never too late."

"Now that is a truly extraordinary thing for a woman to teach her daughter," Claire says, in a tone that makes it unclear if she believes my mother's lesson to be helpful, or even accurate. "And just what is this thing that you're not too late to do?"

I push to my feet. "That's the part I haven't quite figured out yet."

THIRTEEN

The next morning it is still dark when we set out. It's no earlier than usual, but the clouds are so low that eight o'clock feels like the middle of the night. We begin walking in a direction that Tess informs us is northwest, retracing our route and heading back away from the sea. I hope this means things will calm down soon, that we will be able to spread farther apart and begin to walk and talk normally. For now we are packed shoulder-to-shoulder, marching almost in lockstep, a single mass against the shards of cold rain. The conditions are hardly ideal for storytelling, but we have three of them to get through today and we have barely begun our descent from Dover when Tess turns to Steffi.

"You have a tale?" she says, and Steffi nods.

She's ready. Of course she is.

The Tale of Steffi

"When I was growing up," Steffi says, "there was one thing in my family that everyone knew, but that no one was ever permitted to say aloud. At least not in public. It was like my parents believed that if we never talked about it, nobody would notice that my sister was fat.

"For a mother like mine, having a fat daughter was the ultimate shame," she goes on, turning her head from side to side as she speaks and almost shouting over the wind. "It was nice if you were smart, or kind or talented in some way, or if you had a pretty face, but it wasn't essential. Skinny was what counted."

We nod in unison, and wipe the droplets from our faces. It is almost as if the whole group has started crying and merely a few words in, Steffi's story has already explained so much. Just this morning at breakfast they brought us something called a Scotch egg, which had turned out to be sausage wrapped around a boiled egg and then deep-fried. The hard brown ovals had rolled around on each plate like balls and Steffi had said to the poor innkeeper, "You have brought me a plate of death."

A plate of death. It had been a strange breakfast, true, and none of us had known quite how to eat it, but that hardly made it a plate of death. Steffi's food quirks make more sense now.

"My mother had been a model before she married and had us," Steffi says. "Not like Beverly Johnson, not that high up the food chain, but during the seventies she'd been in her share of ads in magazines like *Mademoiselle* and *Glamour* and *Seventeen*.

She was the black girl they always included in every group shot of white friends. You know, the one that's supposed to imply a level of diversity that doesn't really exist. I'm sure that had something to do with why she cared so much how everything looked. When you're the only one . . ."

She stops, pulls a wayward strand of hair from where it has stuck to her heavily balmed lips. "The thing is, nobody had any real idea how much my sister was eating, because she ate alone most of the time. She would carry food into her room, and once I think I even heard her talking to it. Like a friend. Which sounds utterly crazy, if you didn't grow up in my house and never saw how fast a dining room table could turn into a battle-field. My mother would watch everyone while they ate, calculating the calories they were consuming in her head. The damage, that's what she called it. A doughnut had a damage of four hundred and fifty calories. An orange just had a damage of fifty-five. It's funny after all these years how many of her calorie counts I still remember."

"What's your sister's name?" Valerie asks.

"Tina," says Steffi, rather slowly. "Named after my mom, who's Christina, and that made it even worse. You have to understand that my mother would have preferred almost anything else over the stigma of having a fat daughter. A child who was stupid, a husband who beat her, bankruptcy, drugs, affairs . . . any of that would have been better, because any of that could have been hidden. But you can't hide fat. All Tina had to do was walk into a room and the jig was up. She was immediate proof that we weren't some perfectly photogenic black family, like the Huxtables were then or like the Obamas are now, and that we'd never be perfect, no matter how much Mom tried to pretend."

She waits for us to nod before continuing. We oblige. We nod. Nothing sucks quite like being fat sucks, so there's no point in pretending we don't understand.

"Tina's humiliations were endless," Steffi says. "The regular gym uniforms at school didn't fit her. One had to be special ordered. When we went to Disneyland, she had to ride in her Dumbo by herself. Dumbo. She was supposed to be a little girl, but she was too heavy to ride with the rest of us in an elephant. Can you imagine the kind of jokes people made? And if a fat girl walks down the street eating an ice cream cone . . ." Steffi shudders. "Strangers stop and stare and some of them even say things to you. I remember one time the man selling ice cream wouldn't give her a cone, because that was her favorite thing, you see, ice cream, and Mom knew it and wouldn't keep it in the house. So the minute we were on our own, which was rare because my mother watched us like a hawk, we'd head straight for the park. This man . . . he sold ice cream for a living, that's the whole point. He owned the cart. It was his job to sell ice cream, but he wouldn't sell any to her. He held up a cone of strawberry—that was her very favorite—and he said, 'You don't need this,' and he handed the cone to me."

"Did you take it?" says Becca.

"I'm ashamed to say I did," says Steffi. "He was an adult and I was a kid and I didn't know what else to do. I offered it back to her the second we were out of his sight, but by then I had licked it and it had sort of melted. She must have hated me. Felt I was the favored one and thought that it all wasn't fair. And she was right. When you're the fat girl, nothing is fair."

We walk a bit in silence, except for the wind.

"She had one date during all four years of high school," says Steffi. "It was the son of a friend of my father's and a total fix-up. The four parents got together and made him do it. Or paid him, I don't know. He went to a different school, so I guess he figured it would never get back to any of his friends that he'd gone out with someone who looked like Tina, but still, just to be on the safe side, he took her to a restaurant out of town. Some seafood place way down by the beach and he said it was because the fish was fresher there, but she saw through it. Of course she did. So she ate just a little bit, like she knew girls on dates were supposed to do, and he took her straight home afterward.

"When she walked in the kitchen, she was starving. It wasn't just the fact she hadn't eaten that night. She'd hardly had a real meal in weeks, because she'd been getting ready for her big date. My mother had insisted she could knock a few pounds off in time if she tried and she locked the kitchen—wait a minute. Have I told you that part? Mama didn't believe in snacking. She always said that when the kitchen was closed, it was closed, and she would literally padlock everything before she went to bed." Steffi laughs, a hollow sound. "I was in college before I realized that this wasn't normal, that other people's mothers didn't put padlocks on the cupboards and refrigerators."

"Tina came in, about nine, and she was upset. It had been an awful night and she was hungry, but there wasn't anything anywhere. We weren't the kind of family who even kept a bowl of fruit on the counter. She couldn't find anything in the whole kitchen except for dog food."

Steffi pauses, a pause that feels like forever. There's tension within the group. I doubt there's anyone among us who hasn't already figured out that Steffi doesn't have a sister, at least not a fat one named Tina. Steffi's the one who went on the bad date with the boy who was ashamed of her, the one who couldn't buy an ice cream cone, who had to fly solo in Dumbo. She's been talking about herself all along, and the only suspense in the story is how long it will take her to admit that she is both the teller and the tale.

"She'd done it before," Steffi said. "Reached in the big bag of dog food and snatched a handful of kibble whenever things weren't going so good. The Alpo was the one edible thing in the house that our mother had never thought to lock up. But this night was an especially bad one, and she felt like she had to eat. Really eat. You have to understand that whenever she got like this, she was driven by pure compulsion, an addict needing her fix, and when she looked down at the dog's bowl she saw there were the remains of pork chops in it. Which meant that we had celebrated while she was gone, because that's another thing she loved, pork chops. Another food with which she couldn't be trusted to restrain herself. So my mother never served them, except on those rare times when she knew Tina wasn't going to be there. It was just one more additional slap in the face, that the whole family had been eating pork chops while she was off on her awful date, that even the dog was getting pork chops . . ."

Steffi's voice trails off, becomes faint, briefly lost in the wind. "But the worst part is, the boy caught her like that. He'd come back for something. He'd left his keys or a glove or hat . . . who knows? None of us will ever be able to explain why that boy turned around. He had walked her to the door and shaken her hand, then walked to his car, and then for some reason he'd come back. He was looking through the glass panes in the kitchen door, getting ready to knock, and he saw Tina on her hands and knees in front of the dog dish, chewing on a bone."

We exhale as a group. Turn our heads away from the center, afraid to even look at one another. We had known something bad was coming, but I don't think anyone expected it to be as bad as this. Save for Valerie and her slight midriff pudge, which she wears rather defiantly, you wouldn't call any of us fat girls. But yet, in a way, all girls are fat girls. We all have our oversize shirts, our ways of folding in upon ourselves, our instinctual three-quarter turn from the camera. Everybody's trying to hide some sort of ugly, so that image of that boy looking at Steffi through the window, seeing her eating from a dog dish . . . it's a lot to take.

"Why did you say this was a story about love?" Becca says, although even she seems tired of the question. "It's about everything except love."

"But I haven't finished," says Steffi. "Give me time. It's a love story because a man saved her. Broke her out of her prison of fat. Her tower of fat, maybe that's a better way to say it. Because if we're all living fairy tales, Tina was Rapunzel, locked away from the world. The prince was a doctor with a contract from a pharmaceutical company, who was doing a medical study on obesity, and she was one of his guinea pigs. They met three times a week as part of the protocol and then, out of nowhere, on Valentine's Day he gave her a box of Godiva chocolates. No man had ever given her anything, much less Godiva chocolates—" She stops to wipe the collected mist from her brow and I think about the gold box I'd seen in her bag that first day in London. She had seemed so surprised to find it there.

"That's awful. He was trying to ruin her chances before she even finished the study," says Claire. "Because secretly he liked his women fat. I've heard about men like that on the Internet. They call them chubby chasers. Bastards."

"That does seems cruel," says Jean. "You take a man who has some sort of obsession with heavy women, and of course he goes into obesity research. It's a perfect target-rich environment. And he finds someone, this poor girl who has never been loved, not really, who thinks it isn't possible, and he sabotages her. Singles her out, feeds her chocolate, makes her feel special, and keeps her just like she is."

"No," says Steffi. "You're both wrong. Or maybe I've described it wrong, because it wasn't like that at all. Tina never ate the chocolates. She didn't have to. It was enough to know that he had given them to her, that he wanted her to have them. After a lifetime of food being locked away, even her mother withholding . . . No, she just kept them. They were a symbol of the fact that he could see through the fat to the real person inside of it. Because he had done what a normal man does when he likes a normal girl. He brings her candy. It's been fifteen years now, and she still has the box. Do you know what chocolates look like after fifteen years? They turn white. They're like rocks. But she still has them. She knows what they mean."

"What do they mean?" asks Claire. "You've lost me, I'm afraid."

"Maybe this is the story of Beauty and the Beast," says Steffi. "Yes, not Rapunzel, I don't know why I said that. Tina's story was more like Beauty and the Beast, and I don't blame you for not seeing it, because I didn't see it myself, not for years. In order to have the miracle of transformation, something must be loved before it is really lovable."

"Like Sir Gawain and the hag," says Valerie.

"That too," says Steffi. "We're all just telling the same story in different forms. I thought about that last night, when I was in the shower. Because there have been these strange little over-laps, haven't there?" She shrugs, not waiting for an answer. "Okay, maybe it's just me. But the point is that in order for a cursed creature to become beautiful, for the magic to work, someone has to see that she already is beautiful. Because the moment the doctor gave her those Godivas, she lost the taste for them. She never craved chocolate again."

"That's impossible," Claire says flatly. "All women crave chocolate."

"No, all women crave the forbidden," Steffi says. "And when food was no longer forbidden, it lost its power over her. She found, for the first time in her life, that she could think of other things. Because someone had loved her just as she was right then, in the here and now, and not because of what she might be someday if she could just learn a little bit of self-control."

"Well, if that's magic, it's only magical because a man did it," Claire says. "Women love the unlovable every day. We fall in love with a man's potential and then we marry his scruffy, unemployed ass. We treat him like a house we're trying to flip, a fixer-upper, and we convince ourselves all he needs is a little imagination and some elbow grease. That's how we get stuck. How we end up with all those losers sleeping on our couch. But men never fall in love with a woman's potential. They just aren't capable of it—a woman's beauty has to be served right up on a plate for them to see it, and then half the time they still can't. And you're saying this man was a doctor, which means he was successful, which means he could have had anyone he wanted. For a man like that to see past a fat body and fall in love with the woman hidden inside of it . . . I'm sorry, but I find your story completely unbelievable."

Jean is frowning. "But you wouldn't find it unbelievable if a beautiful woman fell in love with an overweight man."

"Of course not," says Claire. "That's my whole point. As a gender, women have a hell of a lot more experience in loving the unlovable."

"It's because we get pregnant," says Angelique. The statement is so her. Out of nowhere and bizarrely genius. She does this. She says nothing for miles and then she suddenly comes up with one of these epic pronouncements, always delivered in her weird Jersey voice.

"What does getting pregnant have to do with it?" says Becca, but Jean is already cutting her off.

"It's true," she says. "Women have to protect a life that isn't quite there yet. Our biology programs us to sacrifice everything for a mass of cells, which is just another way of valuing something for its pure potential. It's what makes us the superior gender. Because there's grace in that, this willingness to love something that you can't see."

"You may find it unbelievable, but I swear it happened just the way I told you," says Steffi, who is still looking at Claire. "He was a man, and yet he loved her even when she was fat. I promise, all of this is true. Or most of it."

"She's thin now?" Jean says.

Steffi nods. "As it turns out, what she wanted all along wasn't food as much as she just wanted permission to eat."

"My father was like that," I say, the words coming out in a rush. "He was an alcoholic, although nobody used that word, because he just drank beer and nobody paid much attention to beer, at least not in an era where there was so much worse stuff floating around. But I guess it must have been a lot of beer, because one day he said to my mother, 'I'm going into the woods and in three days, I'll either come out sober or you'll find me in there dead.' " And all at once it hits me how that must have been for my mother. The cofounder of the commune, designated as one of the keepers of the flame, but yet she was so often alone while my father went off to fight his demons. He was a walker too, like I guess I am, although this is the first time I've ever really pondered this particular similarity in our natures. One time he walked so far that he came out on the other side of the woods disoriented and it turned out he was in a completely different state. He found a pay phone in the parking lot of a truck stop and called my mother collect to pick him up and when she said, "Where are you?" he had to ask some trucker. She always laughed about the time Rich called her from New

York, but I wonder how funny it really was, being left so often on her own with no idea where he'd gone or when he would return. It puts the Davids of the world in a different light.

"Exactly," says Valerie. "That's exactly the point I was trying to make, that whenever you deny yourself something, it turns into an obsession. But if you know you can have it, you don't have to have it, and that's the key to all of life, isn't it? And if a man offered you the one thing you'd always been denied, the one thing even your own mother wouldn't give you . . . of course you'd fall in love."

It's a telling moment. Valerie said "you" instead of "she," but Steffi ignores the shift in pronouns and keeps talking.

"I'm not suggesting it was easy," she says. "She lost a hundred and forty pounds over the course of a year, but the day her doctor gave her chocolate was the start of it. And eventually she went back to school, and moved on with her life, and married the doctor and if you met them today . . . you would never guess that they started out as Beauty and the Beast, you would just think *What an attractive couple.* Oh, and after she had lost the weight she had to have skin-reduction surgery, all over her body. Around the hips and waist mostly, with little tucks in the arms and legs. More than fifteen pounds of skin was removed, can you imagine that? Fifteen pounds of nothing but skin?"

"So her story has a happy ending?" says Becca.

"The happiest," says Steffi. "She now weighs a hundred and twenty-three pounds, and for women I don't think there could be any happier ending. We should rewrite all the fairy tales—Cinderella, Snow White, Rapunzel, and The Little Mermaid. Forget the princes and the castles. Just type the line 'And she weighed a hundred and twenty-three pounds happily ever after,' and we would all close the book with a tear and a sigh."

"How do you know all this?" asks Valerie. "How do you know what she thought and what she felt and how she ate the dog food but she didn't eat the chocolates?"

"I'm being stupid, aren't I?" says Steffi and she stops. Drops her backpack, pulls her shirt from the waistband of her jeans, and lifts it. "Here. You may as well look."

The scars have faded over time to a watery shade of beige, pale slashes across her strong brown abdomen. Two of them, one on the right and one on the left, stretching around her waist from both sides, almost touching in the back and almost touching in the front. It is the body of a woman who, at some point in her life, has been virtually cut in half.

FOURTEEN

Our final lunch will be in a village so small it doesn't have a name. It's no more than a swell in the road, really, a place where a sidewalk suddenly appears beside the main road, but according to Tess it is the site of one of the oldest hospices in all of Kent. She leads us through the shell of an abandoned building and I follow at the end of the line as we walk among crumbling walls and shattered door frames, noting that a tree is even growing in the corner of the largest room. It's taller than I am, pushing its way up through the remnants of the stone floor.

"They called them hospices because you could find hospitality there," Tess is saying, "and over time it evolved into our modern word 'hospital.' Remember that Canterbury was reputed to be a site of medical miracles, which means many of our pilgrims were already ill when they began their journey. It's easy to imagine how the rigors of the trail might prove too much for them. The churches in the various villages along the route opened these hospices as a gesture of goodwill, a thank-you to the travelers who were bringing commerce to their towns and also, in their minds, a way to curry favor with God. If you couldn't afford to undertake a pilgrimage of your own, it was considered almost as virtuous to offer help to those who had answered the call."

She squats down at the roots of the tree and gazes up at the sky before continuing. The day has cleared, the canopy above us having brightened from gray to blue. A shaft of muted sunlight falls across her face as she raises her chin and she closes her eyes for a moment in sheer pleasure before sighing and then going on with her little speech. "Most travelers would only stay at a hospice for a night or two, resting and gathering their strength before once again taking to the trail, but for a few of the most ill . . . that's how these stopping places along the road became the first hospitals. Records show that a fair number of the pilgrims died en route to Canterbury and are buried in the cemeteries of towns not their own, another act of charity. Sometimes the graves are entirely blank except for a cross, because the people who nursed and buried them might never have known their names."

She makes one of her professorial gestures, an elegant little motion toward the largest split in the largest wall, evidently the location that had once held the entrance. Through it we can see a small, ill-kept cemetery. None of us ventures out except for Valerie, and even she is back in a minute. Tombstones that tell the person's life story can be interesting, as are those which offer poems or phrases for contemplation. But each unmarked grave is dispiriting in its own special way, a sign of just one more pilgrim who never told his story.

After meandering through the hospice, we move on to the café next door for an early lunch. It has three tables inside, two of them occupied, but there is a collection of mismatched chairs on the front sidewalk outside, clustered around a long table. The owner springs into action when she sees Tess, who apparently brings groups here regularly, and they begin to speak so quickly that it's hard to understand them.

But she's gesturing toward the street, so it would appear that the woman is directing our cumbersome party of nine to the outside table. The temperature has mellowed since morning, and the wind has calmed, but just in case, the café owner pulls a stack of quilts from behind the bar, thin and worn but folded neatly. We each take one and walk back out the door to choose a chair.

"This is strange," mutters Becca and we all in turn whisper that it's fine even though of course she's right. It is strange.

Tess spreads one of the quilts over her legs and assures us that this café, while small, has the best beef stew in all of County Kent. A bowl will warm us up. We nod, adjust our quilts to imitate her, and stare out at the nonexistent view. Not a single car has driven by since we've arrived in town and the only human activity in sight is a little boy on a bicycle, evidently the owner's child. His mother must have instructed him to keep to the sidewalk, for he is forlornly riding his bike to the absolute end of the concrete, then getting off, pushing it in a U-turn, and riding it as far as possible back to the other end. He probably does this all day long.

The stew is out within minutes, piping hot and as good as Tess promised.

"How's your mother hanging in there today?" Valerie asks quietly as the other women begin to chat and eat.

"Still dead," I say.

"Is that what your story is going to be about?" Valerie persists, handling me a rough loaf of bread to break. It's all very biblical. "Your mom dying?"

"If I can't think of something better. I'm still trying to think of something better." Which is a bit of a lie. I started practicing the story in my head on the walk from Dover. I think I have a good first line. Deceptively simple, but with real emotional punch. *My story begins with the death of my mother . . .* That'll grip them.

Valerie smiles. "Somehow I get the feeling your mom provided you with plenty of stories to tell."

"Oh, she did. When a narcissist dies, it tears a great big hole in the world."

"Your mother was a narcissist?"

"Certifiable."

"Damn. Mine too. What are the odds?"

"Given how the two of us have turned out, I'd say pretty high."

"Che, do you want to order the wine?" Tess asks, and I can only assume that she's joking. A place that doesn't have a food menu likely won't have a wine list, and this poor woman, glancing at her son on his bike as she works her way around the table refilling the steaming bowls, appears to be the restaurant's hostess, cook, waitress, cashier, and dishwasher.

"Bring us whatever kind of wine you have," I tell her. "Red, if possible. Or white. Pink's fine."

"And Becca," Tess says, turning with a smile, "Since we have two stories to tell this afternoon, would you mind starting yours over lunch?" But Becca is checking her phone, or at least trying to, turning it one way and then another in search of bars, and doesn't answer.

"She'd be happy to start," says Jean.

"Come on, Mom," Becca says, still shaking the phone. "She asked me, not you."

"And you didn't answer. So I answered on your behalf."

Becca smiles back at Tess, all sweetness and cooperation. "Of course I'll go."

"Concentrate on your food for five minutes," Jean says. "Then you won't have to talk with your mouth full."

"Maybe I want to talk with my mouth full," Becca says and thus they are off, a mother and daughter having just one more argument about something neither of them can name. There's no point in any of us trying to tell them they should stop for a moment and really appreciate each other, for of course they know their time together is limited, that someday the girl will be grown and the mother will be gone. But for now they must fight with every step along the path. It's a mother's job to say all the words in the world, just as it's a daughter's job not to hear any of them. Each woman must make her own mistakes. To retrace every step of the path her mother walked, and to learn, for the first and millionth time, the untransferable lessons of womanhood.

The Tale of Becca

"Last year, my junior year," Becca says, "I was cast as the lead in my class play. Okay, maybe not. Shit, I guess I'm lying already." She looks around the table, where most of us are on our second bowls of the stew and are tearing off hunks of the bread, smearing it with that strong yellow butter the pubs bring out with every meal. Real butter, and irresistible. I will miss it when I get back to the States.

"I wasn't exactly cast in the role," Becca amends. "I was the understudy and then the girl who they really wanted got sick and I took her place. Her name was Hillary McAllister. Still is, I guess. And when I said 'class play' that wasn't entirely the truth either. We do two plays each year in drama, one for the student body and one that we take to the local elementary schools and that's the one I was in, the kiddie play. *Sleeping Beauty.* And that's who I was. Sleeping Beauty." She looks around the table again. "Jesus. This is harder than I would have thought, trying to tell your own story."

"Hillary was cast," her mother says tonelessly, "and then Hillary got sick. Some form of mononucleosis."

"I didn't think kids got mono anymore," says Silvia.

"Of course they do," says Jean. "Mono never goes out of style, like kissing."

"I think all the old ailments are coming back into fashion," I say. "I even know a woman who recently had her appendix taken out." From the end of the table, Tess makes a face at me.

"The CDC in Atlanta keeps frozen cells of all sorts of ancient diseases," Valerie says. "They have bubonic plague. Which makes you wonder what would happen if somebody, like, dropped the jar."

"Oh, they could probably knock out the bubonic plaque with penicillin now," Silvia says. "They just didn't have anything to fight it with back in the old days."

"You think?" Valerie says. "Penicillin?"

"It's entirely possible," Steffi says. "We have so many more weapons now in the war against germs and we—"

"Hey," says Becca. "Remember how we set that rule that nobody can interrupt the storyteller? And let's go back to how Hillary got mono because this story is all about kissing and how somehow I had managed to make it to eleventh grade without ever having been kissed. That's an awful thing to admit and it makes me sound retarded and save your breath, Mom, I know I shouldn't say 'retarded' like that. I know it's like 'fat,' it's just a word you're not supposed to say. But most girls . . . by junior year, anybody even halfway cute has already had sex and that's just the truth. By the time they were my age they had finished something I hadn't even started and I would have died if anyone knew the truth. Virgins are . . . unchosen."

She stops here and dips a fingertip into a smear of butter on her plate. Takes her time licking it off. It's as if she's expecting someone to say something, like she's waiting for some chorus of protest to rise from the older women. That we will all rush in to say that virgins are not the unchosen, but rather the ones doing the choosing, and that sometimes the best way a woman can take charge of her sexual destiny is by remaining chaste. There's power in restraint—this is what the girl expects us to tell her. That it's smart to wait for the right man to come along. Test him, make sure he's worth it, before you give up the goods.

So Becca lingers over the next bite of stew, her spoon making a scraping sound against the bottom of the bowl. A bottle of wine—red, as luck would have it—has manifested itself at my elbow and I uncork it and begin pouring, but no one speaks.

Each woman in the parliament holds her counsel as to whether or not virginity is a desirable state and, even though Becca has claimed to want a silent stage, I can tell that our refusal to respond has flummoxed her. Ever since we left London she's been waiting for a simple love story and none of us has been able to give her one. She has walked mile after mile, hour after hour, through the English countryside listening to tales of compromise and reinvention, stories of jealous sisters and royal curses and dementia and pornography because once a woman gets past a certain age—thirty? twenty-five? or, God help us, is it even younger?—she's forced to accept that when it comes to love, things will never be simple again. Simple love stories are for virgins or, better yet, those who are utterly unconscious. Of course she played Sleeping Beauty. What else could a girl like Becca be?

"If you're thinking I'm wrong to gloat because Hillary McAllister got mono, get over it," Becca says. "Because she was always mean to me. Mean to everybody. So she deserved to get mono. That's just justice and there's nothing wrong with wanting justice."

Once again, no one steps in to confirm or correct this last observation. There are no debates about justice versus mercy, only the stacked bowls that mark the end of the stew and the gurgles that mark the beginning of the wine. Valerie pushes her chair back and props her knee against the side of the table. Lunch, after all, isn't just our midday meal but also our chance to rest. We've learned to settle in for a while.

"The thing about getting the lead in *Sleeping Beauty*," Becca goes on, when she finally realizes no one intends to take the bait, "is that you're onstage the whole time, but you don't have to memorize many lines. You speak during the first part where Beauty pricks her finger . . . there's that word again, 'prick.' Didn't somebody else prick something, in one of the other stories?"

Eros, I think, *in Angelique's story.* He pricked himself on one of his own arrows just as Sleeping Beauty pricked herself on her spinning wheel. They brought their enchantment upon themselves, seemingly by accident, more likely by destiny. Because that's the real story, isn't it? The one none of us can stop telling. That the end is the beginning, and the beginning marks the end. That no matter how far or fast we walk, everyone eventually circles back. Comes face-to-face with whatever they were trying to escape.

But I don't say anything. No one does. It seems the longer we stay silent, the more powerful the silence grows.

Becca shrugs and fluffs the hair around her face. Normally it's slicked back but today, perhaps in concession to the morning rain, she's wearing it differently. It's brushed forward into bangs and as she peers out from beneath the orangey-red fringe, she looks even younger than usual. "The prince," she says, "was played by Josh Travis, and he's the best-looking guy in my whole school. I forgot to tell you that part, but it matters, that I got a good prince and not a crappy prince. Because in drama class, they don't have many guys so you just never know." Someone has poured wine in her glass and she pauses again, looking down at this unexpected gift with surprise. On previous meals the bottle has never stopped at her, but rather has been passed across her plate, the alcohol flowing from woman to woman but never from woman to girl. It's a moment. She lifts the glass and takes a small sip, taking care not to make eye contact with her mother. Becca is what, seventeen now? Eighteen at most? Too young to drink in an American restaurant, but this is England, where those rules don't apply, and besides, her mother doesn't seem inclined to stop her. She's not even looking at her daughter, merely gazing at the child in the street. It's another unspoken rule of the Canterbury Trail, I suppose, that the storyteller is allowed to drink.

Becca puts the glass down, a thoughtful frown on her face. "So here's where we are. Hillary gets sick and stays sick and I get my chance. Each afternoon in rehearsals I lie there on the bed pretending to be in a coma while the action goes on all around me. And I know that it's building up to the big kiss, even though we never rehearse that part. Our teacher, Mr. Grayson—I think he's gay, Gayson Grayson, that's what all the kids say—he says we'll save the kiss for the first performance because that way it will be fresh. The only note he gives me is that I shouldn't respond too soon. That when Josh bends down and kisses me, I have to remember that I've been asleep for a long time, and that I'm slowly coming out from under the spell that's been cast. 'Emerge in layers,' he would say. 'Like a butterfly leaving its cocoon.' So maybe he was gay, because that's a gay thing to say. But the point is that for most of the play, all I have to do is lie there on the plywood bed the shop class built and wait to be kissed."

Becca runs a fingertip around the rim of her wineglass. "You're all thinking I'm not right to play Sleeping Beauty," she says, with her normal defensiveness, but I for one am thinking nothing of the sort. Behind the bright hair and dark glasses, the oversize ear holes and floppy clothes, Becca truly is a beauty. As lovely as her mother probably was in her own youth, with the same porcelain princess prettiness, the sort that no degree of rebellion can totally eradicate. "But they gave me a long blonde wig and a long blue dress and I think—" She stops. "I can't say for sure if Josh wanted to kiss me. He expected he'd be kissing Hillary and she was the right sort of girl for a boy like him to kiss. They were already going out. They had probably already done it. Done everything. I don't know."

She hesitates again. We're making her nervous, I think, just sitting and staring. She's been put at a disadvantage, having to tell her story at a café instead of on the trail. Apparently it's easier to talk when you're shoulder-to-shoulder than when you're face-to-face. So I shift my weight toward the street and, like Jean, begin to watch the little boy riding his bike. Give Becca a few minutes to finish the wine and pull herself together.

The child is no more than six or seven and he seems to be new to the fine art of balance. It's as if his training wheels were taken off recently and he struggles over the cracks in the sidewalk, weaving first one way and then the other. At times the whole bike tilts and his foot flies down from the pedals, catching his weight at the last possible minute before he goes toppling over. The sidewalk is not only cracked but sloped, with stray tufts of grass poking up in random locations. Hardly optimal for a beginner learning how to ride. He stops for a moment and looks toward the door. It's closed. His mother is inside, at least for the moment.

I finish my first glass of wine, then pour another.

"People think Sleeping Beauty is a silly story," Becca finally goes on. "Simple and stupid, even by fairy-tale standards. The girl goes to sleep, the boy wakes her up. Boom. The end. But I was happy to have the part and happy to know I was going to get a chance to kiss Josh. On the day of the first performance, they packed us up with the props in a bus and we went to the elementary school. One of them. There are seven in our county and we were going to play them all, but this was the first. Hillary came with us. I didn't count on that. She couldn't be Beauty, she wasn't strong enough to be onstage, and of course she couldn't kiss Josh, but she was in the third week of mono by that time and she was well enough that they let her ride the bus and come along to watch. She gave me the evil eye the whole way."

The boy pushes the bike from the sidewalk into the edge of the forbidden street and looks back at us with a guilty grimace. Bites his lip as if he's trying to decide something. Trying to evaluate the significance of our presence in his life. Who are these ladies drinking wine on the patio—allies or betrayers, friends or foe? Will one of us tell his mother that he's broken her only rule?

"Back at the high school we'd only practiced the play in pieces," Becca says. "We'd never run it through even once, start to finish. And so when we set up our props—the spinning wheel and the bed and all the fairies were in costume, and the evil witch . . . it was good. That's the thing. It all came together better than I'd ever thought it would. But then halfway into the play I'm already lying flat on my back with my eyes closed, just listening to the story going on around me and I start thinking, *Oh God, this is it. Josh is going to kiss me. I'm going to get my first kiss right here and now and it's with the cutest boy in school.* And I started trembling. I couldn't control it. I was lying on my bed in my blonde wig and I was trembling so hard that I was sure the kids in the audience could see it and would think, *She's not asleep, she's having some sort of fit.* I tried to think about anything else. I said the alphabet backward in my head. But it just got worse and finally one of the fairies leaned over, I think it was Merryweather, and whispered, 'Are you all right?' I think she thought maybe I was coming down with mono too because I know I was red and it must have looked like I was running a fever. But it wasn't mono. It was the fever of waiting for Josh Travis to kiss me. It was the fever of love."

Valerie and Claire smile at this and Jean turns from the boy in the street to face her daughter, also amused. Is this what a simple love story sounds like? I hate to keep grousing—in fact, I sound like Becca when I do—but nothing about this tale seems simple to me. She was playing Sleeping Beauty while the boy's true girlfriend watched from the wings. And her first kiss, normally a private, even furtive, event was to be played out in front of two hundred squirming children on a well-lit stage. No wonder the girl's notions of romance are so overblown. It hasn't yet occurred to her that a stage kiss is not the real thing.

The little boy is coping better now that he's on the flat street. He's up on two wheels, pedaling straight back and forth in front of us. His view never changes. He sees nothing except the vistas he has created in his own mind. But the wobbles have almost ceased and the only time he falters at all is when he passes the door to the café and looks to the side. He knows that any moment his mother will come out to fill our water glasses and catch him. Then he will be humiliated, grounded. Maybe even stripped of his bicycle and the freedom two wheels can buy.

"The big moment comes," Becca says. "And Josh bends down over me and I feel his breath and his lips were so soft. It was like the ground opened up beneath us and I knew, before he even touched me, that nothing afterward would ever be the same. My life has only two chapters—before Josh kissed me and after Josh kissed me." She laughs. For just a moment it's a woman's laugh and not a girl's. "Mr. Grayson got pissed. Because I didn't wake up slowly like he told me to, I woke up all at once. I think I even put my hand behind Josh's head and held him there for a second and of course the real Sleeping Beauty would have never done that. A real princess never would have grabbed her prince around the neck and practically pulled him down on top of her. But I couldn't stop myself. And Josh . . . Here's the weird part. The part you might not believe. He felt it too."

"Why wouldn't we believe that?" says Angelique. "Do you think we think that men can't feel things?"

"It was the perfect first kiss," says Becca. Her face has taken on a wistful quality and it's amazing that even a girl as young as Becca can already be nostalgic. "It saved me from being unchosen and it saved him from being a man slut. Because before that kiss Josh had been one of those guys who's so cute they can sleep with anybody and so they do sleep with everybody but that moment . . . The miracle is that the kiss changed Josh as much as it changed me."

"So this is your story?" Jean says quietly. "You're telling them that Josh is now your boyfriend—is that the long and short of it?"

"Well, he is," says Becca, her voice sharp. "He comes over to the house all the time. You've met him."

"Yes," says Jean. "He comes over to the house. I've met him."

"And he was my first in every other way too," Becca says, and here her voice cracks just a little. *This is the real loss of innocence in women,* I think. *Not the first time you sleep with a man, but the first time you doubt whatever story you've told yourself about why you slept with that man. She's waking up, all right, but she doesn't always like it.* "What's wrong with that, Mom? Why is it okay for you to have had your one big love and not me?"

"I just don't want you to overromanticize your relationship with Josh," her mother says. She is fiddling with her wedding ring, as she always seems to do when she gets nervous. "I don't want you to make something out of it that isn't there." Jean reaches for her daughter's arm, but Becca pulls back. Squares her shoulders and sits up taller in her chair.

"Right," she says. "Like you don't overromanticize Dad."

The child on the bike is growing in confidence right before our eyes. He still rides in a neat, straight line, but now he no longer bothers to get off the bike in order to turn it. He makes a circle right there on the edge of the street, his face split open with joy and pride, before heading back the other way. And the next time he passes, he does not look nervously toward the café door.

Good for you, I think. *Pedal hard, and when you get to the end of the sidewalk, keep going.*

"Your father," Jean says coldly, "was nothing like Josh."

"Wake up, Mom," says Becca. "I'm not a child. I know everything. I've known it ever since Dave went into rehab." She looks around the table. "Dave's my baby brother, the youngest, and he's already tried to clean up twice. Has she told you that part of our family story? Any of you? I didn't think so."

Jean is flushed. Again. How many times has her face turned this color? I always assumed it was exertion, a woman not used to so much walking, but now, for the first time, I wonder if there is something really wrong with her. "Becca, please. You have no idea what you're saying."

"I know exactly what I'm saying. The file? The one with the family medical history? You left it right on the kitchen table. Maybe part of you wanted me to read it."

"Becca, I'm serious. This has to stop. Right now and right here. You may have read something, but you can't possibly know what it means."

"'Cause Dave wasn't the first addict in the family, was he, Mom?" Becca says, her voice strident and harsh. "There was a genetic predisposition toward drug abuse, isn't that what the file said? Passed from father to son in this case, but I think part of me knew that before I read it."

"You don't understand what you read."

"No," says Becca. "No, Mom, I think the problem is that I understand just fine, which is why you can't say anything else about my relationship with Josh. Not now or ever. Daddy wasn't working that night in Guatemala. And they didn't shoot him because he was trying to protect us." Becca looks from her mother's splotchy face to the rest of us. "The first story we all heard, did you get it? Did any of you figure it out at the time? That the perfect man's ultimate sacrifice was really nothing more than a drug deal gone bad? Isn't that hysterical? The biggest possible joke? Mom built our whole lives around that night. She taught us we should worship Daddy, she turned the date of his death into this . . . this anniversary of mourning when she knew all along that it was nothing but a—"

Jean screams. Despite the fact tension has been building around the table for the last few minutes, despite the fact we all knew something was coming, I startle with the sound, and then Valerie screams too. It is this second scream—louder, sharper, and even more unexpected—that shocks us all out of our reverie. A door opens, then slams, and now the mother is out on the sidewalk too, her face frozen, and in the same instant—one scream, the next scream, and the slam of the door—it all leads up to a squeal of tires, the loudest noise of all. The long shrill shriek of motion interrupted, of a driver frantically trying to stop a car. Trying to rein in the inevitable while it is still in the realm of the merely possible.

Then the final sound. A thud, muted but definitive, and here our story changes, yet again.

FIFTEEN

He has an unusual blood type. The emergency unfolding around us has several components, but this is the first one that arises. The child lying on the edge of the street has B negative blood, a condition that is true of slightly less than two percent of the population, at least in the States. I imagine it is similar in England.

I know this statistic because I have B negative blood.

A burst of activity exploded around us the instant the boy was struck by the car. The driver leapt out, a tall man apparently unknown to the villagers. A nobody, someone just passing through. Four or five of the locals spilled from the café at the sound of impact, one of them rushing to restrain the hysterical mother and the rest gathering around the boy. One of them identifies himself as a doctor, and it will be several minutes before any of us realize he is a veterinarian. But the veterinarian is a decisive man, which in this moment is the most important thing he could be.

The vet waves off the driver's offer to take the boy to the hospital in Canterbury, saying he shouldn't be moved until they've determined the extent of his injuries. Another one of the diners calls for an ambulance and that is when the mother says the boy's blood type is rare. She doesn't have it, his father did. His no-good knockabout father, gone to Spain or Morocco or God-knows-where, and the ambulance must bring B negative blood when they come, for any fool can see that he must be transfused as quickly as possible. Life is seeping from the child's pale, immobile body, the pool of red around him growing by the minute. Blood runs between the cobblestones, and it soaks into the boy's sweater and pants.

But I'm B negative, I tell the doctor. I dig out my wallet, with the Red Cross card I always carry and show him the proof.

No, he says. It's risky. There's no definitive way to measure the flow, to make sure I'm not giving too much, or that I'm not giving it too fast.

We have no choice, I say. Do we? I point at the child in the street.

And thus the table is cleared . . . the empty bowls of stew are knocked off with the broad sweep of someone's arm. They fall to the pavement in a series of clatters, spilling out the last vestiges of carrots and potatoes as the table is moved to the edge of the sidewalk. The doctor has run to his car and come back with a bag. Steffi kneels on the pavement and untangles the line of tubes, then unsheathes the needles, her hands moving swiftly and efficiently. I bare my arm. The rub of alcohol, the making of a fist.

The stick is a hard one. Despite everything, despite the fact that we are all numb with shock, the jab of the needle is so cruel that I make a sound. Release my fist without having to be told to. Like most people with an unusual type, I have given blood many times. I know the drill.

Valerie is clutching my other hand. "Lie back," she says, and I realize I must look terrible, as if I am about to faint. So I let her prop me on the café table and turn my head to see that the doctor is working quickly, too fast for finesse. Blood is flowing from my arm through a tube stretched from the table to the street, where it enters the arm of the boy. And it is somewhere in this process, something about the man's bag or maybe what he pulls from it, that Steffi realizes she has been playing nursemaid to a county vet. In an instant she takes over the situation, standing up and barking out orders, dispatching the small crowd this way and that on various tasks.

How long do I lie like this, with blood moving from me to the child? I don't know. In some ways it seems like merely seconds, in other ways, hours. In the distance I can hear the approach of the ambulance, which has that horrible *wah-wah* pulse of European danger, which seems so different from the high, steady shriek of American danger. *Lie still*, everyone keeps telling me. *Don't try to sit up or move.*

Because the link between my life and that of the boy is a fragile one. He and I are held together by a tangle of tubing and two needles that were designed to inoculate cattle. Despite my efforts to obey their orders, I lose the stew at some point in the process. Jean holds a bowl beneath my mouth while Valerie pulls back my hair and helps me turn my head. It is nightmarish. No sound has come from the boy, and I look to Jean at some point, trying to mouth the words that no one must say aloud. *Is he dead?* I ask, but she's not looking at me.

She's looking both at the child and past the child and I think of that split second just before the crash—Becca's stinging accusation that Jean's story had been a false one. A lie she had told us, just as she told it to her children and herself. I crane my head, trying to see the boy's face, but even that slight motion causes the world to shift and lurch and I know that the vet's hesitation had merit. I'm bleeding out too fast. I think I must lose consciousness myself for a minute, because when I open my eyes again, the ambulance is now parked in the street, that horrible *wah-wah* making it impossible to ask anyone anything.

Wait right there, Valerie mouths to me, as if I have a choice. As if there is anything I can do but lie flat on this café table and bleed, and I know they won't let me bleed to death, not now that the ambulance is here, with blood and medicine and more doctors and human-size needles. And I try to take comfort in that thought because it feels as if I am dying, as if once the life force begins to leave a human body, there's no way to tempt it back inside. I know that it only feels that way, that this is all a woozy illusion, for there is no way Steffi would let me actually die. She's incredibly competent, the fiercest of fighters, and I'm suddenly grateful for her bossiness, the angry way she refuses to make a single mistake. She won't let me die; none of them will let me die. I know that, but it seems as if the whole world is clustered around the boy in the street and the woman on the table has been forgotten.

Forgotten, that is, by everyone except for Valerie. She wraps a green tablecloth around me, since I am trembling. She asks one of the medics if I should have fluids and he looks up and nods. Tells her to give me a beer. Someone brings a pitcher from the bar and she lifts my head and tries to pour it in, right from the spout. But we're a mess, she and I. She's trembling nearly as hard as I am and the beer goes all over the front of my sweater, which is actually Claire's sweater, the cashmere soaked and ruined for sure now, and then I hear a noise, a wail coming from the child, and relief swirls through the group. The sort of relief that follows the cry of a baby who has just been born.

"They think he'll make it," Valerie yells in my ear. "But they want to get him stabilized before they transport him." And then one of the medics is at my side, removing the needle from my vein and helping me to sit up, just a little. He says not to try and stand, at least not for a couple of hours, and then there is some talk of taking me to the Canterbury hospital too, since no one can say with any certainty how much blood I've lost in the past twenty minutes. The shell of the old hospital is visible over the medic's shoulder and in my dizzy confusion, I think that's what he means, that he plans to carry me there to wait for death on the roots of the tree. *They can bury me out back under one of the nameless tombstones*, I think. *The other women can carry my mother's ashes on to Canterbury.*

"I'm fine," I say over and over but when I try to sit up, the earth tilts again and the smell of the blood, both my own and the boy's, is overwhelming. I look at my arm, at the bruise that is already forming, running from my shoulder to the crook of my elbow and I say again, to no one in particular, "I'm fine." But then the scene before me dissolves, the images of the green tablecloth and the ambulance and the boy breaking apart like the pieces of a scattered jigsaw puzzle, and my last thought is *Okay, maybe not so fine*.

I TOLD everyone that I wasn't there when Diana died. That I got the call late at night and rushed to the nursing home but that she was already at peace by the time I arrived. *At peace*. People like that term for death—they like comparisons to rest and sleeping, phrases like "went easily" or "slipped away."

Her hand, I add, *was still warm*.

And that's as much detail as I give them because I'm not like Jean, at least not yet. I haven't had time to add nuance to my fiction. To build in symbols, to know where to pause in the story for greatest effect. I'm sure I will be able to brushstroke all this in later, for it is what we humans do. We lie. Especially to ourselves. An event doesn't even have to be over before we begin telling ourselves stories about it. Softening the edges, eliminating unnecessary characters and minor details, trimming our own unwieldy interior responses into something tidy and acceptable.

And thus our personal myths are born. We know what should have happened, so we convince ourselves that it must have happened, just that way. Society demands official emotions for all events—joy for weddings, sadness for funerals, excitement for graduations, fury in the moment of a lover's desertion. And so if the graduate refuses to leave home, the heir is dancing on the grave, the bride goes fearfully down the aisle, or we are secretly relieved to be free of our dull lover, we edit these inappropriate emotions right out of the story. We all become Jeans, the authors of a fictional life.

How long will it be until I dream about Diana? Because I did make it there that night, in plenty of time. I heard the soft, low rattle of her last breaths. Dried beans in a box, I thought, the sound of the homemade percussion instruments we used to have back at the commune, in those years when she thought the children might form a band. Fewer beans with each rattle and then . . . no rattle at all. Her eyes were open. I stood there and watched the very moment when the light went out. The doctor said, "She's gone," and the priest said, "She'll always be with us," and I stood between them, wondering which one was right.

I thought she would have something to tell me. I thought there would be some final words and that's why when I got the call from the nursing home, I tore out of bed half-dressed and rushed across town without shoes on, running traffic lights and saying out loud, to nobody, "Just let her hold on." And she did hold on, not only until I was there but for several hours beyond that, and I think at moments she was conscious, just a little bit. Coming and going like I am now, her eyes fluttering open, then closing. I guess it was peaceful. I guess she went easily. I suppose she slipped away. That's as good a way to say the unsayable as any, and the only surprising thing is that when it was time to go, Diana died without comment. She put her life down as if it were an afterthought, as if her body were a sweater with a very slight flaw, something she no longer needed. She just tossed it on the bed, turned off the light, and left the room.

Steffi insists I shouldn't walk for the rest of the day and probably not tomorrow either. I insist the others go on without me. Valerie insists she will stay by my side and Tess insists she will find Tim and send him back with the van. There is a lot of insisting going on, for after an experience like the one we've just been through, what else can we do? We are frightened and drained. We have to insist on all sorts of things just to make us feel like we're back in control of our lives.

The ambulance, holding the boy and his mother and the veterinarian too, has departed and the pilgrims and the other diners have moved inside to help clean up the restaurant. Some of them wash dishes and put away the food in the kitchen, others go out to the street with buckets to pick up the shattered dishes and wash away the blood. People from the village, including the boy's grandmother, come dashing in one by one, as they hear the news. They are directed on toward Canterbury hospital.

Through it all I sit and stare. They have positioned me at a table in the corner and Steffi has put her phone in my hand.

"Here," she says. "Relax and check in with everyone at home. Or play Candy Crush or Angry Birds if you want to. Seriously, Che. Distract yourself. I have unlimited minutes, remember?"

Wisps of bubbles are clinging to her hand as she hands me the phone. She has gone from doctor to dishwasher. It's lovely, I think, all of these strangers pitching in to set this woman's restaurant right. We can't help what happened, but at least she won't come home to find her kitchen burned up and her son's blood on the cobblestones. I look down at the phone in my hand. Tap it and let it take me straight to the news of the hour, back to the big, bright world I've done such a good job of avoiding for the last five days. I tap the screen again and again, mindlessly watching the images pop up in my palm.

The Internet is a religion of its own, is it not, and such a perfect prototype of the universe—broad, complex, self-contradictory. Are you looking for recipes, earthquakes, or maybe the score of a hockey game in Saskatchewan? Horrible cruelties, noble sacrifices, political corruption, random acts of kindness? We have them. We have them all. You want porn? Well, lucky you, for as it turns out, the world is full of porn. But it also has babies laughing and puppies trying to sing, more than you can count. Any assertion you wish to make about life, the Internet will provide you with plenty of evidence to back up your claims. Google is the Jesus of our generation. Seek and ye shall find.

"Call him," says Valerie. She has brought me another beer, even though I spilled half of the first one and then puked up the rest. But she has taken the medic's advice they should hydrate me seriously and she sets the stein in front of me with a clatter.

"Call who?"

"Whatever man you've been avoiding all week," she says. "You've been running from someone, haven't you? Ever since London?"

"I wouldn't say running. More like walking. I've been walking away from someone. Ever since London."

She shrugs, willing to let the semantics slide. "And call your own phone," she says. "Maybe it's turned up by now."

I start to argue with her. Tell her that back at the George I phoned my number with the bartender's phone and that it only went to voice mail, but it seems that the fight has gone out of me along with half my blood and besides, I'm a little curious as to whether my voice mail is even still operative. I nod in resignation and call my phone, having to struggle more to remember the number than it seems like I should. And then I hear my own voice, and I say out loud to myself, "If you're the person who has found my phone, please return it to the George Inn in Southwark in London. I will check back for it there on Sunday."

Which is kind of a stab in the dark, but perhaps there is some goodwill left somewhere in the universe. Today has made that idea seem more likely, this odd little tribe of people swarming all over this restaurant, scrubbing it down from top to bottom and probably making it cleaner than it's been in years. Because we all have to do something while we wait to hear about the boy.

Valerie has gone back into the kitchen. And now that she isn't watching me, I feel free to do the thing she advised. I call Ned.

I press my head back against the blue stucco wall of the café while I listen to the numbers beep and drone their way across the sky. Across the ocean, and that great gasp of space that has always separated me from Ned. We were so easy with each other. Too easy, and here is the story I should have told the women. The story of how I mistook convenience for love. I would tell them that despite all the men, despite that shocking number, I've never been swept off my feet. I would tell them that those men were nothing more than bottles of wine that I sampled and rejected. That I opened each one expecting to be disappointed, looking for the subtle flaws, finding them, and then moving on to the next, my palate becoming ever more sophisticated and love becoming ever more elusive.

And then I met Ned. The universe served him up to me, put him right on the treadmill beside mine. Within minutes of our first gasped hello I could see he was everything I'd been looking for. Smart and handsome and funny and well-employed. Taller than my imaginary first husband, with the additional bonus of being existent in the flesh. I took him to meet Diana on our third date. When she hugged me goodbye after that visit, she whispered in my ear, "Perfection." I told myself it didn't matter, that I had long ago outgrown the need for her approval, but of course it mattered. Perfection. That single word. It was a benediction, a sign I had arrived somewhere, that I could stop running at last.

Ned seemed as relieved as I was. He was intoxicatingly quick to commit, using the word "girlfriend" almost at once, introducing me to his friends with the words "Isn't she everything I said she would be?" It seemed like magic at the time—that I not only found something for which I'd long been searching, but that I had also, in just that moment, found myself. And then of course there were those damn sunflowers. I keep seeing them. Sunflowers in a white vase sitting on a plain wooden table at a beach cottage. They stood proof that for four years the universe was benevolent and safe and of course it is hard to let that go. We will divide up the contents of the cottage and I will take that vase. But I'll never put anything in it again. It will stand empty until the end of time.

This is exactly what I'm thinking when I hear Ned's breathless hello.

"It's me," I say. "Che."

"My God," he says. "You're alive."

Barely, I think, but aloud I say, "I'm in England."

"England? Why the hell are you there?"

"I'm walking to Canterbury to scatter Diana's ashes."

It takes him a second to process this, almost as if he doesn't believe I'm telling the truth. And when he speaks, his voice is cautious.

"You didn't bury the urn? Well, I mean, obviously not."

"Her last request was to be taken to the Cathedral. Her note came with the ashes." I can't seem to resist getting a tiny dig in. "The same day as your letter."

He gives me a big transatlantic sigh. "I shouldn't have written that letter. Not when I did. My timing sucked."

"There's never a good time to dump someone."

"But considering that your mother . . . I made my move too soon, I see that now . . ."

I catch a glimpse of my face in the mirror behind the bar as he talks. I am pale, horribly pale, which makes my eyes seem bluer than ever, and there is a new thinness in me too, my skin pulled taut over the edges of my jaw. I have never looked so much like Diana, I think, or at least not so much like she was at the very end. When she was dissolving, losing form, already halfway down the road to the great Somewhere Else.

"I should be there in England with you," Ned is rambling on, his voice cracking and popping with this uncertain connection. "I can still come. I can come now. Did you say you're in Canterbury?"

"Not quite. We stopped for lunch in a bar and after this . . . there should be one more day of walking left."

"You shouldn't be walking alone."

"I'm not alone. I'm with a group of women. One of those touring companies. They call it Broads Abroad. Pretty funny, huh?"

"No. There's nothing funny about any of this. I've been worried sick and I've been beating myself up . . . sending that letter like an idiot when your mother had only been dead a few . . . I tell you what. I'll get a flight and meet you there. Does Canterbury have an airport, or do I need to come in through London? Never mind. I'll figure it out. I want to be in your life, Che. I want you to know you can still count on me. That we will always be friends and nothing can take that away from us. You understand what I'm saying, don't you?"

What I understand is that you like me better now that I'm pitiful, I think. My mother is dead and my voice sounds weak and if you knew that I had just given blood, way too much blood, if you knew I had fainted in the effort . . . well then I would be even closer to the girl you always wanted me to be.

"I was too strong," I say out loud. "Was that it?"

"What are you talking about? Of course you weren't too strong."

"But I never really fell, did I? Not in love or anywhere else. I never let myself be swept—" and here I gesture toward the sight of Becca lugging a rug to the open door. Jean is following her with a broom, so they are evidently intending to beat it, but of course Ned can't see any of this. He's back in America sitting behind his big heavy lawyer's desk, frowning into his phone. "We fell in love with the perfection and tried to make it enough," I begin again, "but love isn't supposed to be easy. I see that now. We're supposed to fall in love with the mess."

"I don't know what we were supposed to love. I only know that you don't sound good. You sound like you're lying down.

Where did you say you were? Just outside of Canterbury? What's the name of the town?"

"It doesn't have a name."

"Come on. Everywhere has a name."

"I don't think so. I heard them tell the ambulance driver—"

"Ambulance driver? What the hell's going on, Che?" His voice is high now, strident with fear, and I see Jean and Becca dragging the rug back in. They are smiling, both of them covered in dust.

"The ambulance wasn't for me," I say. "And I don't need you to come. This town doesn't have a name so you probably couldn't find it if you tried and I don't think Canterbury has an airport and besides . . . I'm moving on. Or at least I will be, as soon as they let me walk. I was really just calling to tell you I'm fine. I have to go, in fact. There aren't a lot of bars here."

"I thought you said you were in a bar."

"I mean not a lot of bars on my phone."

"But this isn't even your number, is it? I started not to pick up but I've been so worried. When you just disappeared like that, my mind went wild. I even thought that maybe you had—"

"No. Not even close."

I click the phone off and look down at it there in my hand. I sort of just hung up on him, didn't I? And it was surprisingly easy to do. Of course over the long run it won't really be quite so simple to rid myself of Ned and his legacy. It's like Silvia says—the world makes it easier for men to move on than for women and I know what's ahead of me. Months of therapy, years of first dates, decades of self-recrimination, an empty white vase.

But it still felt damn good to be the one who broke the connection. To press the long red bar that says END.

THE NEWS comes back from Canterbury along with the veterinarian. The boy has a broken femur, several broken ribs. A perforated intestine, that's the worst of it, and he needed additional units of blood once they got him into triage. "But we did the right thing transfusing him," the vet adds, his eyes falling on me. "I'll admit I wasn't sure at the time."

With this resolution, the manic energy in the group deflates. Tim has come back with the van and for a minute everyone debates climbing into it and simply riding to the next destination, but then Silvia says no, that we should finish the route of the day. Well, not me, of course. I'm still woozy and Valerie is still determined to be the one to escort me on to the inn and put me to bed. She and I climb into the seat right behind Tim and wave goodbye to the others—the women who are ready to set back out and the villagers who are now our foxhole friends. And the vet who says to me, through the window, "Sorry I was so rough on the arm, love. Lots more ice when you get there, right?"

And then we are gone, enveloped in the van's soft roar. When I finally get into bed tonight I know I'll sleep for hours, maybe days.

"I know the truth," says Valerie. "You planned all this just to get out of telling your story."

"You got me," I say. I hadn't thought of it yet, but I don't have to tell my story now. I've earned a free pass to Canterbury with the spilling of my blood.

"But if memory serves," I say to Valerie, "you didn't tell your story either. You told a story, but you didn't tell your own story and thus you're in the same boat that I am."

"True," she says. "I'm a coward."

"So tell it to me now," I say. "Not something about King Arthur and Sir Gawain, but your own rock-bottom truth, something so dark and disgusting you dare not confess it, even in the company of sisters."

She cracks the window to let in a little air. It blows into both of our faces, making us blink, keeping us from sweltering amid the roaring heat vents supplied by the well-meaning Tim. She looks out for a moment, taking in the green fields, the stone walls. The sheep and meadows, this sweet and drowsy world.

"My story is a secret," she says.

"That's all right," I say. "It's all right to have a secret."

"You won't tell the others?" she asks.

"I won't tell anybody."

"Because I'm a bit of a buzzkill."

I thought that was my job, to be a bit of a buzzkill, but I shake my head to reassure her again that I won't give her up to the rest of the women.

"I won't tell," I say.

"Okay," she says. She rolls the window open a little more. "I'm dying."

SIXTEEN

The next morning Valerie and I do not walk into Canterbury with the others. They take the longer, more circular route that Tess promised yesterday, the one that enters the city from the same angle as Chaucer's pilgrims. Perhaps they will see more than us, perhaps less.

The fiction is that I'm still weak from my bloodletting and, like most fiction, there's some truth in it. The other women accept this explanation readily, just as they accept Valerie's offer to stay behind and escort me into the gates of the city. I am the one who is officially ill, but now that I've studied her more closely, I can see just how much this walk has cost Valerie, day by day. She had a round of chemo just before leaving the States, she says, an especially intense protocol that her doctors believe might buy her a "bonus round," and she'd been encouraged by the fact she was able to keep up with the rest of us. Not only have we not had to make special concessions, but no one has really even realized that she's sick. For her this has been a true pilgrimage, much like the one Diana envisioned. A last-ditch stab at a medical miracle, which, if denied, she is prepared to turn into an appeal for forgiveness. The chance to make peace with herself before she enters the final stage of her illness, now that the cancer has moved from her breast into her bones, progressed from something that a woman can live without into something she can't. And so Tim is pressed into service once again, and even though we will not take the full lap on this final day, Valerie and I shall enter Canterbury by foot, and that's all that really matters.

The whole thing makes Tess nervous. She doesn't like it when the group splits off and she gives me and Valerie precise instructions on how to get to the Cathedral. We listen patiently and then Valerie says, "But there are signs, aren't there?" and Tess laughs and says, "Oh, of course. Signs are everywhere." And I say, "And you can see it, can't you?" and she laughs and says, "Of course. It's the only large thing in a rather small town."

The van drops us off right at the gate of the city and once again we wave madly as Tim seesaws in the street, turning back to take the others to the beginning of their own trailhead. As they fade from sight, Valerie says, "Do you feel like we're missing something?" and I say, "Not at all."

Compared to the villages we've walked through in the last few days, Canterbury is metropolitan. It's home to four colleges and thus young people are everywhere, zooming past us on bikes and skateboards, playing music and laughing. It's a beautiful place, the perfect size, halved by a river so gentle that it's almost a stream. Full of bookstores and tiny, trendy cafés. The smell of olive oil and garlic wafting from one of them nearly stops me in my tracks.

"Don't get your hopes completely up," I say, "but I think the

restaurants of Canterbury may offer more than cod and potatoes."

"You're limping," Valerie says. "Is it where you hurt your
heel?"

I shake my head. "These boots have never quite fit."

"What size is your foot?"

"Eight. The most average in the world."

"I'm an eight too. Want to switch shoes and see if that
helps?"

"Are you kidding? I'm not going to give you bad boots on top
of everything else."

She shrugs. "They might not be bad boots on me. Sometimes a shoe that rubs one woman raw fits another just fine."

We stop at a bench and I unlace my boots, then hand
them to Valerie one at a time. Hers are softer, more broken in,
the footwear of a woman who had the good sense to prepare
herself for a sixty-mile walk, who didn't just flee in the moment because she was afraid to face her own life. I pull on one
and sigh before I can help myself. They feel like bedroom slippers.

"Did she say anything?" Valerie asks.

"Who?"

"Your mother. In the last moments. Was she one of those
people who talked about white lights and long halls? Grandparents waiting for her, that kind of thing?"

I consider lying. Offering up some sort of false comfort, but
then I've never been much of a liar and this doesn't seem like
the right time to start. "You said your mother was a narcissist?" I
finally say. "Give me an example."

"She stabbed herself on my sister's wedding day."

I burst out laughing. I can't help myself. "How did she manage to do that?"

"No one's exactly sure. She went in to talk to the caterer and the next thing we know, the wedding has to be postponed while the ambulance comes."

"That's good. I'd give that at least a seven."

"Just a seven?" She leans back on the bench and begins lacing the second boot. "Top it."

"There was a time when some Russians came to our commune to talk about . . . you know, communism. The real kind, not the fake Pennsylvania kind. And just before they were due to arrive, Diana locked herself in her bedroom over the weekend and emerged fluent in Russian so she could greet them. Well, not fluent, I guess. But she managed to learn enough to seduce the man and his wife into a three-way."

"You're kidding. You knew that at the time?"

"Not really. I knew something was going on, but I was only about twelve or so and I didn't put it all together until much later. So she was a different sort of narcissist than your mother, more 'look at me' than 'poor me.'"

Valerie double knots her boot strings. "I'd give that a seven too."

"Where did she stab herself?"

"The kitchen at the country club."

"No, I mean where on her body?"

"Right in the center of the chest."

"Damn. Near the heart is risky. Maybe I'll adjust my rating up to an eight."

"You should. It was one of Susan's better moves." She sighs. "Sometimes I call my mother 'Susan.'"

"It's okay. Sometimes I call my mother 'Diana.'"

"Do you think it helps? Gives you the right kind of distance? Like Silvia telling a story in the third person?"

"I'm not sure. Where is Susan now?"

"In rehab. She'd been clean for years, but she relapsed when her daughter was diagnosed with cancer."

I stand up. The boots feel great but I can't tell Valerie that. This isn't some Civil War battlefield. I can't pull the boots off a dying woman. She stands up in mine too and takes a few steps.

"They feel fine," she says.

"You're lying. Besides, it's hard to tell how shoes feel all at once."

"How are those on you?"

"Heaven."

"Then let's go on for a few minutes like this. We can always switch back if either of us starts hurting. Why did you ask me to tell you about one of my mother's stunts?"

"Oh. Oh yeah. You'd asked me what happened the night Diana died. But that's the weird part. Here was a woman who had approached life flamboyantly, who had . . . well, you know how they say you should live every day as if it might be your last? Diana, for all her faults, really did that. She made these big dramatic statements, and she undertook these big fuck-the-world challenges, just as if every day she was lying on her deathbed. Right up to the moment when she really was lying on her deathbed. And then, at the one point when all her drama would have finally been justified, on the one day she was most entitled to do something drastic . . . she didn't. Her death was almost casual."

"She didn't say anything?"

"For once, no."

We have come to an intersection, with a small park and a visitors' welcome kiosk on the other side. I glance right and step into the street and Valerie has to grab my arm and pull me back. She has enough sense to glance to the left, to see the cars rumbling toward us. I made exactly the same bonehead move on my one morning in London, stepping off a curb and nearly getting hit by a cab coming from a direction I didn't expect. I visit Europe often, but not England. They don't have much wine here.

"I didn't used to be afraid of the dark," Valerie says, as if we had been discussing fear, which I guess in a way we were. "Not until I was diagnosed. Or actually rediagnosed. It was gone and then it came back . . . Now I sleep with a night-light. I have them all over the house at home and I bought one here, in a hardware store in London, before I met the other women in the George. So it would use the right current, you know, so it wouldn't blow up like an American hair dryer. The dark is the only thing I've ever really feared. Look. There's a city map beside the visitor kiosk. Tess gave me the address of our hotel for the night. Do you want to go there first and drop our bags?"

"First?"

"We're going on to the Cathedral, aren't we?"

"Just the two of us?" I say, as we drift toward the map.

"We don't have to wait all day for the others. Tess called ahead. She's arranged for us to be greeted at noon by a priest named Matthew. You're okay with that, aren't you? Being blessed by a man instead of a woman?"

I nod. It doesn't matter a flip to me who or what blesses us, just so long as we're blessed. Valerie runs her fingertip along the laminated map of the city, starting with the star that reads YOU ARE HERE and tracing it to the Cathedral, which sits in the dead center of Canterbury, like a castle in a board game.

"Wow," she says. "The hotel really does look like it's right on the grounds of the Cathedral. Tess said it was as close as you could get, but I thought . . . Look. We'll be sleeping right here."

I nod again. I'm a little thrown. I had thought we would spend the afternoon eating at some city restaurant that cooked its food in olive oil and garlic, shopping for souvenirs, maybe checking into the hotel for a shower and a nap. I didn't expect to enter the Cathedral quite yet. Despite everything, it feels too soon. Premature. Like I'm not quite ready to let go of the last of Diana after all.

"What's wrong?" Valerie says. "Are the boots hurting?" I shake my head and she frowns. "Are you dizzy again?"

"No," I say, "but it wouldn't hurt us to eat. Somewhere with olive oil and peppers and spice and things like that. And then, yeah, I'll be ready for the Cathedral."

"Are you nervous?"

"Why should I be nervous?"

Valerie turns away from the map. "Because this is what we've come for. All this time, all this way, all the weird shit that's happened. This is what it's been leading up to, isn't it? Our appointment with God."

CANTERBURY CATHEDRAL is enormous. That much is obvious. That much is to be expected. It's the first thing a visitor notices and I'd imagine it's the last thing he forgets. Wall after wall of Gothic ornamentation, a crown of spires, a dozen places to enter or exit. But there is very little yard around it, not much of an approach. Once you are through the gates and on the grounds, it is right there upon you, looking down.

Despite the fact that we stopped on a side street for gyros and despite the fact that we dropped our bags off at the surprisingly large and modern lodge, Valerie and I are still early. We give our names to one of the elderly ladies working the group tour desk and she says she will call Matthew. We tell her not to worry, that we're the ones who are off schedule, a remark that seems to confuse her.

"But you have walked, have you not, from London?" she asks. Apparently most tourists come in by bus or train and now, in this modern age, those rare pilgrims who arrive on foot enjoy an elevated status.

The woman consults her computer screen again. "And one of you is ill?"

Evidently she's referring to me. Valerie steps away from the window, which looks just like the will-call booth at a theater, and I step up. "I'm fine now," I say through the little hole in the glass, but Tess must have been very thorough when she called this morning with her instructions, for the woman is still staring at the computer screen, her lips moving slightly as she reads.

"Lovely thing you did, my dear," she says, her small, red-rimmed eyes flicking up to me with respect. "Matthew will be here in a jiffy."

A jiffy? It's hard to imagine a priest doing anything in a jiffy, and Valerie and I both revert back into our daughter-of-an-interesting-mother routine, falling all over ourselves to assure this woman that we will wait, that we expect no special treatment, that the schedule of this priest should not be shuffled around to accommodate our unexpected early arrival. But this lady's having none of it. She waves her hand to shush us and picks up a phone. The big retro kind, black and heavy. She talks to someone and when she puts it down she says, "Ten minutes."

"Do you want your boots back?" Valerie says as we wait. We've sprawled on the grass, our heads resting on our backpacks. There's no sense of religious formality here on the lip of lawn that circles the Cathedral, but rather the air of a picnic, with schoolkids and tourists lounging about.

"They suck, don't they?"

"No," she says. "They haven't bothered me at all and I'll take them back if you like when the tour is over. I just thought that if the priest is going to wipe the dust from our boots as part of the ceremony, it might be nice if, you know, if it's our own dust that he's wiping off our own boots."

"When was the last time you were in a church?"

"My niece got baptized. You?"

"Diana's memorial."

And with that the shadow of Matthew falls across us. We

both look up, squinting, but the sun behind him makes it impossible to see his face. All I can make out is the bright outline of a large man wearing a dress.

"It will be my honor to lead you through the Cathedral," he says. "Intones" might be a better verb, for he has the voice of a movie priest—low and calm and certain—and God help me, that's all it takes. I'm already tearing up, even as he extends two hands down to help pull us from the grass. He looks from me to Valerie, then back again. "Which one of you is ill?"

"We both are," Valerie says. "In different ways, of course."

He nods. "Of course."

We follow him through an unassuming side door leading into a chapel, which is a good thing. I'm not sure I could handle seeing the entire expanse of the Cathedral at once. Better to sidle up on it, to come to the center incrementally, and Matthew says we will start our tour in the chapel where Becket was killed. It's one small cell within the great body of Canterbury, an edifice that probably has a dozen such crannies. But this one, where the saint met his doom, is the most famous.

I know the story by heart and I suspect Valerie does too, but Matthew tells it to us anyway, guiding us from spot to spot within the chapel while he talks. Thomas Becket started his life not as a priest, but as the friend of Henry II, a notorious womanizer and rake. By all accounts, Becket matched the king thrust for thrust in their debaucheries and together the young men enjoyed all the perks of fame and wealth.

But as Henry progressed through his reign, he became frustrated by the fact that the Catholic church held as much power in England as did the monarchy. This was long before Henry VIII broke from the Catholic church and established the Church of England, before church and state were effectively merged, Matthew says. We have a bit of the background, do we not? He says this with uncertainty, for he knows we are Americans—which, after all, rhymes with "barbarians"—but both Valerie and I hasten to assure him we're up on our English history, or at least on those fascinating Henrys. We've read Philippa Gregory; we've seen every episode of *The Tudors*.

Matthew believes us and cranks his story into a higher gear. The point is that when Henry took the throne in 1154, he often felt that his power was eclipsed by that of the church, specifically the archbishop of Canterbury, who was practically a royal in his own realm. When the old archbishop finally died, Henry named his friend Thomas Becket to the post, thinking this was his chance to gain control over the church. "But things," Matthew says gravely, "did not turn out as the king planned."

Here in the darkened chapel I can see him better, and Matthew is quite a vision. He is wearing a white cassock, tied with a rope belt. He has a broad, honest face and he is younger than I would have guessed, probably no more than thirty, with deepset blue eyes and straw-colored hair that is quite a bit longer than current fashion. His wife, he has already informed us, also works for the church, as do about three hundred other people. Her specialty is glass restoration and there is plenty here to keep her busy. The Cathedral is one of the major employers of the town, along with the universities. In other words, little in Canterbury has changed since the 1100s. Tourism is still the big business.

Valerie and I sit down on a pew and Matthew paces before

us. Not nervously, but more in the manner of an actor or a professor. No, he says, nothing ever turns out quite like one expects, does it, not even if you're the King of England. Because almost immediately after being named as archbishop, Thomas Becket pulled a Diana de Milan. He got religion. True religion, the most improbable and inconvenient kind. To the king's great dismay, Becket took his role as archbishop seriously and in fact advocated for the church so enthusiastically that the two former friends were soon at odds. They may have once been lads together, drinking and carousing, riding shoulder-to-shoulder through the land that Henry ruled, but then Thomas repented. Changed, and no one likes it when their friends change. No one likes it when his friend grows up without him, precedes him down that thorny path to adulthood. The man who Henry had assumed would be an unquestioning patsy had turned into a powerful adversary and one day, in a fit of exasperation, the king muttered, "Who will rid me of this troublesome priest?"

Here's the thing: he didn't mean it. Despite their recent differences, Thomas Becket was still the king's best friend and on some deep interior level, Henry even admired him. It was a momentary outburst.

But the irony and the tragedy is that the slightest outburst from a king can have immediate consequences. A couple of minor-league lords, eager to ingratiate themselves with their monarch, rode to Canterbury vowing to put the archbishop to death.

Becket knew they were coming. A man who rules a great church has spies of his own and besides, even if it hadn't been this particular band of fools, others very much like them were certain to eventually attack. He had spoken out against the throne too many times and he must have known his day of reckoning would eventually arrive, even if he didn't know precisely how or when fate would find him. And then one night, as Becket was at vespers, came a pounding at the door.

Matthew says the line just like that, "came a pounding," a rather awkward and old-fashioned phrase he must have read somewhere, and then he nods solemnly toward the door where we entered. "We do a reenactment," he says, "each year on the anniversary of the archbishop's murder. Our little theatrical ends with that same pounding on the door and guests tell us that they find the moment quite dramatic."

But not, I suppose, as dramatic as it would be if the church didn't cut the scene there, but rather attempted to replicate the bloodbath that had followed the knock. For the monks of Canterbury tried to persuade Becket to bar the door and hide, but he said no, that the doors to a church must never be barred. And thus he stood a willing victim. The intruders rushed him as a group, slicing off the top of his head with their swords, and he died on the spot.

"King Henry was devastated," Matthew tells us. "So the historians say, and I believe them. He had never intended for his comment, said in a moment of impatience, to be taken as a royal edict, and now his boyhood friend was dead." Matthew pauses. He is like Tess, professionally doomed to tell the same stories day after day but, also like her, he has made an art of it, weaving in little beats and asides to the audience. In this case, his audience is only Valerie and I, but we are still getting the full-throttle performance.

"Can you imagine the horror of having that sort of power?"

Matthew is saying. "The sort of power where a comment made against a friend could result in his actual murder? How many people might we have spoken dead with our words throughout the years? The king's guilt was enormous and the canonization of Thomas Becket was the fastest in all of church history, the process beginning almost as he still lay bleeding in front of this altar."

He now directs our attention toward the shrine of Becket, but after all this buildup, the altar itself is a rather humble affair, probably just like dozens more within the Cathedral. "The monks were busily wiping up the gore even as Becket lay dying," Matthew says, "already certain they could sell any scrap of cloth that was dotted with the archbishop's blood."

"That's sort of like what they did with Elvis Presley," Valerie says. "His promoters would take the sheets that he slept on during his tours and cut them into little squares and sell them to his fans."

Great. I like her better now, know her better now, but still . . . She has a knack for saying the most inappropriate and god-awful things in the world, always in that same cheerful tone of voice. But Matthew seems to be taking her seriously, as if Valerie were a fellow theologian, come from America on foot to discuss the mysteries of sainthood.

"Just so," Matthew says. "Precisely. Becket was the medieval equivalent of your own Mr. Presley. Everything that touched him was rumored to have holy power."

"My mother had a square of Elvis's sheet, but she always told me she got it the honest way," Valerie says.

"The honest way?" asks Matthew.

"She claimed she slept with him. Do the Brits say it like that? You know what I mean. Had carnal knowledge."

"Ah," said Matthew. "That would indeed seem to earn her a scrap of his sheet."

"I don't know how it's possible," I say to Valerie, "that you and I would turn out to have the same mother. Because that sounds exactly like something Diana would say."

"I've always thought perhaps all American women of a certain age once slept with Elvis," Matthew says. "And that perhaps all their daughters were his illegitimate love children, scattered across the land. It's the only way I've ever been able to make sense of your country."

"People go to Graceland," Valerie says, "to be healed, so I guess it's the American version of Canterbury. They say it has the same magic."

I'm not sure she should have called it "magic." I understand the point she's trying to make, but I wince again. Because "magic" is a dismissive word, implying that Canterbury is more scam than salvation, more tourist trap than house of worship.

But Matthew seems unperturbed. He brushes back his pale bangs and looks up at the shrine with a small smile. I guess there's nothing we could say about Canterbury that he hasn't thought of first.

"I'm sorry," Valerie says softly, as if she realizes she's been disrespectful, but Matthew shakes his head.

"No, you're quite right. It's just as you say, that Becket became a celebrity. History's first rock star. The blood of the martyr went up for sale and the claims of miraculous healing began almost at once. There was a stampede of the lost and broken, all heading to this one particular shrine, just as Chaucer tells us in his *Canterbury Tales*."

"'The holy blissful martyr for to seek,'" Valerie says, maybe showing off to regain any ground she's lost. "'So he would helpen them when they were weak.' Or I think the prologue goes something like that."

"Quite good, very good," Matthew says. "For there is weakness in everyone, is there not? Have not all of us been drawn here to the shrine of the martyr because, consciously or unconsciously, we seek some sort of help?"

It's just the opening I was waiting for. I get up and wander over to the altar, presumably to study the inscriptions, but actually to give the two of them a moment alone. Because this would be the perfect time and place for Valerie to tell Matthew why she has come to Canterbury. I don't know if she will, or what she might say, but they need a moment of privacy.

Besides, it's also a good opportunity to drop a pinch of Diana. There's not that much of her left, so I'm going to have to be judicious and I don't want Matthew to see what I'm doing. There's undoubtedly some sort of ordinance against it. I mean, let's face it, a rather high percentage of people in the world eventually die and you can't have all their relatives dragging them to Canterbury and throwing their ashes around the Cathedral. The place is big, but not that big, and while Matthew seems like the kind of priest who might be sympathetic to my mission, I don't want to put him on the spot.

I fish out a few grains, then let them drop at the base of the shrine.

A cat comes up. He rubs against my legs and looks at me

expectantly, as if experience has taught him that sometimes pilgrims carry kitty treats. He notes the crumpled fish-and-chips bag in my hand with special interest, but just then I see Matthew and Valerie walking toward me. It's only been a minute or two and it's hard to determine what she's told him, if anything, but his face is changed. Thoughtful, almost somber.

"Off with you," Matthew says gently. "Move along." It takes me a minute to realize that he's talking to the cat. "There are several of these furry little creatures living within the Cathedral," he adds, this time to me and Valerie. "One of them likes to sleep curled up on the tomb of the Black Prince just beside the main altar. The ladies who run the restoration council find it a bit scandalous, but—"

"I like them," I say, thinking of the purple dragon back in that small church where we stopped two days ago. The chapel around us is filling. A large tour group has come in and another waits at the door behind them. The shrine of Becket is one of the most popular spots within the church, and Matthew notices them too and begins herding Valerie and me toward one of the halls.

"This way next," he says. "Toward the rear a bit."

Matthew steps between us as we walk along the side flanks of the Cathedral, glancing left and right at the various nooks as we pass. Some are dark and free of ornamentation, while others practically assault you with their displays of glitter and gold. The center section, where Matthew tells us that seven daily services are held, is raised and bright and full of the curious, as well as, I suppose, dead princes and sleeping cats. It is the place for great proclamations, the most public face of the Cathedral. But these side sections of the church, with their mazes of small rooms and narrow hallways, seem meant for a different purpose.

We stop seemingly at random in front of a cluster of pews. I guess this is the rear of the building. I'm turned around.

"We can do the blessing here, if you like," Matthew says. "It's private. It has access to water in case you . . . I should have thought to ask before we began. Do either of you call yourself Christian?"

"I do," I say. I say it so fast that I think I startle all three of us. I certainly startle myself. Where the hell did that come from? Have I been dazzled by the setting, the splendor, the gentle drone of an organ in some distant hall, the story of Becket's sacrifice, or by the mere fact that Matthew is kind? For he is kind, and this has not been my experience with most holy men, not at all. The cat has followed us. I don't realize it until I sit down and he jumps on my lap.

"Don't feel you have to say that to please me," Matthew says. He makes a halfhearted swatting gesture at the cat, who looks back at him with contempt before settling into the valley of my legs. "Canterbury offers a variety of blessings, suitable for all sorts of travelers. I was only asking if you wanted communion in addition to the prayer and foot-wiping."

"We want the whole package," Valerie says, sitting down beside me. "I call myself a Christian too."

Matthew disappears. Valerie and I wait with the cat.

"Oh God," she mutters under her breath. "Are we going to hell? We've just lied to a priest."

"And a nice one," I whisper back. "I think that's worse. But I don't believe in hell. I'm not sure I believe in any of this."

"Then why are you whispering?"

"I don't know. Just in case."

"It's easy for you to blow it all off," she says. "You haven't gotten a look at your own expiration date."

"Did you tell him?"

She nods. "You should tell him too."

"Tell him what?"

"About your mother."

"I don't think I'm supposed to be throwing her around in the church."

"Why not? They let cats in. You should talk to him. Seriously. He's different. He looks right at you when he prays."

"I know."

He's also back, coming toward us with a basin, a towel, and two bottles. He has a bottle, in fact, stuck under each armpit, even though one of them presumably contains holy water and the other one communion wine. So far our Canterbury blessing has not been what I expected.

Matthew places the accoutrements of his craft on the stone floor before us. "Why do people pilgrimage?" he asks.

I assume the question is rhetorical, the start of some prepared speech or prayer. But Valerie sees what I don't, that he's really asking us. As he begins to pour water in the basin, she gives him the same explanation that Tess gave us back in the George Inn.

"They come seeking forgiveness and healing," she says.

"And which do you seek?" he asks.

"Both, I guess," she says. "Aren't they the same thing?"

He looks up from the bowl and winks at her. But a priest

wouldn't wink at a dying woman, would he? Of course not. I've been teetering on the verge of a full-blown hallucination all week, what with the swarming bees and kisses in the smoking garden and children being struck by cars in the middle of an empty street, and if I didn't know better I would swear I had somehow gotten myself drunk again. But I guess Matthew might wink at Valerie, that it's possible they've shared something during their brief private talk that I'm yet incapable of understanding. Which at this point could be just about anything, because I'm feeling very stupid and I've even started crying again. And I don't know if I'm crying because my mother is dead or crying because Valerie's cancer has come back, or crying because someday I will be dead too. Death feels realer than life in this place and despite the fact that Matthew has poured water into the basin, he is now picking up the other bottle, the one with wine. So apparently we are to have communion before our blessing, sharing before absolution. He pulls a plug from the top of the earthenware bottle and a plastic cup from where it has been wedged onto the bottom. This is simultaneously the most humble and most exalted of ceremonies. Valerie looks over at me, and this time the wink is definitely real. What wine will this be—what vintage and what grape? Is God's sense of humor broad enough to send redemption in the form of a nice white zinfandel?

But instead it is a red wine, blood-colored and serious. Matthew's hands enfold the plastic cup, and as he moves toward me I can see he has a bump on his third finger, the type of cyst a child gets when he is first learning to write. He raises the cup to my lips and I take a deep breath to pull in the aromas, more from habit than anything else, but there is nothing before me but grapes and alcohol. It feels warm and thin on my tongue.

"This is the blood of Christ," he says softly, "spilled for you."

I struggle with it. Dip my head too far and when he tilts the glass I nearly choke. It rushes at me, not a sip but a swill, and I know that whatever I'm feeling is not because I am dazzled by the Cathedral. Not by the riches of Canterbury or even its history. What would happen if I began to laugh hysterically during this communion, here in this holy place? Probably nothing. Matthew would continue with the sacrament. He's that type. He would soldier on without judgment, no matter what his pilgrims do. The Cathedral is ancient and enormous. Everything that can happen to a human being has undoubtedly happened here at some time or another. People have laughed and cried, died and been born, choked on Jesus or accepted him without question, made love and made murder, all within these walls.

I close my eyes and pretend to pray. Hear the murmur of Matthew offering the wine to Valerie, her own smaller and more ladylike slurp. *This is it, Mom,* I think. *I've got you all the way here and if this isn't enough, then we're both of us sunk. Because, God knows, we've got no plan B.*

When I open my eyes, Matthew is back on his knees before me, which seems overwhelming too, and somehow wrong. If it's hard for a modern woman to bow, it is even harder to be bowed before. To accept the fact that this man has dropped to his knees and is taking my boot in his hand. Or rather Valerie's boot, for we never bothered to swap them back. He dips the cloth into the basin of water, then wipes the leather with a single damp corner, smoothing away the dust of the trail and a little of Diana too, I'd imagine. Even though this modern version of foot washing is not quite so intimate as the original, it's still touching, and as he moves to Valerie he continues to murmur something softly. Apparently this is the blessing, and I can't catch all of what he's saying. Something about "the circle of life," but surely that's wrong, too Elton John and Broadway, and then he says, quite clearly, "May the broken world ride on your shoulders," and I lean back in the pew and exhale.

It's a real exhalation, the kind you make only a few times in your life. I sneak my hand into the bag in my backpack, which is balanced on the pew beside me.

The cat's ears rise hopefully at the reappearance of the white fish-and-chips bag. He is probably thinking *Yum*. I try not to rustle the paper. Valerie and Matthew need their moment, and he has taken her hands in his now. She is bent forward and they hover, their foreheads nearly touching, completely absorbed. I ease the baggie from the bag, slip my fingers inside of it, and then slowly expand them, pushing the walls apart.

The bag tears. Easily. It has been held together by Band-Aids and desperation for some time now. It is more than ready to break. As my fingers continue to open, the plastic gives way, and the last of Diana's ashes run down my palm, falling to the stone floor.

My mother is gone. My mother is everywhere.

This would be the logical time to cry. The logical time to give in to the emotion I've been tamping down all morning. All week, all year, all my life. So of course I don't. Now that my great quest has been completed, the energy seems to go right out of me. I sit back against the pew. Watch Matthew and Valerie, still forehead to forehead, his lips moving and then hers. I close my eyes too.

Is this enough? Enough for Diana or even for me? Life will always be a mystery. Whatever you think you own can be taken from you in an instant and—even more confounding—all the things you once thought were lost can come rushing back. The veil that hangs between worlds has felt very thin to me lately. As easily ripped as a ziplock bag, and almost illusionary, like maybe death isn't so awful or even so far away.

I open my eyes and look around me, at the great windows in the distance, high and colorful, full of saints I can't name and I know that my body, this body I now sit in, dusty and tired, is just one more thing that I will someday lose. And when that day comes, whether it is fifty years from now or tomorrow, whether I'm sleeping in a nursing home bed or looking the wrong way as I step off a curb, I hope I will die exactly like my mother did. I hope that I toss my body aside just as she tossed hers, with no more thought than Claire throwing one of her many sweaters across a rented bed. I hope I leave this world gracefully, like a pilgrim slips from the back of his donkey at the end of a long ride, like a traveler disembarks from an airplane that has carried him across a great ocean. The way a letter slides from an envelope once it has finally been delivered.

SEVENTEEN

Y ou never got to tell your story," Tess says.

It's another thing that frets her. One more loose end. There are certain experiences she tries to provide for her guests on each guided tour and she's afraid she's failed with this one. Already she's apologized twice for the fact that Valerie and I had to walk into Canterbury unescorted and, even worse, that we were forced to receive absolution from the hands of a man.

This afternoon has had a great deal of coming and going. When the other women arrived at about three, they'd stopped by the lodge first, only to find Valerie and me bedded down in our separate rooms, both sleeping off the effects of our spiritual bender. Then they had walked over to the Cathedral and had their own ceremony with a priest named Virginia, who'd evidently been quite a hit. When Angelique had asked her, "Where do I go next?" Virginia had said, "Home," and this had set off their own collective crying jag, followed by what I gather was a couple of rather large checks written to the Canterbury Preservation League, courtesy of Claire and Jean. It is just past six now, and the women are all back in the lodge, putting ice packs on their faces and preparing for their final dinner together. When Tess stops by my room, she seems alarmed by the fact that I am still dozing.

"Seriously, don't worry about it," I tell her, sitting up and propping pillows around me. There are plenty of them here in this bed, overstuffed and heavily tasseled, covered in gold-and-burgundy brocade, the colors of royalty. "I promise on my mother's grave that I got everything out of the trip I needed."

But she's still distressed, perhaps because I've told her I won't be joining them at the final dinner, when they will crown the winner at Deeson's. She stops just short of pushing me on the matter. She says she understands that I might rather rest. I must have been quite a sight yesterday, lying on that café table giving blood. I must have looked either exceptionally noble or exceptionally pathetic, because the women have changed in the way they're treating me. They look at me with big wide eyes now, as if I might suddenly take flight.

Although I point to the chair, Tess continues to stand. The poshness of our rooms at this final lodge is a sign, I suppose, that our journey truly has come to its end. Our reward for completing the trail comes in the form of duvets, coffeepots, well-lit mirrors, and pulsating showers with unlimited hot water. And there's a whole closet for Claire, a walk-in, with thick wood hangers. All the rooms have enormous picture windows looking straight at the Cathedral, or at least some piece of it. We're positioned too close to get any perspective on the whole thing, but a lovely expanse of stone is outside my window.

"Join us just for a drink," Tess says, pausing in her pacing.

"Or an appetizer, perhaps. You can tell your story and then come back straightaway to bed."

I start to say something about how giving blood to the little boy was perhaps my version of a pilgrim's tale. Which would be total bullshit, of course. The fluke of having B negative blood is not a story. Or I could recite the first line I've been practicing in my head the last forty-eight hours. *My story begins with the death of my mother . . .* Either of those things would make Tess feel better. She's haunted with a sense of unfinished business, of eight women walking but only seven stories told. So it would be a kindness to give her something, anything, some sequence of words that would allow her to check my name off the list.

"The priest who blessed us today," I finally tell her, "was really good at his job. And while he was serving the communion—"

"Communion?" she breaks in, with genuine surprise. "That isn't part of the blessing."

Just a little bonus they throw in for the dying, I think, but out loud I say, "I don't know what the standard deal is. I only know he offered and we accepted."

Tess is frowning, trying to reconcile just one more irregularity in her mind. "I didn't know either one of you were practicing Christians."

A bell from the Cathedral strikes. A single gong, and Tess and I both look at the clock on the bedside table. 6:15.

"It's loud, isn't it?" she says. "I sometimes wonder why we stay here, so close, despite the view. There's that big boom every quarter hour and of course when midnight comes, the whole lodge is shaken awake. It sounds as if all the angels of heaven have declared war on earth at once."

"I think it's magic," I say, rolling over in bed to face the window. "Everything about it. Valerie used that word today in Becket's chapel and at first I was afraid she would offend our priest. But now that I've slept on it, I can see it's exactly the right word, and maybe all places are magical if you stop to pay attention. I mean, look at how many miracles we encountered along the path. They're all around us, even the way that hops turns into beer . . ."

But Tess is still frowning, her head tilted and her arms folded across her chest. She looks like a buried monarch. She came here expecting me to say something, but this evidently wasn't it. I try again.

"My trip wasn't incomplete," I tell her. "I had to get all the way to the end to see that the end wasn't what counted. Because the trick isn't being able to recognize the holiness of Canterbury. I mean, look at it. It's practically standing there in the window screaming, 'Wake up, woman. Get out of bed. I'm holy.' But the real trick is seeing the holiness in everything. Everything along every step of the trail, the whole broken world. You get that, don't you? You must. It's why you lead these tours."

Tess hesitates. She's more comfortable asking questions than answering them. "I'm not entirely sure why I signed on with Broads Abroad," she says. "I enjoy meeting the women, of course, and it's extra income during the weeks when university's not in session."

"Oh, come on. It can't just be that. I doubt they pay you that much money."

"You're right," she says, glancing out the window. "The salary's an insult and yet I keep signing on for just one more tour. How many times have I been here now? Twenty or thirty? Likely more. I always imagine that this is the trip that will be different. What you Americans call 'the one.' Oh, the Cathedral is architecturally marvelous, of course. No arguing with that. And the historical significance is profound . . ."

Her voice fades. So there we have it. The Tale of Tess, the shortest of them all and in some ways the most poignant. She leads tours to a destination she herself can never reach. But she shakes off this singular moment of vulnerability, like a dog shaking off rain, and asks, once again, "But you're satisfied? You found what you were hoping to find here?"

It's actually more accurate to say I lost what I was hoping to lose here, but there's no point in telling her this. It would only confuse the matter more, so I nod vigorously and smile.

"When I was in the chapel I made myself a promise. That tomorrow and going forward I'm going to take a few steps toward Canterbury, every day, no matter where in the world I happen to be."

"Well, that's quite marvelous," says Tess. "Really, very good. Do you mind if I write that last bit down, the bit about walking toward Canterbury every day? Perhaps they'd like to use it on the Broads Abroad website."

"Be my guest."

Tess makes one more halfhearted stab at trying to convince me to come to dinner with them, but when I beg off a third time, she lets it go. I tell her all I want to do is order room service, soak in a tub, and make it an early night. And it's true enough. The symmetry appeals to me. I was not with the women on the first night of the pilgrimage and I won't be with them on their last.

She pauses at the door and looks back. "And your mother?"

"All gone."

She nods. "Good. So that's one thing we've managed to finish off properly, at least."

AFTER TESS leaves, I do everything exactly as I said I would. I order a mushroom flatbread and a Diet Coke in a can, relishing the carbonation like a crack addict. Put some of the lovely ginger-scented bath salts in the tub for soaking, and afterward go straight back to bed, wearing the terry cloth hotel robe. The sun faded while I was lingering in the bathroom and the Cathedral looks especially dramatic at night. It's lit from below, with golden light pulsating upward like water from a fountain, throwing strange shadows over the facade of the building. I chew on the remnants of the flatbread crust and contemplate the fact that I will probably never dine with another view like this one, at least not from my own pillow.

But it's not yet eight. If I go to sleep now, after spending half the afternoon in bed, I will awaken at three in the morning and that's not good. Tomorrow is stacking up to be a hell of a day: the break-of-dawn goodbyes, the train to London, a dash across town to the George on the off chance someone has returned my phone, then six hours on a plane back to

America. Fetching Freddy from his kennel and beginning the long slog of making sense of my post-Ned life. It exhausts me just to think about it. If I don't get a good night's rest now, I'm ruined.

So I decide to get up and take a few laps around the Cathedral, forcing myself to stay awake at least until ten. The longer I've lain here, the more I've grown curious about what Canterbury feels like at night. The main gates are said to be closed at seven, so the only people on the grounds are worshippers straggling from evensong and those of us staying in the lodge. Even circling the perimeter of the building should be a decent walk, and when, if ever, will I be here again? Besides, this morning I went to Canterbury for Diana, to fulfill my final promise. I still haven't gone there for myself.

I only have one set of completely clean clothes left, put aside for the flight home, so I drag a somewhat smelly sweater and dusty jeans out of my suitcase and pick up Valerie's boots. Just looking at them makes me feel guilty. If she could buck up and make it to the last dinner, it seems like I should be able to. Find my way to Deeson's and join the women at least for a drink or two. Congratulate the winner. I'll do that, and then take my evening stroll of the grounds.

I walk down the wide, carpeted hall, past the lobby where a group of businessmen is checking in for a conference, through the well-tended garden, and out the front entrance, which leads me into the city. Tess said the restaurant is on Sun Street, which I noticed coming in today, and I can always ask for help if I need it. More people are out than this morning, college students walking by in packs, tourists taking pictures. A young man is handing out flyers for a boat tour of the city the next morning. I take one.

I should stay longer, I think. *I should have tacked another day onto the vacation, taken the time to relish a bit of Canterbury now that I'm finally here. Maybe I would like to take a rowboat down the Stour, that romantic little river with its unromantic name.* But I'm booked back to America on the noontime flight. At least that's what I believe my phone said, so I have little choice but to show up with my passport and half-assed explanations and hope they let me on the plane.

I have no trouble finding Deeson's, which takes up a broad expanse of a building. The night is fine and the patio is charming, with barrels of what appear to be herbs growing amid the sleek slate-top tables. No one is smoking. I find my friends on the inside, arranged much as they were at our first meal back in the George. One notable change. Becca is now beside Jean. They smile and wave when they see me enter the restaurant, all except for Tess, who wails, "Oh dear, we've already ordered."

"And I've already eaten," I tell her, pulling out the only empty chair. "I just came by for a glass of wine."

While walking over, I'd decided to buy a bottle for the table, not something merely good enough, but something great, a send-off for our last evening together. The wine list comes in a heavy leather folder, page after page of thoughtfully chosen varieties, and my extended consultation with the sommelier—a real sommelier, for we have somehow managed to return to 2015—clearly amuses the other women. I settle on a Châteauneuf-du-Pape and say, "Okay, who won?"

"Tess won't tell us," says Steffi.

"Only because I haven't decided," Tess says. "I want to hear what all of you think."

"I'd say Jean," says Angelique, carefully pouring the olive oil and then the balsamic until she has made a bit of a flower pattern on her broad white plate. She dips a crust of bread into the heart of the daisy, like a child playing with her food. Since arriving in Canterbury, Angelique has found her whole face again and painted it on. If I'd passed her in the street I'm not sure I would have recognized her.

"I'd agree," says Jean with a laugh, "if for no other reason than the fact that I told twice as many tales as anyone else. You two missed it," she adds, turning toward me and then Valerie, "but I came clean yesterday afternoon. Becca was quite right with what she said at lunch, just before the accident . . . Do you even remember what we were talking about? It all became such a mad jumble there in the street, with everything happening at once."

"I remember exactly," Valerie says, probably to the surprise of no one. I'm the snob and she's the blurter and Becca's going to sulk and Angelique has on enough makeup for ten women and Tess is going to fret the details and Claire sleeps around while Jean writes big checks and Silvia squints and Steffi's a food freak . . . and it's all okay, because that's just who we are. In fact it's more than okay, it's perfect. This whole night has an air of perfection about it. It sits here rounded and complete before us, like an unbroken egg.

"Right before the boy on the bike got hit," Valerie is saying, "Becca was saying that her father was really shot during a drug deal. When you screamed, for a minute I thought that was why."

Jean nods. "Precisely. My first tale was a complete lie. Yesterday afternoon I finally screwed up my courage enough to tell everyone what it had really been like living in an affluent suburb with three children and all the time trying to hide the fact that your husband's an addict. To give you the short version, Allen's drug use started legally, as I gather these things often do. Prescription painkillers and the like, but when he got the chance to go to Central America . . ." She shrugs. "I was afraid he took the job just to give himself better access, and that's why I was so insistent that we all had to pack up and follow him. And once we were there, I bribed our driver, Antonio, to keep an eye on him, but as it turns out Allen was bribing Antonio too, to keep the truth from me, and since Allen was paying more . . ."

It all makes sense now. Jean's frantic desire to hold together the illusion of the perfect family, Allen's late-night rides through the dark parts of a dark city, the gunshot, the splash. She has broken off her story because the appetizers have arrived. They are dainty and delicate, little towers of scallops and salads shaped like fans, and the wine is here too, hovering just over my shoulder, waiting for my nod.

So I nod, the sommelier pours, I swirl, then sniff and taste. It is deep and subtle. Exactly what I want, and what I want to give the others. Glasses are being brought around too—thin-lipped, deep-bowled ones, proper glasses for a proper wine—but I notice how many of the women have seafood appetizers and wonder if I should have gotten a white as well. No matter. Nothing is perfect. This is close enough.

Becca, in fact, is beaming, looking around the trendy restaurant with satisfaction, before raising the goblet to her lips. "Canterbury's awesome," she says to Tess. "Is it hard to get into school here?"

"There are several colleges and universities in town," Tess says, "some more demanding than others . . ."

"She got a fifteen-forty on her SATs," Jean says, pride in her voice. "And she's number two in a class of five hundred." Another surprise, but why shouldn't Becca be smart? She has hung with us extraordinarily well on this trip, considering her age, and I've been too quick to put each woman in a little box, I realize. They are all bigger than my mnemonics. They carry many tales.

"The UK has its own admissions tests," Tess says, "which are utterly different from those in the States, but I could give you some information if you're truly interested."

"Look at this," Steffi says, tilting her salad plate. "Artichokes, spinach. Red and yellow peppers. Phytonutrients. Antioxidants. Fiber. I'm in heaven."

"We should stay a day longer," says Claire. "It's such a charming little town. Why didn't we all plan to stay a day longer?"

"They have river tours," I tell her.

"River tours," she repeats slowly. "And what do you see?"

"Mostly the river, I'm afraid," Tess says with a laugh. "But I suppose that can be romantic, if you're the kind of person who likes rivers. It's the same one we crossed a few days ago, back at a much narrower point. The Stour. Nice enough little trickle. It just sort of runs, you know, from here to there."

"Oh dear," says Jean. "I seem to have lost my napkin."

"Sit tight, Mom," says Becca, twisting to reach down beneath the table. "I'll get it."

"Taking nothing away from Jean," Steffi says, "I found Angelique's tale of Psyche compelling as well. And Valerie, with the Sir Gawain story. What do women want? That may really be the most powerful question of all, don't you think?"

Silvia is nodding. "I was about to say the same thing. That question has haunted me for the last two days. In my opinion Valerie should get the free dinner."

"Hear, hear," says Claire, raising her glass for the toast, but Valerie is already shaking her head.

"I won't accept," she says, "because I'm the only one who ducked the challenge. You all told the truth about your lives, more or less, except for Che . . ."

"Hey," I say. "I bled."

"Yes, you bled," Valerie concedes. "All over the place and that buys you a pass. But I just repeated a story I read in a book, so I don't deserve to win. Not when I'm sitting among women who—"

"Then tell us something true," Jean says. "About yourself. Right now."

"Yeah," says Angelique, spearing a piece of candied violet with her fork and popping it in her mouth. "Your story asked what women want, so tell us what you want."

I sit back. Scan my slow and systematic way around the table, my eyes coming to rest on Becca. She is watching the other young people in the room, college students on dates, and still smiling, like a girl who is getting a glimpse of her future and likes what she sees. When Jean's shoulder brushes hers, she does not flinch. Something has shifted between them, something as small as the mother dropping a napkin and the daughter picking it up. Or perhaps that's huge, I don't know, and I'm not foolish enough to think Jean's confession has healed every wound. They will fight again, hard and soon, but for now a new equilibrium has been established.

And I'm conscious that I'm holding my breath, waiting for what Valerie will say. Claire's glass is still raised. Angelique picks a stray petal from her lip. Silvia has brought her hands together like the Mona Lisa.

"What I want," Valerie says, "is a thousand more nights like this one."

"Exactly," says Claire, and Steffi clinks her glass against hers. The conversation starts up again, one woman saying something to the person seated next to her, the subtle vibrations of companionship, and I remember a news show I once saw back in the States. They were interviewing the NYPD's most successful negotiator and they asked him how he did it. How he got the kidnapper to release the hostages, the suicide to come down from the ledge, the terrorist to reveal the location of the bomb. And he'd said that he started each negotiation the same way, by saying to the other person: "Tell me your story," because we want to tell our stories, all of us from criminals to priests. It's perhaps our deepest need—to speak and to listen, even if we don't always know what the stories mean. Somehow we know that just the telling can have enough magic to bring us here, to this holy place, to this circle of friends, to this happy end.

The servers are swarming the table to remove the appetizer

plates, making way for the entrées. I look out the door. I should be going.

But first I drain my glass. Catch the eye of Valerie, who is sitting at the far end of the table. "This wine," I say, and I have to raise my voice to be heard above the chatter of the others. "What did you think of it?"

"I think it's fine," she calls back. "In fact, I think it's one of the finest things I've had in a very long time. Thank you."

THE GATES to Canterbury are locked. Truly locked, with an old-fashioned chain and padlock woven through the iron bars. I walk back through the hotel, nodding at the desk clerk, and down another hall, this one leading to the Cathedral grounds. The door snaps shut behind me as I exit the lodge, followed by a frightening little buzz, the sort of sound you hear in prison movies. They've said my room key will get me back into the hotel and I try it, just to be sure. It works, but I'm still jumpy. It's dark out here on the Cathedral side and the transition from the modern world to the medieval is too abrupt. I take a few tentative steps away from the hotel, flinching as my foot leaves the level sidewalk and sinks into gravel. It's not just dark, it's very dark, with all the ambient light muted in order to make the Cathedral shine even brighter in contrast. When the bells chime nine, a shudder runs through me, top to bottom and then back again, as if my spine has become a lightning rod.

But I have come here to walk, and so walk I must. I start out resolutely in the opposite direction from the path Valerie and I took today, and there is no sound anywhere except for the steady crunch of my boots in the gravel and the faint echo of re-verberation from the bells. *I'm being ridiculous,* I think. *I'm not alone out here. The church grounds are never empty. Matthew said as much today. Literally hundreds of employees and volun-teers, dozens of services a week, an army of a cleaning crew, in-cluding one laudable fellow who simply washes the windows all day long, week after week, moving in a never-ending orbit around the Cathedral. Some of these people are bound to be merely steps away.*

This is what I say to myself, what I think, but the truth is, it feels empty. Empty and dark.

And then I see him. A single man, walking toward me.

Well, all right, maybe not toward me. That's dramatic. He's probably doing nothing more than what I'm doing, giving in to an urge to walk around the Cathedral at night, and it's only by chance that he happens to be coming from the opposite direc-tion. I can't see his face, but the outline of his body looks ordi-nary. He's one of the businessmen from the lodge, most likely, or just another tourist. His hands are in his pocket . . . reaching for a gun? But no, of course not, I'm being crazy. This is En-gland. He'd be reaching for a knife. But no, that's crazy too, people don't get raped on the grounds of Canterbury, and it's only by chance that it's just me and him out here in the dark-ness, a mere fluke of timing that I can look in all directions without seeing or hearing anyone else. That is what we're pay-ing for in the lodge, after all, this sense of isolation and privacy. And I haven't managed to encounter a killer, not here within the holy stillness of Canterbury—although let's face it, the safety record of the place isn't exactly unblemished, is it?

I have two options now. I could turn and walk toward the lodge, but that would mean that the man and I would be moving in the same direction, all the way back, and I would have to stay scared, never sure if he was going to catch up with me from behind. So maybe it's better to pass him face-to-face, just like I'm about to do, because I'm being silly. There's nothing scary about this man, not really. I've let my imagination and the events of the last few days run away with me, make me convinced that every moment has portent. We are closer now. No more than twenty feet apart, and I look directly toward him, toward the shadows.

"There you are," he says.

Here I am.

"Lucky, isn't it?" he says. "Amazing luck, that I would find you just like this, on my first walkaround."

He steps toward me and for the first time I see his face. There's a shard of illumination bouncing off something, shining through the glass face of some saint or another, or maybe somewhere somebody has opened a door. But a slant of light shoots across the gravel path and I see the man from London, the one from the George, the man with the closely cropped hair. He reaches into his pocket and pulls out my phone.

"I believe you may have been looking for this," he says.

IT'S A grand gesture. Bringing the phone all the way to Canterbury just to return it to me in person.

Or so I tell him, as we sit on a bench looking up at the Cathedral. He reminds me that trains run from London to Canterbury on the hour.

"That's right," I say. "You can pop down and then pop back. You told me that yourself."

And then he fills in the rest of the story. How as he was paying his tab he saw I'd left my phone but by then the women and I had already departed. He started to turn it in to the barkeeper, but something stopped him. It's mostly kids who work there, he says, kids who'd love to have an iPhone. It hadn't been hard to play detective. He'd woken the phone up and been greeted at once with Freddy's picture and he'd remembered how old I said I was and my dog's name. My password was most likely some combination of the year of my birth and the name of my pet. People are predictable that way. They use the same random facts over and over as identification and any code that's easy to remember is likewise easy to crack. That's how he'd found my itinerary. Known not just that I would end up in Canterbury but also the hotel where I'd be staying and the date I'd arrive.

"You could have just sent the phone ahead to the hotel," I say.

"Yes," he says. "I could have. I thought of that."

But when he'd gone back to the George for lunch a few days later the bartender told him I'd returned and that I'd become, in the words of the boy, "actually quite hysterical" when I had found my phone was missing. "At that point I knew I'd botched it," he says. "I should have left the phone at the restaurant that first day, or tried to send it by messenger to one of your stops along the way. I decided that the safest thing—"

He breaks off, looks at the phone in my hand. I still haven't unlocked it. I'm not sure exactly what he's done, but it's not the safest thing. By coming here he's thrown us both into uncertainty, and the thought is strange and thrilling.

"That's how I decided to deliver it myself," he says. "I know it means a lot to you."

I swallow, not sure how to respond. If he got into my mail enough to see my itinerary, he has likely seen my whole life. Not only where I was going but why, and with whom, and who has tried to contact me and who has not. It would seem he must know everything about me now, not just the name of my dog and the date of my birth but all my little secrets and hopes, locked within the vault of my phone. He pinches his lower lip between his thumb and forefinger, tugs it a bit away from his face. He made that same gesture, six days ago in the George. I remember now. It's what he does when he's nervous. He is as unsure of me as I am of him.

"What's your name?" I ask. "You know so much about me, and I don't even know your name."

"Dylan."

"Dylan?"

"After Bob. Bob Dylan, your American folksinger. My parents were the most dreadful sort of hippies. The sort who end up turning their youngest child into an accountant. Chased me right into the world of numbers and ledgers, just so something would make sense. But I suppose it could have been worse. My brothers are called Arlo and Seeger. Why are you laughing like that? You think I'm daft for coming here, don't you?"

"Wait just a minute," I say. "I'll be right back."

I take my phone and walk farther down the path. Find one of the nooks within the wall, wedge myself beneath a window. Wait for my mother to butt in like she always does. To give me one of her predictable pep talks. *Che,* she would say, *there are*

times when a girl's got to take a chance. And not just any chance,
baby. Take this one.

But Diana is silent. She's gone off somewhere, distracted by
one of her bright shiny things. I press on my phone. He's
charged it. The screen lights up immediately, as bright as Canterbury. The little purple microphone snaps right to attention. I
stare at it for a moment, then cut the phone off and walk back
to the shadowy bench where Dylan is waiting.

"All is well?" he says.

"I don't think you're daft for coming," I say, sitting back
down beside him. "In fact, I'm glad you brought the phone here
yourself. It was a grand gesture, but sometimes a person needs
to make a grand gesture."

"I've been looking at the Cathedral," he says. "What's it like
inside?"

"Big."

"I've never been here. Mad thing for a Londoner to say, I
know."

"Perhaps you should stay until tomorrow. Make a holiday
of it."

"But you're going back to America?" he asks. "Sunday noon,
that's the plan? I know that's what your schedule demands."

I grind my toes into the pebbles beneath the bench and let
the dust rise. Valerie's boots are going to have to be cleaned
again. "I'm not sure," I say. "Not entirely sure what I'm doing.
I've heard this town has a river."

"I believe so," he says cautiously, his eyes never leaving the
glow of the Cathedral. "I may have seen a sign saying you can
rent boats."

"Apparently it's not much of a river."

He pinches his lip. "Most likely not. But there's only one way to know for sure."

And so we sit, Dylan and I, shoulder-to-shoulder, looking up at Canterbury. A few minutes pass. And then a few more. At 9:15 a single bell will ring. But for now, the silence is fine.

ACKNOWLEDGMENTS

To research this book, I walked the Canterbury Trail, an undertaking that would have proven impossible without the (literal!) guidance of Jane Martin, the mastermind behind Tours of the Realm. Jane organizes and leads private tours based solely on the interests of the traveler, and she helped me bring authenticity and realism to Che's journey.

I am also deeply indebted to my agent, Stephanie Cabot of the Gernert Company, and my editor, Karen Kosztolnyik, at Gallery Books. *The Canterbury Sisters* would not have been possible without their loyalty, support, and counsel.

My gratitude goes out to the entire team at Gallery, starting with those at the helm: publisher Jen Bergstrom, president Louise Burke, and associate publisher Michele Martin. The publicity department couldn't have been more helpful, especially publicity director Jennifer Robinson and publicist Jules Horbachevsky. Special thanks to those in marketing: director Liz Psaltis, manager Melanie Mitzman, and online marketing manager Diana Velasquez. Thanks to Becky Prager, Karen's editorial assistant, who answers all the questions. And at Gernert, thanks to Anna Worrall, who gives such great advice to authors, and most of all to Ellen Goodson, who sends the checks.

THE CANTERBURY SISTERS

Kim Wright

INTRODUCTION

From the critically acclaimed author of *Love in Mid Air* and *The Unexpected Waltz*, *The Canterbury Sisters* is a warm, compulsively readable novel about how one woman's mission to grant her mother's last wishes ends up taking her on a pilgrimage that changes her life.

Che de Milan's life is a mess. Her longtime boyfriend has just announced—in a letter—that he is leaving her for another woman, and Che's eccentric mother has recently passed. When her mother's ashes show up on her doorstep with a set of instructions that require a trip to Canterbury Cathedral, Che reluctantly packs her bags and embarks upon a pilgrimage. The eight women in the tour group swap stories along the length of the Canterbury Trail in the best Chaucerian tradition, vying to see who among them can describe true love. Armed with wine, ashes, camaraderie, and the magic of Canterbury itself, these unlikely pilgrims help Che find a sense of peace and hope that has always eluded her.

QUESTIONS AND TOPICS
FOR DISCUSSION

1. In the opening pages, Che loses her mother, Diana, and describes herself as an orphan: "I've always been an only child, and now I'm an orphan as well, and the time has pretty much passed for having children of my own. Not that I ever particularly wanted such a thing. The bumper sticker on my Fiat reads, I'M NOT CHILDLESS, I'M CHILD-FREE, but still, to find myself utterly alone in the world, at least in terms of blood relations, has hit me harder than I would have guessed" (pg. 6). What does the loss of her mother represent to Che? As the story progresses, how does Che reconcile with her loss?

2. When Che first sees the Broads Abroad, she remains on her side of the pub, observing from a distance rather than approaching the group. What about this trip makes her reluctant to sit down with the women at first? How does a stranger in the pub ultimately convince her to go on the journey? Describe her initial reactions to the women and how her opinions change over time.

3. *The Canterbury Tales* include pilgrims who are men, whereas the Broads Abroad is a group made only of women. Discuss how this affects the sort of stories that are told during Che's pilgrimage versus the one Chaucer would have experienced in the Middle Ages.

4. Before the women officially begin their journey, each person briefly mentions her marital status. Che blurts out, "I was married once, but so long ago that it's like it hardly happened" (pg. 48). Describe the role of secrecy, lies, and "personal myths" in the novel. Whose secrets are the most surprising?

5. Jean's tale is a good example of how self-blame permeates the women's lives in *The Canterbury Sisters*. Discuss how other characters blame themselves (or others) for events that have occurred. Are they able to liberate themselves from this self-blame? Why or why not?

6. In chapter five, Che checks her email after a day without her cell phone. After seeing more than a hundred unread emails she thinks, "Would it be such a crime to be unreachable, to hold my silence for just this once?" (pg. 77) Consider what this statement means in relation to her recent breakup with Ned, the loss of her mother, and her overall experience on the pilgrimage.

7. Because of the reality television show she stars on, Angelique's entire relationship is the most exposed and seemingly the most brutally honest. Why does she choose to illustrate her relationship through the myth of Psyche and Eros?

8. In chapter six, Che reveals how one of her mother's lovers ruined Cinderella for her as a young girl. What is it about this memory at this point in the book that causes Che to react so strongly and to finally cry? What is it about Valerie's presence that causes her to flee?

9. After Claire's tale, Tess says, "We aren't sharing these stories to entertain each other" (pg. 131). What is the purpose of the tales on this journey? Discuss what the storytelling represents in this novel.

10. Valerie chooses to tell the tale of Sir Gawain and the Loathly Lady instead of the story of her own life. The tale has an important message: above all, women wish for the chance to make their own decisions. Were you surprised to learn Valerie's secret at the end of the novel? Do you think the chance to make decisions is what women truly want most in life?

11. In chapter eleven, Silvia reveals that her seemingly perfect marriage was devoid of love and that ultimately, both she and her husband find true love once they are no longer following The Plan. What does your plan look like? What do you think about Silvia's decision to start a marriage and a family with a path already set forth?

12. On page 223, Claire asks Che, "What did she teach you? Your mother, I mean. Girls always learn something from their mothers, even when they try not to." What did Diana teach Che? Discuss with your fellow book club members what you've each learned from your own mothers.

13. The accident comes as a big shock in chapter fifteen. How does this change the dynamics of the group? Describe how each woman reacts to the accident.

14. One of the major themes in *The Canterbury Sisters* is the importance of company. Discuss how sisterhood—or the lack thereof—in Che's life plays a role in her participation in the trip. Do the other women lack sisterhood? Consider the relationships between Becca and Jean, Claire and Silvia, Che and Diana. Do you think the group comes together by the novel's end? Why or why not?

15. On page 290, the priest asks, "Why do people pilgrimage?" Share your initial reaction with your book group. What would you hope to gain from a similar experience?

ENHANCE YOUR BOOK CLUB

1. Read some of Chaucer's *The Canterbury Tales* with your book group. Do you see any characters from *The Canterbury Tales* echoed in *The Canterbury Sisters*? Are there any particular scenes that appear in both books? Consider the influence of Chaucer's themes on *The Canterbury Sisters*.

2. Read Kim Wright's other two novels, *The Unexpected Waltz* and *Love in Mid Air*. Do you notice similar themes, characters, or plot points? Discuss these similarities and differences with your book group.

3. Take a trip to a historic site or scenic hiking trail in your area—and leave the phones at home! Invite your fellow book group members to tell the tales of their own romances or love stories that have touched them throughout their lives. Or have a "walk and talk" book club meeting and get exercise and insight all at once.

4. For your next book club pick, select a memoir or biography about someone who travels on a trail or specific path, such as *Wild* by Cheryl Strayed or *Tracks* by Robyn Davidson. Do you see similarities between these books? Why or why not?